Book of the Three Dragons

Kenneth Morris

Now back in print in the United States — and for the first time anywhere, with the author's never-before-published original ending!

Book of the Three Dragons

Kenneth Morris
Introduction by Douglas A. Anderson

Cold Spring Press

Cold Spring Press

P.O. Box 284, Cold Spring Harbor, NY 11724
E-mail: Jopenroad@aol.com

ISBN 1-59360-027-5
Library of Congress Control Number: 2004109829
– All Rights Reserved –

Printed in the United States of America

Contents

A KEY TO THE PRONUNCIATION
OF THE WELSH NAMES IN

The Book of the Three Dragons

which it would be a good plan to look into either before starting to read the book, or whenever you come to a name that puzzles you.

A is pronounced like the *a in father; e* like the a in *mare; i* like the ee in *sheep; o* like *oa* in *oar; u* like the French *u* in *une* or the German *ü* — or you may make it like *ee* if you don't know that sound. *Y* in the last syllable of a word is the same as the Welsh *u* — call it *ee* if necessary; in syllables other than the last it has the sound of *i* in *fir;* and *w* is pronounced like *oo* in *moon.*

Ai, ae, au, ei, eu, all have much the sound of *i* in *dine; wy,* that of *ui* in *ruin; yw* and *iw* and *uw,* that of *ew in* few; *aw* that of *ow* in *cow; oe* that of *oy* in *boy. I* before another vowel becomes a consonant like the English consonant *y;* thus Taliesin is pronounced Tal-yes-in.

B, d, l, m, n, p, t, are pronounced as in English. *C* is always pronounced like *k; ch* is a soft aspirated guttural, as in the Scotch *loch; dd* has the sound of the *th* in *this, that, breathe. F* is pronounced like the English *v; ff* like *f;* the words *of* and *off,* in English, are spelt as if written in the Welsh, and not the English, alphabet. *G* is always hard, as in *egg* or *give* — never soft as in *age* or *gender. H* is always aspirated- never silent. *Ng* is pronounced as in *sing* — never as in *longer* or *singe.*

Ll is an aspirated *l.* Bishop Thirlwall, when he was appointed to the see of St. David's, learnt Welsh and became a great preacher in that language. His teacher taught him to make this sound: he said, "Your lordship must put the tip of his episcopal tongue to the roof of his ecclesiastical mouth, and hiss like an old goose!" Try that method and you will succeed in pronouncing the *ll.*

R is well trilled on the tongue as in Scotch or Italian — never left out as in southern England, nor burred gutturally as in English dialects

BOOK OF THE THREE DRAGONS

and parts of America. *Rh* is the same well aspirated. *S* is as in *hiss* or *so* — never as in *lose*. *Th* has the sound of English *th* in *breath* and *think* (*breath* would be written *breth* in Welsh, and *breathe* would be written *bridd*).

The stress or accent falls on the last syllable but one of all words you are likely to meet with.

Let us take some of the names in the book, and see if we can make the sounds of them clearly understood. First there is the hero: whose name to begin with was

Pwyll [Pooeelh], and then

Dienw'r Anffodion [Dee-ENN-oorr An-FOD-yon]; — the syllables on which the accent falls are in capitals — and lastly it became

Manawyddan [Man-ow (as in *how*)-OTH (as in *other, brother*) - *th*an]. The *th* in the last syllable is italicized to show it is like the *th* in *that* and *this;* not the *th* in *breath* or *think*. Then there is

Hu Gadarn, — as you have no *u* modified in English, you could call him Hee GAD-arrn. Then there are, among the Gods, the Three Dragons after whom the book is called; they are

Plenydd Brif-fardd Prydain [PLEN-neathe BRIEVE-varr*the* PRUD-dine],

Gwron [you had better call him GOO-ron] with the same titles, Brif-fardd Prydain and

Alawn [AL (to rhyme with *Hal*) -awn (to rhyme with *down]* Brif-Fardd Prydain. They are the three Prif-fardd or Primitive Bards of Britain. [No, the type-setter has made no error: it's *Prif-* when it stands alone, and *Brif-* when it follows their names.] Then there are the three sons of Don:

Gwydion, the first syllable of whose name rhymes with *sir* as the English pronounce it, with the r dropped out; or again you might call him GWUD-yon — the *gwud* rhyming with *bud;* it does not look so pretty, but is very nearly right —

Amaethon [Ah-MY-thon — the *th* as in *think*], and

Gofannon [Go-VAN-non]. There is

Bran the Blessed or **Bendigaid Fran;** [Ben-DIG-ide Vran] or **Bran Fendigaid;** once Crowned King of London.

8

Gwerddonau Llion [Gwairr-*TH*ONN-igh (to rhyme with *high)* LHEE-on] in which the Seven found him; there are the three Persecuting Foemen of the Island of the Mighty,

Gwain Llygad Cath [GWEE-own (to rhyme with *down)* LUGH-gad CAHTH] the **Forleidr** [VORR-lyder] —Gwiawn Cat's-Eye the Sea-Thief,

Llywd Ab Cilcoed [Lhooid ab KILL-coyd], and

Tathal Twyll Goleu [TATH-al (rhymes with *Hal)* Tooeelh-GO-ligh]. And there are the Goddesses

Ceridwen [Care-ID-wen], and

Arianrod [Arr-YAN-rod]; and there are the

Cymry [KUM-ree or Welsh], also called the

Brython — of which the first syllable rhymes with Cuth- in *Cuth*bert — or Britons, Ancient Britons, as you may say; and their language, the

Cymraeg [Cum-RYGUE]; and many more, which I think will not be difficult to guess.

Hirewin Frith [Here-RAY-win (with the stress on the ray) Vreeth]

However, an excellent plan is just to decide for oneself what one will call each of the people in the book, and stick to that. Thus if you elected to call Pwyll simply *Pwil,* and called him that every time his name cropped up; m why, *you* would get along charmingly, and he wouldn't mind in the least, It doesn't sound so nice as *Pooeelh* perhaps, but then — !

INTRODUCTION
by Douglas A. Anderson
editor of *The Annotated Hobbit* and *Tales Before Tolkien*

In her 1973 landmark essay, "From Elfland to Poughkeespie," Ursula K. Le Guin singled out three writers as master stylists of fantasy: J. R. R. Tolkien, E. R. Eddison, and Kenneth Morris. Tolkien's writings are well-known, and E. R. Eddison's first novel, *The Worm Ouroboros*, has considerable renown. But in 1973 the writings of Kenneth Morris were unknown to most readers. We owe it to Le Guin that, in the years since her essay was published, Morris has gained some of the acclaim that he deserves.

Morris was born in Wales in 1879. Even as a child his imagination was nurtured by Welsh folktales and by the *Mabinogion*, the primary collection of Welsh mythological stories surviving from medieval times. Usually published as a book containing eleven tales, only four (each of which is named as a separate "branch") are considered to be part of the *Mabinogion* proper. Morris's father died when he was six, and the family moved to London, where he was educated at the famous school Christ's Hospital. In 1896 he visited Dublin and encountered the Theosophical Society, which he joined enthusiastically. Morris remained devoted to theosophical ideals, like the universal brotherhood of all mankind, for the rest of his life. In 1908 he moved to southern California to teach at the International Headquarters of the Theosophical Society. He stayed there—at Point Loma, near San Diego—for twenty-two years. In 1930 he returned to Wales, where he died in 1937 at the age of fifty-seven.

Morris was a prolific writer, publishing a great number of essays, poems, dramas, and stories in various Theosophical magazines. With regard to fiction, Morris wrote three novels and about forty short stories. Two of the novels, *The Fates of the Princes of Dyfed* (1914) and *Book of the Three Dragons* (1930), are imaginative re-workings of Welsh mythological stories. His other novel is a fantasy of the ancient Toltecs of central Mexico. Titled *The Chalchiuhite Dragon*, it was first published in 1992. Of Morris's short stories, ten were collected in 1926 under the title *The Secret Mountain and Other Tales*. All of his short stories, ranging through the mythologies of the world (Celtic, Norse, Greek, Roman, Taoist, Buddhist, etc.), were gathered in *The Dragon Path: Collected Tales of Kenneth Morris* (1995).

Morris wrote both *The Fates of the Princes of Dyfed* and *Book of the Three Dragons* around 1910-14, but only the former was published at that time. It was not successful. In the late 1920s, when Morris returned to *Book of the Three Dragons*, he was critical of the style of the first book: "I was in a very Welsh mood when I wrote the *Fates* —in 1910-1911—and managed to write as if it were Welsh. Of course very few in Wales are interested in it: a few are. That piling up of adjectives in English is a dangerous ploy: the worst American after dinner ranters do it ghastlily. But there, with the robes of my Welshness and Welsh moods of thought on me, I walked along gaily oblivious of my peril." Having re-read *Fates*, and having "found the ornament so thick in places I lost the thread of story in reading," Morris determined that should not be the case with *Book of the Three Dragons*, and went to it "with a severe blue pencil, cutting out ornament left and right." Morris was correct to do so—*Book of the Three Dragons* shows a maturity of style well beyond that in the earlier book. It is also considerably more imaginative. *The Fates of the Princes of Dyfed* is a fairly close retelling of the first branch of the *Mabinogion*, telling the story of Pwyll and his journey to the Otherworld. *Book of the Three Dragons* is Morris's recasting and reshaping of the other branches into a story of his own.

Inexplicably, when it was first published, the ending of *Book of the Three Dragons* was simply lopped off. The surviving correspondence is unclear, but evidently the publisher felt that the book was too long. This edition of *Book of the Three Dragons* publishes for the first time Morris's ending, his fifth and sixth branches, amounting to approximately one-third as much again of what was originally published.

Book of the Three Dragons appeared in September 1930. It was chosen as a selection of the Junior Literary Guild, and achieved more notice than any of Morris's other books. Favorable reviews appeared in the *New York World*, the *New York Herald Tribune Books*, the *Atlantic Monthly*, and the *Horn Book*.

Morris's true achievement went unnoticed for many years, but with his two books, and especially with *Book of the Three Dragons*, Morris essentially invented the sub-genre of modern Celtic fantasy. In "From Elfland to Poughkeepsie," Ursula K. Le Guin described *Book of the Three Dragons* as "a singularly fine example of the recreation of a work magnificent in its own right (the *Mabinogion*)—a literary event rather rare except in fantasy, where its frequency is perhaps proof, if one were needed, of the ever-renewed vitality of myth." Le Guin's comments are precisely correct, and thanks to her championing, *Book of the Three Dragons* has also achieved the status of a modern fantasy classic.

Here is
the Bringing-in of the
BOOK OF THE THREE DRAGONS

THE Seven Chief Chieftains of the Cymry were out on the wave in their ship, with Ireland on their right hand and Wales on their left; and making their way toward the Island of the Mighty. The marvel they had in the ship with them was the Wonderful Head of Bran the Blessed, son of the Boundless: and here is why they had it and why they were out on the wave at all:

At that time there was no Crowned King in London; and for lack of one, often there would be confusion and the failure of crops. So the Six Chief Chieftains consulted among themselves who should get the crown. Taliesin the Chief of Bards was at the head of them: his forehead shone like the Morning Star.

"If you will take advice of mine," said he, "the one to wear the crown will be the Blessed Bran."

"The best advice in the world," they agreed, "if there be any getting him." He had been Crowned King of London none knew how many ages before; and there would be no finding him but in the Islands of the Blessed in the West of the World; and the journey thither they were for making.

"It would be beneath his dignity to have less than seven men come to him on an embassy," said Heilyn ab Gwyn Hen. (He was the most impatient of all warriors and horsemen.)

"That is true," said Taliesin Benbardd. "We shall meet the seventh in Mon as we go forward; and he will be a son of the Boundless as Bran Fendigaid is; and he will be at the head of us?"

13

In Mon they met Manawyddan; and all could see that he was to be their leader. Now here is who this Manawyddan son of the Boundless was.

I. The Story of the Nameless One with the Misfortunes and of His Coming into the Caldron of Ceridwen the Mother of the World

IT HAPPENED of old that the Gods of the Island of the Mighty desired to raise auxiliar godhood from the ranks of the Cymry, the men of that island. So Hu the Mighty called them into council; and in the council they decided that Pwyll, Prince of Dyfed in Wales, should be the man they would make a god of, if he were capable of it. So first they sent him to reign in Annwn, the Great Deep; and a year and a day he was king there, and undergoing the trials incident to the place, and nowise failing in them. Then they sent one of their own divine kindred, Rhianon Ren the daughter of Hefeydd, into Wales to become his wife; that she might help him towards godhood as only a goddess could.

But it was when his son Pryderi was born that they put the heaviest trial on him; and in that he failed. So they did what they had to do by him: took the memory from his mind, and himself from his kin and his kingdom; and cast him loose on Wales and the world. Whatever misfortune they could devise, they brought him deep into the midst of it, and poured it out over the head of him, and set it howling and fanged at his heels; and all for no reason but that bound they were to make a god of him, and to have him fighting in their ranks with them against Hell and Chaos along the borders of space.

He knew nothing, at that time, of his having been Pwyll Pen Annwn; Lord of Dyfed and the Great Deep; style or title he had none; the best name there was for him was Dienw'r Anffodion, the Nameless One with the Misfortunes; and to get a better he would have to come into Pair Dadeni, the Caldron of Ceridwen the Mother of the World; but he knew nothing of that. In it the dead come by new life and the nameless by a name; and the Gods were guiding him towards it always, by the shortest path there was. For Hu Gadarn sent Gwydion ab Don, the God of Wisdom and Laughter, to guide him; and by reason of that,

14

towards Pair Dadeni his face was set. Gwydion ab Don was beside him on all his wanderings: through Europe and through Africa and the Islands of Corsica, and through Sach and Salach, and Lotor and Ffotor, and India the Greater and India the Less, and Powys and Meirion and Arfon.

And there, one day, he was traversing the mountains towards Mon and Ireland; and it seemed to him he had never been anything but fortunate, compared to what he was then.

It was long since he had passed any habitation, or looked on the faces of men. The fields bore no mushrooms for him, nor the thorns blackberries, although it was the beginning of Autumn; and if there were eels or trout in the streams, he could get no news of them. Three days before he had shot an old lean rabbit; and had seen neither bird nor beast to shoot at since. Nothing was left of it but the right hind leg; and the best that could be said for that was that it was dry and tough and withered. He was shoeless and in rags; and lame with a wounded foot a sharp rock had torn the day before and that now was festering.

He had risen from the heather at dawn after a night of rain and fever; and thought that death could not be far from him. Now and again hunger tormented him; but he took no thought for the rabbit leg in his wallet. Through the morning he limped on, and the rain drove down on him; and the thoughts in his mind were either numb and silent or else fantastic and beyond control; and the one thing he hoped for in his heart was death.

And then suddenly he became aware of that which had already driven the clouds from the sky, and the rain from mid air, and now the grief and confusion from his mind. It was harping and song that filled the mountain world with wonder, and made the morning wholly beautiful, with sunlit raindrops sparkling everywhere on the fern. The rabbits came hurrying from their burrows to listen, and paid no heed to him as he passed. An old gray wolf, sauntering down the hillside, turned, and stood still with trembling ears. Three eagles came down out of the sky, and lighted on boulders, intent. Wild goats on the crags above stood motionless. Nothing living moved but himself; and he, as best he could, hurried forward to come to the heart of the enchantment.

A hundred paces brought him to it. A youth sat on a rock, his harp at his breast, floating out the music on the sunlight. A motion of his eyes bade Dienw be seated; and so he kept him until the song was sung. It was healing and happiness to listen to it. The singer was hardly more than a boy; yet had the blue robe of an Institutional Bard of that island on him.

He ended the song and set down the harp, and picked up his wand of alderwood studded with gold. "The greeting of the god and the man to you, pleasantly and kindly!" said he. It was the best greeting Dienw had had, so far as he knew, during the whole of his life.

"And better be it with you than it is with me — better and more copious!" he answered. "It would be a delight to me to remember, in after times, the name of the one who could so ingratiate these mountains with his harping and his vocal song."

"As to the name, it will be Goreu fab Ser," said the Bard; and clear it was he would be of starry lineage, and few his betters throughout the worlds. "It was foretold to me that I should meet here the man I desired to meet; and I made the music to attract him to me."

"It would be pleasant to know who that one might be," said Dienw.

"It is a Prince of the Cymry, a Son of the Boundless, to go with Taliesin Benbardd into the Western World. Is it you who are the man?"

"Dear help me better!" said Dienw. "Is it the look of a Prince of the Cymry or a Son of the Boundless is with me?"

"Whether it is or not," said Goreu, "the fate is on any man who heard the music, that he shall accompany me today until I find that man; if it is all Arfon and Mon itself I must travel."

"I will do that gladly," said Dienw.

"That is well," said Goreu fab Ser. "We will go forward."

They journeyed on; and what with Goreu's songs and his stories, and his laughter and diverting conversation, Dienw had no memory of his sorrows and pain; and was happy for the first time in his life, so far as he knew. At noon Goreu stopped, and said:

"The hunger of the world has overtaken me. Is there food with you in the wallet?"

Dienw remembered the rabbit's leg, and was overcome with shame. "Such food as it is," said he. He opened the wallet and brought out what it contained.

"Dear, a miserable provision is this, for such a one as I am," said Goreu. "In your deed, is there nothing better with you than this poor and dilapidated meat?"

"There is not," said Dienw, sighing.

"Detestable to me, truly, is loathsome hunger; abominable an insufficiency of food upon a journey. Mournful, I declare to you, is such a fate as this, to one of my lineage and nurture!"

"Well, well," said Dienw'r Anffodion, with the bitter hunger awaking in him again; "common with me is knowledge of famine. Take you the whole of the food, if you will."

"Yes," said Goreu; "that will be better." With that he ate the meat and gnawed the bone and flung it from him. "Now that I have partaken of food," said he, "I am refreshed, and grief and fatigue have forsaken me; and I am filled with a desire for music. Play you the harp for my diversion!"

Dienw took it, and played *The Little Mountain Bird* on it, sing-hag the song as best he could. When he came to

God fired with song his wild, prophetic tongue

Goreu fab Ser, groaning piteously, snatched the harp from him.

"Music I desired, and not this soul-piercing cacophony!" he cried. "A poor return is this for my kindness! Listen you now, and be silent."

Then he struck chords from the harp and began singing; and hurried forward as he played and sang; and the harping was a ruthless torment, and the song, hideous screeching: the birds in the air hearing it fell dead, and the rabbits perished in their burrows; the wolves fled howling, and the winds of heaven moaned and mourned. And as for Dienw, his pains and sorrows came back to him a thousandfold, and there was nothing for him to do but mourn and follow: over the mountains and the wild places, by sharp crag and raging torrent: his legs jerked miserably into speed by the harping; his mind and body in anguish.

"Come!" cried Goreu fab Ser augustly; "I am refreshed with food and glorious music; I loathe this dawdling unenterprise; it is a poor return for my kindness to you, that you should delay me thus on the road!" Thus he dragged him on and never spared him; keeping neither to road nor path, rabbit run nor goat track; but to gorse-grown level and jagged steep; trailing the way with crimson from Dienw's wounds, but going weightless and dauntless himself: until they came to the shore of the Menai and the house of the ferryman.

"Soul," said Goreu fab Ser; "is there food in the house with you, to appease the enormous hunger of the world that afflicts me?"

"Such as it is," said the ferryman; "and little enough of it." He brought out half an oatcake and a thumb's weight of cheese; and it was Goreu who took them from him.

"Better for one to be filled than for two to go hungry," said he to Dienw. "Is it grudge me the provisions you do?"

"Not I," said Dienw. "Hunger and famine I am familiar with."

"It will be the better for you," said Goreu; and compassion in his voice instead of mockery and merriment; if anyone had been listening for it.

The ferryman launched his coracle, and the three of them went into it and began the crossing. And now a mood of restlessness came on Goreu, and he became wilder and merrier than ever he had been; yet losing nothing of his augustness of mien and tone. Night was drifting westward at that time, and the deep gray of the twilight over the waters of Menai.

"Dear help thee better!" he cried, leaping to his feet, "behold yonder!" What was there to be beheld, none was to know: for no man may leap to his feet in a coracle without overturning it. The three of them were in the water; the ferryman swimming back towards Arfon, and pushing his boat before him as he swam.

"Peace now to drown and forget," thought Dienw with the Misfortunes. But there was no peace for him. "On me is the sorrow of all my race!" cried Goreu son of the Stars. "Never have I feared anything so much as death by loathsome drowning — a watery and evil death, and to end my life beneath Menai waves. Were there one here better than a poltroon and a braggart, he would quit his extreme selfishness and save me from the fury of the deep sea!"

"I am here," gasped Dienw; "it is not fated that you should drown." He gathered what strength he had, and made the best use of it, and held Goreu up in the water, and began swimming with him towards Mon. Whilst he swam, Goreu struggled and encumbered his limbs, and made no end of his august lamentations and reproofs. "If I save him, it is as much as I shall do," thought Dienw. "As for me, there will be peace when the waves have closed over me." Night fell, and the stars shone fitfully through gaps in the clouds. "I will save him," thought Dienw; "in my deed to Heaven I will." Then he thought, "It is a hundred miles between me and Mon;" and with that a wave lifted the two of them, and cast them up upon the beach. Mind and thought were gone from him, as if death had taken him.

Goreu son of the Stars arose, and lifted him beyond reach of the tide, and laid him down in a hollow between the sand-hills; and then the likeness of human flesh and bone departed from Goreu, and he took fire-form and god-form, and rose up flaming into mountain stature till the peak of the Wyddfa was less lofty than he; and turned his face southward and east toward that holy mountaintop; and he said:

"Lord Mighty One, he is ready; the breath is gone from him; the Nameless One with the Misfortunes is ready; Pwyll Pen Annwn is ready at last."

Out of the peak of the Wyddfa rose Hu Gadarn, who was appointed in those days to be Emperor of the Gods and the Cymry of Ynys Wen. He too flamed skyward, his crest burning among the stars of Capricorn, his eyes shining with wisdom and beneficence, his White Shield better than seven moons in the heavens.

"I commend you, Lord Gwydion ab Don," said he. "Let him be brought now into the Caldron of Ceridwen my daughter; let his body be laid in Pair Dadeni, that new life and name may be his."

From the midst of Mon, light streamed up into the sky; flame-flakes of rainbow hues; and thence came nine dragons through the air, and lighted down among the sand dunes, and became the Nine Faery Princes that watch the fires under Ceridwen's Caldron. They picked up the body of the Nameless One, and bore it to the Caldron.

IN THE morning when Dienw awoke, not an ache nor wound was in his body, nor any sorrow in his mind. One stood over him of immortal beauty, whose forehead shone like the Morning Star; five others came up the beach toward them.

"The greeting of heaven and man to you, Manawyddan son of the Boundless!" said Taliesin the Chief of Bards.

"And better be it with you than with me, Lord Taliesin!" said he, arising from the sand. "And better be it with the other five Chief Chieftains that are approaching us. It is I who will go with you into the Western World."

"Yes, it is you," said Taliesin Benbardd. "Behold here, the seventh who will be at the head of us!" said he, "Son of the Boundless, as befits the Blessed One's dignity!"

He went with them towards the Malltraeth; remembering how he had come by the name Taliesin had called him by, in the Caldron of Ceridwen in the night. "Goreu fab Ser," said he; "the Best One, the son of the Stars; and Gwydion ab Don he was, whatever. And I that was Pwyll Pen Annwn, am Manawyddan son of the Boundless." Then as he went, he repeated to himself the words of the hymn:

> *Many the enchantments that*
> *Of old time overcame me;*
> *Ere the Mighty set their will*
> *To slay me and re-name me!*
> *Then was I enchanted thrice*
> *By Don's son, by Gwydion;*
> *Purity I had from him,*
> *The Purifier of Brython,*
> *And Eurwys and Euron,*
> *And Euron and Modron,*
> *And Five Battalions of the Seers*
> *The Gods had set their seal on.*

II. The Wonderful Head

THEY TOOK ship at the Malltraeth in Mon, where, they say, there is always a Ship of Glass waiting for such voyagers; and were seven years wandering the lonely sea. Then in the gold and cool of the evening they came to the Isles of the Blessed —shining, lost Green Places in the wide plain of the sea.

No one could come to land in those islands, and his body and mortality still encumbering him. The earth there is subtle and luminous, and always breaking into a foam of flowers whose odor, blown westward to the world, is the fulfilment of aspiration, the kindling of bardic dreams. It was appointed to Bran the Blessed to be Crowned King there, at that time.

Under the headland, where the bloom flowed down to the shore, they saw One, gigantic, grave and beautiful, pacing the honey-colored sand. Courteously they gave him greeting from the ship; and with even greater courtesy he greeted them again.

"And you also, whence come you?" said he.

"We are an embassy from the Island of the Mighty," said Manawyddan. "Seeking Bran the Blessed, the son of the Boundless, we come."

"Lord Brother," said the Blessed One, "speak you your message without concealment. I am that Bendigaid Fran."

"A Crowned King is needed in London; and no king is better than you are."

"Well," said he, musing; "it was foretold I should take that sovereignty again, at the end and head of ages."

"What was foretold, let that befall," said Manawyddan.

"Yes," said Bran the Blessed; "but there will be conditions. No one could leave these islands, head and body of him together. A bodiless head I should go with you; and bodiless I should be the thirteen years of the journey."

"Equal with us, that bodilessness, to your having the best body in the world," said Taliesin. "We should serve you and guard you."

"And I would be telling you the lore of these islands during those years: I would be imparting learning to you, and you my pupils."

"Gladly and proudly we should listen to you; proudly and gladly we should learn."

"Well," said he, "we will make trial of it. It may be that I shall come at last to London with you, and a body with me by that time, the best in the world; and that I shall wear the crown of London. It may be that no evil will befall, to prevent my coming there."

"What evil would prevent it?" they asked.

"You to be neglecting my counsels during the thirteen years," said he.

"Fear you nothing as to that, Lord Blessed One," said they. "In our deed to the Mighty, the Compassionate, the Wise, may the stars fall if we neglect your counsel!"

In that way they pledged themselves.

"I will come with you," said Bendigaid Fran. "But it will not be easy for you to obey me; and it will not be easy for me to come by that sovereignty."

With the word, the body melted away from him, and the Wonderful Head of him rose like a seagull in the air, and lighted down on the prow of the ship.

Away with them, then, eastward toward the island of the Mighty. Over sunlit and mist-hid seas they sailed; and it was equal to them, having the Wonderful Head for their companion, to having seven score bards, the best in the world at songs and story-telling; and to having seven score pilots and sea-chieftains, knowing all the secrets of the salt deep; and to having seven score druids of Ynys Enlli and Ynys Mon, Kinsmen of the Dragon. By reason of this, it took them no more than a year to journey from the Islands of the Blessed to the Island of the Mighty; and during the whole time the Wonderful Head sang to them, and conversed with them, and unfolded to them the whole marvel of story-telling; and foretold to them the fates and destinies of the Island of the Mighty from that out until the day of doom.

They came to Harlech High-above-the-wave, in Ardudwy. "We will go to land here," said the Wonderful Head. So they made fast their ship with seven beautiful anchors, and landed, and made their way up the hill to Caer Harlech. They came to the gates of the caer, and there was neither porter nor dog to withstand or to welcome them. They went forward by court and corridor, voiceless places full of silence and sunlight. On the walls were pictured hangings: the mighty of old, scarlet-raimented, moving in the greenwood, moving by the shores of the sea. Proud faces, white as ivory, wary-eyed, looked out: as if, at a sudden spell a moment since, the power of motion had gone from them. Hall and court and corridor, all was mute as a song just ended; all empty, as if the singers had but now gone down to the sea.

They came into a hall at last, the largest in the world so far as they knew then; and found feasting made ready in it: cups of carved beechwood inlaid with silver and ivory; meat and mead in plenty; fruit from a thousand orchards; and seven thrones at the board, and on the dais, a pillar of unhewn crystal for the Wonderful Head. "We will take food now," said Bran Fendigaid. So they sat down, and the food they ate was better than anything they had eaten before. They were in great contentment, and had no desire for speech.

The sun drew toward his setting: they could see, through the open arches of the hall, the glory of the sky over Ireland. Then they heard low, melodious music, drifting in from the sea. They saw three moons rising over Ireland, better than the common moon of heaven. Out of the gloom and splendor of purple, out of the gold and vermilion waning in the west, those three wonders rose; and about them sky and sea burned mysterious, twinkling and somber with rapture.

One of them was pearl-white, swan-white, snow-white; one, blue like the turquoise; one, dim with a myriad colors and all the beauty of the rainbow intermixed and interfused. They were winged and arc-like, radiant; moving to and fro on quivering pinions through the dreamy evening over the glittering heaving of slow waves. They filled the vast, dark-rimmed world with music better than any harping. To the ones that listened, all other music they had heard seemed to have been harsh, and dull, and uglily repugnant.

But Manawyddan listened with more delight than the others did: because he knew that they were Aden Lanach and Aden Lonach and Aden Fwynach, the three Birds of Rhianon his wife, the three Singers of Peace: birds out of Faërie, the proper possessions of a Goddess such as she was. He had heard no tidings of them since they were stolen by Llwyd ab Cilcoed the Enchanter and he himself had been exiled from

Dyfed. Now the news he got from the sight of them was that Pryderi his son would have grown up a man and returned to Arberth in Dyfed and to his mother, after having freed them from their captivity with Llwyd.

"The Daughter of Hefeydd sent them," said Bran the Blessed; "she knew the need I would have of them." He bade the seven remain silent, listening to the birds; because the first part of all learning is through music and vocal song. So they leaned over the table, watching and listening. They saw the birds winging, poised, darting: to and fro, up and down, over the waters. They heard many poems from them, and the smooth harmonies of music — the delirious harmonies of music. They heard the birds overcoming the winds, and gathering the Four Waves of the West, hushed and wondering, to listen: the Wave of Ireland, the Wave of Fannau, and the Wave of the North; and even the fourth of them, that proud sea-sweeper, the Wave of Gwalia of the warlike hosts.

And now the glimmering sea-face would be white-flecked, now all silvery; now it would be hued like the gentian, now like the forgetmenot, or rosy lilac rippling into gold, or cold on the rim with a dust and wan smoke of pearl and amethyst. It appeared to all the seven that the whiteness and silver would be strewn from the triumph of Glanach; that the blue would be poured from the throat of Llonach; that the gold and roses and rainbows were all from Mwynach: they did not realize the passing of dawn-mists and noon-blueness; the flame and sad glory of the setting sun. Morning and midnight were one to them, because of the beauty of the birds, and their mysterious singing over the sea. Blue was the wave with June; gray with raging November; white-streaked with howling January on the leaden grayness; over it all was the arcane, unwearying song. It grew blue again, and the foam whitened with March.

It seemed to the Seven that they would have been listening an hour, or some part of an hour.

Then they heard lapping and falling waters, the crooning wash of the waves far off and below: slowly the sea-sound crept in on them. They saw the birds, star-like, vanish southward, glimmering faintly in the haze and noon sunlight; they heard the music drift into silence and cease.

Then they rose, and went down to their ship, and aboard, as the Wonderful Head directed them; and Went forward toward Gwalas in Penfro.

"In Gwalas we shall be till the thirteen years are out," said the Wonderful Head. "There I shall be teaching you: the music having prepared you to learn. There is a hall there with three doors in it; and therein we shall abide. The first of the doors looks westward toward Ireland, and through it we shall go in. The second looks eastward toward the Island of the Mighty, and we shall go out through it when the time comes. Those two doors are open, and open they shall remain. But the third door looks toward Aberhenfelen and Cornwall, and has been shut since the sea and the sky and Caer Walas were made. And none of you will open it, if he will do my will."

"What would happen if it were opened?" they asked.

"You would remember every sorrow and loss you have known, and they would seem glad and advantageous beside the loss that would come on you then."

They came in sight of a rock rising skyward out of the sea, and a vast caer at the head of it that had the look of being equal in age to the sea and the sky. "It will be Gwalas in Penfro," said they. "We will go to land."

The sea ran green, and white-flecked under the precipice; gray the sky over the gray caer. They threw out thirteen anchors and furled their thirteen sails; and took the steep path through the gorse to the cliff-head; long they were climbing it, and the caer towering immense above.

At the gate was neither porter nor watchdog; none on guard but olden silence. This had been a house of giants formerly: its peaks were familiar with the clouds and stars. They passed through vast halls and corridors, where all was ancient, gigantic, mute. On the walls hung armor that none but giants could have worn; it was dinted with blows taken in chaos before the worlds were made, yet was no rust nor tarnish on it. No dust had settled anywhere; no wind blew in the salt, wet, iron-corrupting breath of the sea. No wave-sound came there. It was a mute, gigantic loneness, ancient as the sea.

They came at long last to a hall that seemed not unfamiliar, as if they had heard news of it of old, or had dwelt in it in forgotten lives. "Ah," said Manawyddan, "this will be the hall." "This is the hall," said Taliesin Benbardd. For there were three doors in it; whereas in the others they had passed through there had been two, or four, or many. The first was that through which they came in: it looked out toward Ireland. The second, clearly, they would go out by: its aspect was eastward toward Wales. But the third door looked toward Aberhenfelen and Cornwall; and the moment their eyes lit on it, all knew it had never been opened since the sea and the sky and Caer Walas were made.

"Here we shall be," said Bendigaid Fran.

Seven thrones were at the table, and on the dais a pillar of silver and dark sapphire for the Wonderful Head. When they were seated, food and drink were set before them, though no servitors were visible, nor ever a footstep heard. Strange light, not of the sun, filled the hall; and a wandering sound of indefinable harpstrings, better than mortal.

So there they feasted pleasantly, conversing on what had been and what should be. They had reached the Island of the Mighty, and deemed all danger passed.

"Now," said Bran the Blessed at last, "I will tell you the things I know; you shall receive the instruction I promised you."

So he began; and it seemed to them they had never heard anything from him until then. From the Top of Infinity to the Bottom of the Great Deep, he revealed the secrets of time. They had tidings from him of the Lonely One that slumbered in Ceugant: who arose, and chanted the Threefold Name; whereupon the worlds and systems flashed into being more swiftly than the lightning reaches its home.

They had tidings of the Gwynfydolion, the Host of Souls; and of their indignation when they saw the gulf between them and the peaks and splendors of Ceugant from which they were banished; of the war they declared on the Lonely One in Ceugant, for love of Him; and of the oath they swore when they went forth heroically to take Infinity by storm; of the flaming of their long-scythed, starry war-cars that took the untravelled roads of space, and of their war-shout, the grand *hai atton* they cried among the stars. The Seven Chief Chieftains heard it all; and seeing and hearing it, their souls were exalted within them, and their memories loosened from the thraldom of time.

"When was it we came in here?" said the Wonderful Head, breaking off.

"An hour since, or two hours," said Heilyn ab Gwyn.

"Put your hands to your chins," said the Wonderful Head.

Their beards, that had been close-shaven when he began to teach them, now were flowing down over their knees. They looked at each other marvelling; it was the first news they had had of the growth of them.

"A year and a day I have been teaching you, and now I desire rest," said he. "Be in silence now tonight and tomorrow, musing over what you have heard."

Till that moment they had known nothing of changing daylight and darkness, because of the marvels they had been hearing; and because of that unknown light in the hall that made things even; and beyond that, because of the light from the eyes and forehead of the Wonderful Head. But now Bran the Blessed was silent, and veiled those radiances; and it was dark in the hall between nightfall and dawn, but for what light came from the brow of Taliesin Benbardd, and from the wan moon and stars. In that hush and dimness they brooded on what they had heard from the Blessed One, turning and turning it in their minds; storing it, as the bees in their skep the gathered honey. So again during the day; until for wisdom, valor and insight, they wondered were they indeed the same men they had been when they came there.

"It is evening," said the Wonderful Head; "and time for feasting again, if you are to keep your health."

With that, fresh food was set before them; and it was even better than what they had had the year before; and even less did they know whence it came, or how. Until midnight they were at conversation; but one by one grew silent, leaving his turn for speech to the Wonderful Head of Bran the Blessed, who then began revealing his wonders again, making his secret glories known. The wandering music rose, and hummed and rippled to his chanting; and the light shone through the hall, bright or dim according to what he told. From the Top of Infinity to the Bottom of the Great Deep, worlds on worlds flowed forth before their vision on the soaring hwyl of his speech. They heard the grand *hai atton* of the Blessed Ones; they saw their long-scythed chariots gleam as they rode forth from the Circle of Gwynfyd and Bliss. They saw them take the steep of Abred, daring the untraversable void — and the waters of Abred that rose and encompassed them, so that their beauty was fouled and their magnanimity encumbered with oblivion. They saw the worlds and starry systems spin forth winging out of hollow nothing — and the Host that rode forth, imprisoned in the worlds, taking shape on shape through many ages, until they attained their congenial human form. Magical words were framed between the tongue and palate of Bran Fendigaid; it was all made clear to their vision; it was not like hearing a tale told.

He would have been speaking barely an hour, they thought, when he broke off again. "Go you to your musing and meditation," said he. "The second year is passed."

So the twelve years went by, and he teaching them; and eleven of the twelve days over and above, and they brooding on what they heard; until he had given them at last all that was written on the Three Hazel Rods that grew out of the grave of Einigan the Giant; and that, heaven knows, is all that can be known.

"There will be this one night of musing and meditation further," said he; "and then I shall reveal to you the Three-fold Name itself. And when the sound of it is framed between my lips, I shall have a body, the best in the world; and in great joy we will go forward to London. And I shall hold sovereignty in London from that out through the ages until the coming of my son, Arthur Emperor. The Cymry will be fortunate: all shall have their just reward."

THE NIGHT passed; and immense joy with six of them; they thinking of all they had learned, and the grandeur that was to come. Morning came, and with it their joy increased. And afternoon, and soon, they would be hearing the last wonder and mystery of the world, the Threefold Name for the crown of their wisdom. The sun was very near the rim of the sea; the fall of dusk was at hand.

But there was that Heilyn ab Gwyn Hen: he was the most impetuous of warriors and horsemen. "Why do we wait?" thought he; "with this wisdom one might conquer worlds. Evil on my beard if I wait!" He rose from his throne at the table, and lurched towards the door nearest to him; eager to be enveloping the world with his wisdom. And in an instant he put forth his impetuous strength, and flung the door wide upon its hinges.

A gray bird flew by screaming; the shrill scream filled the hall and wailed through the palace afar. Hollow was the noise of falling armor; hollow and mournful through halls and corridors: the ancient armor of Caer Walas clanging and shattered on the flagstones. The rain-wet wind blew in, salt-laden, from the melancholy, gray-green, heaving leagues of the sea. Ruin had come upon Gwalas in Penfro: crumbling on the stones that were mortared before the world was made. Worst of all, the beautiful life and the glory were gone from the Wonderful Head.

In a moment they were aware of hostile presences in the hall; and none knew whither to turn or how to oppose them. Then they saw what had befallen: they looked out southward through the door Heilyn had opened: they looked out toward Aberhenfelen and Cornwall, through the door that till then never had swung on its hinges since the day the sea and the sky and Caer Walas were made.

"It is failure," whispered the Wonderful Head. "Go you now in haste to London. And bury the Head in the White Hill in London, and the face turned towards France. I shall not come by reigning in the Island of the Mighty until the end and head of innumerable ages."

So they went forth, according to his bidding. They went, remembering all the losses they had ever known. Nothing seemed to them to have been evil in comparison with the loss of the Wonderful Head.

Here is the First Branch of it, namely
THE WYDDFA MOUNTAIN

I. The Gorsedd of the Gods

WHILE the seven Chief Chieftains were with Bran the Blessed on the sea between Harlech and Gwalas, the Gods were at Gorsedd on the Wyddfa. For the sake of the Cymry, and to guard the Island of the Mighty, they held their Gorsedd. They knew what depended on Bendigaid Fran's coming into the kinghood. So Tydain Tad Awen, their Archdruid, called them to the Gorsedd Circle, the morning the Seven and the Wonderful Head set out from Harlech.

"*A oes Heddwch?*—is there Peace?" said Tad Awen from the logan stone. When the Gods held Gorsedd, Tydain had precedence over Hu the Mighty himself.

"Peace!" they answered; and the Gorsedd went forward. By virtue of their Godhood, they were all Institutional Bards.

At that time Math fab Mathonwy was the Chief of the Ovates, because none was better than he at magic and science and learning. "Better to put some wonder in the hall at Gwalas," said he. "It would be a protection for the Seven."

"The White Shield might be put there," said Hu Gadarn. It was Hu who was appointed to be Emperor over the Gods and the Cymry; and it was by virtue of the White Shield he held his sovereign power. It was the chief and holiest of the treasures of the Gods of the Island of the Mighty at that time.

They did not hear his proposal with acclamation. "Lord Mighty One," said Ceridwen the Great Mother, "if there should be failure?"

"If there should be failure, and the Shield lost, it would be the end of our dominion in the Island of the Mighty," said Tydain Tad Awen.

"Part you not with the Shield of our Preservation!" said the Gods.

Plenydd, Alawn and Gwron, the Three Primitive Bards of the Divine Gorsedd, were standing by the logan stone, as the custom is with them at Gorsedd, whether of gods or men.

30

"Lord Archdruid," said Gwron Gawr, "let not the treasures of the Elder Gods be imperilled. Leave you the guarding of Caer Walas to my two brothers and me!"

If one of those three had spoken, it was as if all had spoken.

"What would you three Prif-feirdd do?" Tydain asked.

They answered in order, the three of them:

"I would put my breastplate in the hall there," said Plenydd. "Well known are its powers and peculiarities,"

"Yes they are well known," said Ceridwen. "But is there anyone who might steal it? Among the hellions and the men of Uffern, is there anyone?"

"None but Tathal Cheat-the-Light," said Plenydd. "And there is no door open through which he could come into the Island of the Mighty."

"No," said Math; "but he could come in through the door in Caer Walas that looks out towards Aberhenfelen and Cornwall, were it opened."

"No one has opened it," said Plenydd, "since the sea and the sky were made."

It seemed to all that it would be a good protection; and Hu Gadarn himself was not averse to its being used. "Although," said he, "there may be danger."

"I will tell you," said Alawn the Songs, he who presides over Music and Hearing, as Plenydd does over Color and Sight, "there would be less danger were the harp there also. Well known the powers and virtues and protective peculiarities of this little three-stringed harp."

It could bring sleep or waking, whichever were desired; and it could so exalt the soul that the body would have little need of food while it was being played.

Said Ceridwen Ren again, "Is there anyone might steal the harp? For every strength there is a weakness."

"No one," said Alawn, "or as good as no one. None in all these worlds save Gwiawn Cat's-Eye the Sea-Thief; and he has no power to set foot in the three Islands of the Mighty or in the three islands near thereto, nor in the Island of Ireland There is no door by which he could enter."

"There is the door that looks out towards Aberhenfelen an, Cornwall," said Math. "Whenever that door may be opened he will come in."

But it seemed to them that there would be very little danger at Caer Walas, with the breastplate there, and the harp also.

"I give permission for it," said Hu the Mighty; "but there will be danger, and grave danger."

"Sure you now, Lord Mighty One," said Gwron Gawr, "there will be no danger at all when my two gloves are there likewise. I had it from Arianrod Ren that by them the Sea-Thief will come by his defeat. Here's how it will be with the Seven, and these three treasures in the hall with them. Plenydd's breastplate will be light for them day and night, and insight, and causing all they hear with Bran the Blessed to become visible before their eyes. Alawn's harp will be waking and vigilance for them, and their nourishing with music; and no need of a hand to be on the strings. As for my gloves, they will be strength and endurance –"

"The Seven are not weak or fickle, Lord Heartener of Heroes," said Gwydion. "They are the best of the Cymry."

"Yes," said Gwron; "but there may be impatience, over-eagerness, careless and excessive ardor. Common those faults, among the Cymry; and these gloves would be the restraining of them."

"Is there danger of theft?" said Ceridwen. "Is there any man gifted to steal the gloves?"

"Llwyd ab Cilcoed could steal them," said Gwron. "And I would recover them when they were stolen."

"The peril is great," said Tydain Tad Awen. "Llwyd ab Cilcoed is in these islands already; he may go where he will through Dyfed, since Pwyll failed on Gorsedd Arberth. Were the gloves in the caer at Gwalas in Penfro he would steal them: he could go in through either of the opened doors. And it might be a thousand years before you recovered them, with all Uffern for him to hide in."

"Were we three on guard at Caer Walas there would be little stealing for any of the hellions," said Gwron.

"On guard there you may not be, nor any of us," said Hu Gadarn. "It is the Cymry who must carry this out, and not the Gods. Success comes never when we do too much and men too little. I withhold my permission to put the gloves in the hall. The breastplate yes, and the harp yes; for we may lend men insight and the inspiration of music; but the gloves no, for the strength must be their own."

Gwron Gawr sighed. "Well, well," he said, "it is always the Cymry who set bounds to our power."

Then Plenydd and Alawn rose, two beautiful dragons in the air, and sped through cloud and clear from end to end of Wales, and left their treasures in the caer at Gwalas, and came again to the Wyddfa.

During the twelve years the Gorsedd went forward. The Gods left nothing undone that they might do. At last they saw the door that looked towards Aberhenfelen swing wide on its hinges; such far-seeing is little, with them. They saw ruin come up from the sea and lay hold on Gwalas in Penfro; they heard the clang of the armor when it fell and was shattered; they saw the crumbling of the stones that were mortared before the world was made.

"There will be trouble out of this," said Hu Gadarn "What news is with you, Alawn the Songs?"

"The harp is stolen," said Alawn. "I saw Gwiawn Forleidr go in through the door that looks toward Cornwall; he will have full power now in the Island of the Mighty. For me there will be nothing better than idleness, and to abide alone in Dinas Alawn: no service for the Gods, and none for the Cymry. Beyond vile enchantments, there will be no music in these islands until the harp is recovered; and no power with me to recover it."

"Nor with any of us," said Hu the Mighty. "What is lost through the deed of a Cymro, the deed of a Cymro must regain. The Gods have no power in this."

So Alawn the Songs went out of this world.

"What news with you, Plenydd Splendid?" asked Hu Gadarn. "None good," said Plenydd. "I saw Tathal Twyll Goleu rise up from the sea, and go into Caer Walas by the door that looks towards Aberhenfelen and Cornwall. Now he will work his will in the Island of the Mighty; and I shall be as those Gods are who never came into the world. I shall abide lonely in Caer Ysplenydd, without my rights, serving neither Gods nor men. Contemptible cheatery will be worked against the Cymry; all their insight will be darkened until the Breastplate of Light is recovered. And not with me is the power to recover it."

"Not with you, nor with any of us," said Hu Gadarn.

So Plenydd Splendid took his way out of the world for that time; and the Gods mused on the narrow limits of their power.

"Little can we do for the Cymry," said Hu. "Wage our wars for them we may, from the birth of the world to the death of it: woe is me that we may do no more!" In that way he was musing and considering. "No victory for the Gods, unless the Cymry fight on their side with them," said he. "And now it is the Cymry who must wage this warfare – if there is anyone among them who will desire to do so, and the soul in him great enough."

Then spoke Gwydion ab Don: he is the most laughter-loving of the Immortals, and he has most dealings with men, for some reason. "There is one that will desire to do it," said he; "and that will be great-souled enough. If he sets out to do it, he will come by success."

"Perhaps indeed," said the Mighty One. "Who will it be, Lord Gwydion ab Don?"

"Manawyddan son of the Boundless it will be," said Gwydion. "The one for whom we planned to gain immortality, the time I took stag-form from the wand of Math my Teacher."

"He failed three times on Gorsedd Arberth, when we made trial of him," said Tydain Tad Awen.

"Unknown whether he would come by success in this," said Math fab Mathonwy.

"It is doubtful, in my deed," said Mabon ab Modron.

"Not doubtful, in *my* deed!" said Nefydd Naf Neifion the Prince of the Sea. "He will be remembering Arberth in Dyfed, that he has not seen these many years; and nothing else will seem to him desirable. Common with the Cymry to be hankering after their own land."

"Well," said Hu Gadarn, "it may be that he will be desiring to get back the breastplate and the harp –"

"Lord Mighty One," said Gwydion ab Don, "I pledge to you my wand of alder, and the nails of Welsh gold in it, that he will desire to get them back! He will undertake it of his own free will. Let him but hear of these three Persecuting Kinsmen, Gwiawn, Tathal and Llwyd, that are out against the Cymry, and he will be for going against them, without request or suggestion made to him. He is one to forgo praise and delight, renown and glory, kingship and honor, for the sake of the Gods and the Cymry. Better than the world with him, is doing service for these two races. Let trial be made of him, and you shall see."

"It would be Godhood for him, if he came by success in it," said Hu Gadarn. "It would be the immortality we planned to gain for him, long since."

"Come by it he shall," said Gwron Gawr. "My two gloves he shall wear on his hands, and my strength shall flow through his limbs; and for the one blow he strikes, I will strike two."

But Hu the Mighty gave no heed to Gwron Giant at that time. "Where is Arianrod Ren ferch Don?" he asked.

"I am here," said Arianrod. It was she that turned her wheel in the heavens, to know what should be and befall.

"Turn you the wheel, if it please you," said the Mighty One, "to know shall we make trial of Manawyddan."

She turned the wheel and read the fates from it. "Here is what shall be," said she. "Let the trial be made: let news be given Manawyddan of the three Persecuting Kinsmen. If he is for going against them, well enough: let him know that it is they who have stolen the harp and the breastplate. But if there is anything else he wants besides the news and the knowledge – that will not be well."

"What will it be?" said Gwydion. "Make known what it will be."

"Here's what it will be for you, Lord Brother," said she. "It will be loss of the wand you pledged to the Mighty One; and loss therewith of your godhood and immortality."

Said he: "If trial is made of Manawyddan, and he is willing to go against the Persecuting Kinsmen, but desires help from us first; and that help to be given by us, and not earned and won from us by him: I am to lose my wand and my godhood and my immortality?"

"Yes," she said; "that is what will be."

There was consternation with the younger Gods at that. "Run you never this risk!" said they. "Serviceable is that wand of yours; delightful is your presence here in the Wyddfa. Long mourning would be for the Island of the Mighty, Gods and men, were you to lose your immortality and your godhood."

"Is the fate acceptable to you, Lord Gwydion?" said Hu Gadarn. "You yourself must say how it shall be."

Gwydion laughed. "Yes, sure, Lord Mighty One!" said he. "Acceptable and more than acceptable."

Therewith he parted with his wand and his godhood; and death, they say, might have taken him at any time then.

"And attend you now," said Hu Gadarn. "I will put obligation on the Dragon Kin; on you, Lord Gwron Giant, and on all of you. The fate of the Island of the Mighty shall not depend on the Immortals in this. We shall make trial of Manawyddan; if he succeeds in the trial, and goes forth, and brings back the harp and the breastplate, and saves the Cymry from their ruin, he shall do it without help from us. Ungracious it would be in us to enfeeble their long generations to come by interfering now."

They considered it would be some old wrong-doing of theirs before their immortality was gained, that was the cause of such restrictions being put on them. All were silent except the Prif-fardd Gwron.

"Great was my desire to help Manawyddan, and to have my gloves on the two hands of him," said he.

"Withhold the gloves!" said Hu Gadarn. "Help not, but rather hinder him: put labors on him, and it will be better. If he come to you for the gloves, let him win them from you difficultly in battle or not have them at all. And come to you he well may; for he will need good equipment for the work that is out before him."

So the council of the Gods ended. But Hu Gadarn called Gwydion to him after the rest had gone. "Lord Gwydion," said he, "I am in need of your services, whether you are immortal or not."

"Have them you shall, pleasantly enough," said Gwydion.

"Here is my need then," said Hu Gadarn. "Let the Yellow Calfskin Mat be put in the Cave of the Trials, and let Manawyddan be led to the cave."

Gwydion went on his way, eager enough to be obeying the Mighty One. There was no taking dragon guise for him now: no journeying brilliantly through the blue of heaven. Wandless, on foot, and mortal he went.

Then Hu Gadarn fell to his musing again. "Immortality itself I will offer Manawyddan," said he. "That will be the trial."

II. *The Yellow Calfskin Mat*
in the House of the Spinning-Woman of Arfon

THEY BURIED the Wonderful Head on the White Hill in London, and the face toward France; as Bran the Blessed had directed them. No word came from one of them as they went down from the caer in Gwalas, and boarded their ship, and landed presently, and rode with bowed heads to London through the rain.

After that, Manawyddan fell to remembering Dyfed, his own land; and wondering would he be allowed to go back there at last, after all those years of his absence; and about Rhianon his wife and their son Pryderi; and how it would be with Pendaran Dyfed his penteulu, and the men of his household, and with the Dimetians his people. He would make trial of going back, he thought; although there was no knowing. He parted from his companions, and rode into the west.

At the Ford of Hafren a Youth overtook him, and greeted him pleasantly and kindly with the greeting of the god and the man; and Manawyddan searched his memory where he would have seen that Youth before. But he could get no news of it at that time.

"Is it to Arberth in Dyfed you will be riding?" said the Youth.

"It is," said Manawyddan; "if I shall."

"With whom, shall you or shan't you?" said the Youth.

"With the fates," said Manawyddan, "and with the Mighty Ones in the Wyddfa."

"Well, well; come you with me, and we will make trial of it," said the Youth.

Manawyddan thought by that, that his companion would be riding into Dyfed with him; and the trial would be, whether they should come there or be turned aside by the way; for if the fates and the Gods were against it, turning aside there would be. So much Gwydion's saying meant to him; but Gwydion himself had another meaning. So it happened, as they went forward, that if Gwydion was riding on the left, he would be edging his horse to the right; and if he were riding on the right, he would be half turning northward ever, and causing Manawyddan to follow him. But such were his conversation, his singing and laughter, that he might have led an army south that desired to go north; and not one man in it would have known or noticed.

So they came, the second evening, among lofty mountains; then Manawyddan drew rein. "Soul," said he, "into Arfon, not into Dyfed, we have come."

Between Dyfed and Arfon is the length of universal Wales. A great gloom of clouds hid the sky entirely; above them in the pass, the pines tossed under the shrieking wind.

"Arfon?" said the other — "Arfon?" and then, "Evil on my beard (he was clean-shaven), the way is unknown!"

Darkness covered away the great heights of Eryri; and those two wandered through the darkness and the blinding storm leading their horses. The wind howled down the pass, and their cloaks were blown out wide over their heads or back from their shoulders; rain beat and beat against them. They stumbled on and upward; and presently must leave their horses under what shelter they could get from a rock. Hard and soft, rock and bog, it was hateful travelling for them, heaven knew! At the worst of it they saw a glow and flicker above; and soon, in a sheltered windless place, the door of a cottage open.

Within, and facing the fire, and her back and right shoulder to the doorway, a woman sat at her wheel, spinning; beyond her, on one side, was the like of a sleeping-bench, on the other, the flicker and shadows running away into darkness; so that there was no telling whether the place was large or small.

"Soul," said Manawyddan without entering, "the greeting of heaven and man to you, courteously and kindly!"

"I greet you," said she; not looking up nor turning from her spinning.

Wild was the storm he had come through; the room was poor enough: the walls without hangings, no skins covered the earthen floor. A free Cymro would go in, at any time, into the house of slave or freeman, noble or chief; and would be expected to go in, and ill-considered if he did not. But there was an aspect of dignity with the Spinning-Woman; and some kind of hesitation took Manawyddan, as to whether it would be fitting for him to enter.

"Is there coming in, and taking shelter here?" he asked.

"If a riddle is guessed," said she.

"Of your courtesy, propound you the riddle."

"It is, *A Nettle for the Nameless,*" said she.

"Not difficult to know that, since nameless I have been, and came by nettles," thought Manawyddan. Then he answered her: "Before the nameless can come by a name he must be in the Caldron of Ceridwen. Therein, I know, are nettles; and they are for sorrow."

"Enter you," said she, "and be at peace."

So he went in and stood drying his cloak at the fire, facing the Spinning-Woman, and the fire between them. As for the Youth that had come with him, he was not there, and Manawyddan had forgotten him. With the Spinning-Woman's bending over her wheel, and the uncertain light, and the smoke of the burning chaff, he could see little of her face, to know was it mortal or immortal; but he thought it would hardly be mortal. He wondered had any of the Cymry seen it, since the day the mountains were made.

Thus he stood, deep in his musings and puzzled by some mystery: he might not be in her presence, and unhaunted with august unimaginable things. The croon and whir of the wheel grew upon his hearing, until he was no longer aware of the wind in the pass, the storm at leapfrog with the mountains. The wheel sounded to him like the march of time, like the hurrying of years and cycles and ages. The croon and murmur of the wheel possessed him: it drifted to him music uninterpretable by the mind. She turned the wheel and spun, making nothing of his presence. Whenever she drew the thread, he heard what seemed to him an undertone of whisperings from all the quarters of the world.

"Soul," said he at last, "what secrets are written on the thread? What poem is the wheel singing?"

"What was, what is, and what will be," said she.

"Is it allowed to ask?" he said.

"Yes, to ask," said she.

"Will there be, for me, returning to Arberth in Dyfed? Will there be kindly welcome for me from Rhianon and Pryderi?"

Turn and turn the wheel she did; in the flickering fire. light deep mystery surrounded her. He could not tell whence she drew the threads that fed the spinning: out of the gloom and flicker they flowed to her, suddenly glimmering into sight from the unseen.

"Answer you this riddle, and it shall be known," said she, "*The Vervain of Virtue: the Virtue of the Vervain?*"

"Not hard this one, after the other," he thought. Then aloud, "It is the second herb in the Caldron of Ceridwen; and its virtue, sleep and the oblivion of sorrow."

The crooning of the wheel swelled and swayed, like a solemn palpitation of wings. "Sorrow is known, and the end of sorrow," she murmured, as if she were giving the news to the wheel. "The vervain is known, and the virtue of the vervain: there should be gaining this information." Then she glanced up, and he caught the quick shining of her eyes out of the shadows.

"Sleep," she said; "and you shall know."

So he lay down on the sleeping-bench, to which she pointed, and drowsiness came on him. It seemed to him that he slept, but heard always a rumor from the wheel. And presently that the sound drifted from inarticulateness and croon and murmur into human voices and speech; and in his sleep or half-sleep he listened, and heard conversation like this:

"Wherefore is there no entering? Inhospitable is this, and unlike the Gods and Cymry of Ynys Wen. To exclude guests upon a night of storms!"

He heard the voice of the Spinning-Woman making answer: "None may enter until a riddle be guessed."

"Ah, propound the riddle! Propound it—for the wind blows and the rain drives down. Propound it, I beseech you, and let me in!"

It was a low, frightened voice that spoke, with a kind of whimper in it.

Through the croon and murmur of the wheel, Manawyddan thought he heard the Spinning-Woman repeat the riddle she had first asked him: *A Nettle for the Nameless.*

The one at the door replied, "It is not for me; in my deed, it is not for me! Not nameless am I: Tathal Twyll Goleu am I, out of nether Uffern." The voice rose into boasting and braggart pomp. "I stole the Breastplate of Plenydd Splendid, when the door at Caer Walas was opened; and now there is no light nor vision among the Cymry, nor shall be from this out through the age of ages."

A great wind rose, and the voice ceased, as if the speaker had been blown away. Manawyddan at last was able to shake off sleep, and started up.

"Soul," said he; "who was it that spoke? What news was it he gave you of some dreadful stealing?"

"You are here, and I am," she said. "What other is there? Sleep you on: perhaps you were dreaming."

He lay down again, seeking further remembrance of what he had heard. Tathal Cheat-the-Light — Tathal Cheat-the-Light: he was sure he had heard that name. And though his head had been unlighted and his eyelids over his eyes, it was as if he had seen one at the door with white face and round staring eyes m a little man, with strands of uncombed black hair fallen over his forehead, and the ends of his toes and fingers very broad and great, but his limbs thin and ill-formed. And this one had given news of some black peril that threatened the Cymry; and there was stealing in it; there was —

But the croon and murmur of the wheel bore him away into drowsiness and sleep or half-sleep — and at long last drifted into voices again; first, one from the door, with a ripple of laughter in it:

"I need it not, truly: I need no herb for my exploits, vervain or another! Why should I forget? I stole the Harp of Alawn when the door was opened at Caer Walas; I am Gwiawn Llygad Cath the Sea-Thief; since I have the harp, I need no vervain to put sleep on the world with it. Ha! ha! music is lost to the Gods and the Cymry, because I stole–"

A howling of the storm, and the voice was lost on it; and Manawyddan awoke.

"Soul," said he; "who was it stood but now at the door? Who was it gave news of stealing —?"

"Sleep you further," said the Spinning-Woman of Arfon. "It may be that you were dreaming."

He lay clown again, but his mind was in great anxiety. It seemed to him that he had certainly seen a shadowy man at the door, and heard news of some perilous stealing; and he was under apprehension for the Island of the Mighty, as if the whole fate and future of the Cymry were threatened. He turned his face from the light, and forbore to close his eyes. "This time I will not sleep," said he.

But there was that croon and murmur of the wheel to take account of; and its insistence was hardly to be opposed. It was winning upon him and winning upon him; with peace and peace; and oblivion and oblivion; and then, with anxiety and anxiety, until it broke into words:

"What is oneness to me? I came here not for oneness but for sleep. For sleep upon the Yellow Calfskin Mat; that I may break into the Palace of the Gods, and steal the Gloves of Gwron Gawr. Tathal has stolen the breastplate; Gwiawn has stolen the harp; when I shall have stolen the gloves there will be sleep enough for the Cymry, and an end in this Island to the reign of the Gods. Llwyd ab Cilcoed am I —"

On that word, up with Manawyddan, and he leaping towards the door with his sword drawn. But no man stood there.

He turned to the Spinning-Woman. "Soul," he said; "sure you now there was one Llwyd ab Cilcoed at the door demanding entrance?"

"I bade you sleep," said she.

He went towards the sleeping-bench; and hesitated; and came again to the fire. "Ill dreams come to yonder bench," said he. "Three times I have dreamed of peril."

She looked up, and met his eyes with hers. "There is better sleep to be had here," she said quietly, "were a riddle answered."

"Of your courtesy, propound it," said Manawyddan.

"The Three Leaves that are One Leaf: the Third that is for Oneness."

"It is the third herb in the Caldron of Ceridwen; the green shamrock for oneness with the Mother of the World."

"Beyond the fire is a Yellow Calfskin Mat," said the Spinning-Woman. "Sleep you on that, and ill dreams shall not trouble you, but you shall find what you seek."

So he went whither she pointed, and searched through the dimness of the room, by the waning firelight; and wandered on and on, and found no mat; and came to no wall or limit, but only darkness was before him; and turned back at last, and saw the fire far off, a little glow in the vast room, and made his way towards it.

"Soul," said he, "I can find no mat here."

"For whom is the Heal-all?" said she.

"The Mistletoe is for the Mighty One," said Manawyddan. "It is the fourth herb in the Caldron of Ceridwen, and the most wonderful. As they say, *The holy Heal-all is for Hu.*"

"Dost thou see it, now?" she said.

There was a ripple and a twinkle of very dusky gold at his feet. "I see it," said Manawyddan.

It was the Yellow Calfskin Mat; and even among the Gods of the Island of the Mighty there were few better treasures. It is a main privilege for anyone to lie down and seek sleep on it; as now Manawyddan lay down, and drew the edges of it about his shoulders.

III. The House of the Dragon

THE WHIR and croon of the wheel melted into beautiful voices at conversation, and called Manawyddan from his sleep; so that presently, he opened his eyes, and saw the solidity of things about him flowing and changing, and taking new forms and conditions: a mystery that bewildered him for a little.

He rose up quickly, before he should be noticed by the beautiful people in the hall, whose faces and forms were alive with immortal beauty. Only the Spinning-Woman remained of the room in which he had lain down; but now she had the guise of the mightiest of queens.

It was not night but noon; although Manawyddan was certain that he had been on the Yellow Calfskin Mat but a moment or two. Between the pillars of the hall on all sides, and low down to the ground, shone skies brighter than noonday. It was a fair palace on the top of the highest mountain in the world: delightful to be in: an abode of happy kings.

The ten that greeted Manawyddan, as he advanced out of a vanishing darkness into the light of it, were ten Crowned Kings of greater dignity, and much greater, than the Kings of London of old. It was a wonder to his eyes to behold them. Youthful, or in the prime of their manhood, or white with age, there would be no equalling them, nor nearly equalling them, even in the Island of the Mighty. Brighter the eyes of the oldest and wisest, than the eyes of the thrush at song, or sunlight on the sea in June. More nobly aspected the brows of the youngest and merriest, than the brows of Cadair Idris or the Wyddfa or Pumlumon. Majesty and kindly demeanor with them all; but whatever praise might be spoken of any of them, much more would be for the Chieftain at their head.

Heaven knew what memories might be with him; what sorrows he might have known; what wisdom and victories won in the childhood of time and the world. The carved arms of his throne were in the form of two oxen; of the two Exalted Oxen, Nynnio and Peibio, that ploughed Ynys Fel. Above him on the pillar hung a shield without pattern or design: whiter and brighter than Pumlumon in the snow on a cloudless, frosty morning in January.

He rose up, and came forward, and greeted Manawyddan pleasantly and kindly. "The knife is in the meat and the mead is in the horn," said he. "Fortunate in my deed is your coming here now!"

Courteously the others greeted him, and with equal courtesy he returned their greetings. A throne was set at the table for him, and he took his place at the right hand of the Chieftain, and meat and drink were set before him.

"Fortunate is your coming, and pleasant to us," said that one.

"But the manner of my coming is not clear to me," said Manawyddan.

"You shall know," said the other. "Once in every hundred years it is given to a Cymro to come here upon the Yellow Calfskin Mat."

Manawyddan started; remembering suddenly the house of the Spinning-Woman of Arfon, and all that he had heard there: until that moment he had forgotten it. There was something that disquieted him. He put down the food he was lifting to his mouth.

"He who comes here upon the Mat," said the Chieftain, "it is a main privilege for him. He may partake of the food that nourishes ourselves and the immortality in us, and the divine fire that is the blood in our veins. Eat you therefore, and drink; there are many peculiarities with the viands. They are the quenching of unrest and desire; the kindling of godhood in mind and limbs. Who partakes of them, the world in ruin would not shake him; his path is towards the stars, and all below is forgotten by him."

But unrest and lack of ease were on Manawyddan at once; he keenly remembering the three that had come to the door of the Spinning-Woman's house; and remembering it ten times more clearly than he had heard it at first.

"Lord," said Manawyddan, "I heard news in the Island of the Mighty, and must be gone."

"What news heard you? Not well, I warn you, to forgo this feasting."

"Courteous the invitation; courteously it is declined. Not half the praise of the viands will have been spoken. But there are three Persecuting Kinsmen out against the Cymry, and I must oppose them: food and drink will be loathsome to me till I go. Here are who these three are: Tathal Twyll Goleu, and he has stolen the Breastplate of Plenydd, and insight is gone from the Island of the Mighty. Gwiawn Llygad Cath the Sea-Thief; and he has stolen the Harp of Alawn, and there is no music there. A door was opened at Caer Walas in Penfro, and they came in and stole those treasures. And there is a third of them: Llwyd ab Cilcoed from Nether Uffern: he seeks to steal the Gloves of Gwron Gawr. Plenydd, Alawn and Gwron: if you have heard no tidings of them at any time, they are the three Primitive Bards of the

Island of Britain; Bardic brothers, proud and beautiful, the three Disciples of Tad Awen, princes on the Wyddfa with the family of Hu. It was through the deed of a Cymro their treasures were stolen; and therefore a Cymro must win their treasures back for them. They, being Gods, are powerless in this. And so I must hasten back to the Island of the Mighty, wherever I am now; because it is I who must regain the treasures for the Gods and the Cymry."

"Consider you not the Gods and the Cymry!" said the Chieftain. "Forget you the Island of the Mighty. None may have rest or peace, who is given to musing on those things. Eat you with us, and be as we are!"

"Peace and rest I desire not," said Manawyddan; "and I will not have them. Unless I remember the Island of the Mighty, and unless I consider the Cymry and the Gods, evil upon me through the age of ages! It may be they are unknown to you, those two proud races; but they are not unknown to me."

On all sides round were those countless pillars of silver and alabaster; and between them, only the far, deep blue of the middle sky. And now, as he sought a way out, white and blue and silver melted together, and danced, and all was uncertainty about him, and no way clear. So he stood there, eager to go, but not, knowing where to turn. But the Crowned Kings sat with bowed heads and sighed.

"Go not now," said the Chieftain; "it is not the time for going." What magic was in his words, who could say? But the world melted about Manawyddan, and became a silver mist; and when the mist vanished he was seated at his place again. Then the Chieftain said:

"Let these viands be taken away: there would be no taking pleasure in them, and this lordly Brython unsharing. Let stories be told to amuse him, lest we be called inhospitable."

So one came forward; and it seemed to Manawyddan he would have seen him some time; but there was no knowing when or where. "Is it a story you will tell?" asked the Chieftain.

"Yes," said the Youth, "and it will be a good one."

They all applauded at that; knowing well what manner of story it would be, if he said in advance that it would be good.

"Begin you telling it!" said the Chieftain.

"Ah, lord," said Manawyddan, "let it not be begun till you have set me free! Discourteous indeed is breaking away from the hall when the word is in the bard's mouth; but how can I sit here and listen while those three kinsmen are out against the Cymry?"

"I marvel at this," said the Chieftain. Indeed they all marvelled. "Is the skill of the teller known to you? Is the nature of the story to be told?"

"No," said Manawyddan; "but the nature of the Gods and the Cymry is known to me; and there are those three Persecuting Kinsmen."

"Few attain hearing the stories that delight us through the age of ages," said the Chieftain. "Few attain hearing them, while still encumbered with their mortality. And here is one to tell the stories, without his equal at it from the Top of Infinity to the Bottom of the Great Deep."

There was magic in the Chieftain's tones; his voice wound itself round Manawyddan like a spell, till the desirable nature of the stories was made known to him, and more than made known. He was convinced of it as the Chieftain proceeded:

"He will narrate them, and expound them, and cause them to take form before the eyes of the listeners; so that it is better with these, hearing him tell the stories, than it would be to see them enacted by the Gods or the Cymry, or the men of the Emperor Arthur of old. So great is his skill and bardic science, that when he has a mind for telling stories, and prophesies in advance that they will be good ones, the ten words will barely be out of his mouth before the winds of heaven themselves will grow calm to listen to him the better, and this on the wildest riotous morning in March; and the waves of the sea will come peaceably to hear him when the tempest is raging in November.

"Indeed to you now, there is more than this: I have seen the Regents of the Stars lean down from their thrones to heed his chanting; and leaning down they would be, their chins resting in the palms of their hands, during seven times seven ages until the story was told and ended. When he has spoken three words it will be the same to you whether there are three Persecuting Kinsmen, or three times three-score; or whether the Gods retain their dominion, or are hurled into the abyss. Sorrow will be forgotten, and the Cymry will be forgotten, and the Island of the Mighty will be forgotten: the Gods themselves will be forgotten, and all their wars with the demon races."

"It may be," said Manawyddan. "But I am a man out of the Island of the Mighty; I am a Cymro out of Gwalia of the warlike hosts. Were the Gods forgotten, there would be no virtue or beauty in Ynys Prydain. And forgotten they would be, if those three foemen flourished. Dishonor would be better with me than listening to such stories as would make me forget the rights and dignities of the Gods."

"Churlish is the answer!" said the Chieftain. But the nine other Crowned kings sat with bowed heads, and the tears dropped from their eyes. "Churlish is the answer: I marvel at it. There must be compulsion, and stern compulsion."

Manawyddan rose and drew his sword. "Hospitable you have been, O Noble Ones!" said he; "woe is me that I should make war on the hospitable host. Yet for the sake of the Gods and the Cymry, if compulsion is attempted, vigorous resistance shall be set up against it. In my deed to heaven, I will not forget the Gods."

The Chieftain muttered in his beard, "You shall not; and much less shall they forget you." But Manawyddan got no hearing of that.

Then the Youth who would have told the stories stood forth. "Mighty One," said he, "grant to him the beholding of your ring that gives vision. In consideration of his stubbornness, let this privilege be granted him."

The Mighty One mused a little. "Lords Brothers," said he, "shall my ring that gives insight be shown? Is it your opinion now, that vision of immortality shall be granted to the Son of the Boundless-without-Utterance?"

"It is our opinion," said they.

"The ring shall be shown," said the Chieftain. "But not the ruby in it that gives memory of the vision." He turned the ring on his finger, that the ruby might be hidden, and lifted his hand.

A light flashed forth, encompassing the universe. Knowledge broke upon the mind of Manawyddan: his two eyes became gifted with insight. The hall and the silver and alabaster pillars became all wrought of empyreal immaculate flame. He beheld the flamy forms, the august splendor of his companions. He knew the Chieftain for Hu Benadur Byd. He knew Tydain Tad Awen, the Archdruid; and Math fab Mathonwy, the Enchanter of the Gods. The three disciples of Math he knew: Gwydion and Amaethon and Gofannon, the three magnanimous sons of Don. He saw Gwron Gawr the Heartener of Heroes; but Plenydd and Alawn he saw not. And Menw the son of the Three Shouts, who first awoke at the Chanting of the Name. And Idris Gawr the Marshal of the Stars; and the Blessed Bran fab Llyr; and Nefydd Naf Neifion the Prince of the Sea.

Other Gods he beheld there, with azure plumes and crowns, with wings of silver and orange and purple: Einigan the Giant; and the Sons of Nudd, and the Sons of Nwyfre, and Lludd with the Silver Hand. And Mabon the son of Modron (at three nights old he was stolen from between his mother and the wall; and after seventeen ages of captivity he was released by the Men of Arthur and the five Ancients of the World). And the golden-chained Princesses of the Immortals, and the Mothers of the Masters of the Mountains: Ceridwen Ren ferch Hu, and Malen Ruddgoch the War-red War-Queen, and Arianrod the daughter of Don, the Spinning-Woman of Arfon, and Don Ren herself. Modron the mother of Mabon, and Creiddylad the daughter of Lludd; Gwenllian Deg the Majestic Maiden, and Branwen the daughter of the Boundless.

With his two eyes he beheld them all, and kindly affability on their eternal faces. As for the palace, he knew it now for the Wyddfa Wen, the House of the Unperishing.

"Now," said Hu the Mighty, "God-life and immortality begin for you. From this out there will be no more need for you to wander among mortals, nor to toil on behalf of the Cymry: no more need to sweat and sorrow as a man in Ynys Wen."

"Lord Mighty One," said Manawyddan, "I request of you a boon."

"Name you it without fear or hesitation," said the Mighty One. "Whatsoever you desire you shall obtain."

"Here it is then," said Manawyddan. "There are three Persecuting Kinsmen out against the Island of the Mighty; and the harp and the breastplate are stolen by them already, and there is peril of their stealing the gloves also. I should take little delight in immortality, thinking of those losses."

"What is it you desire?" said Hu Gadarn.

"Mortality again, if it please you to grant it to me," said Manawyddan. "To go forth armed through the Island of the Mighty, and to overcome the three Foemen, and to restore their treasures to the Prif-feirdd. Were the Gods to suffer loss, I know what it would be for the Cymry."

"Look forth upon this palace, and these companions, and this land," said Hu Gadarn.

"I behold them," said Manawyddan. "Glorious are the faces of the Gods: but it would be a sorrow to me to gaze on them, remembering sorrow on the faces of the Cymry. Glorious is this palace; unequalled in the worlds; having the pure beauty of the sun. But I should have no peace of mind in it for dreaming of grief in the cottages of Ynys Wen. Better the delights of this region than anything in the world; but better than them all, with me, to cross the silver wave of the Teifi, and to set foot in Emlyn or in Cemais of Dyfed, the knowledge in my heart that you, the Immortals, had suffered no loss, and that none was left with magic to oppress the Cymry."

"It would be well to take thought," said Hu the Mighty. "Were such a choice made, there would be waning from the eyes of their present vision, and ebbing of immortality from the limbs, and memory blown from the mind of all that had been seen here. There is much for any man to consider, in making such a choice as this."

With that, such vision came on Manawyddan, and such knowledge, as Hu Gadarn desired. He looked out over the mountains of Arfon — and they with their divine aspect, as the Gods behold them when they desire to behold wonder incomparable; not as they appear to the imperfect eyesight of man. There was little that was not disclosed to him, from there up to the utmost, tremulant, gleaming throne of Loveliness Eternal. He felt the immortality in his veins: there was no part of him, limbs nor mind nor heart nor imagination, that was not filled with an onrush of delight: delight in his whole being, like the sea-wind swelling and singing in the ship-sail when sunlight is glittering on the foam-capped wave. And he remembered mortality, and the little knowledge that is given to it, and the deceits imposed on it, and the continual impingements of pain and grief.

"Indeed there is much to consider," thought he.

"Will it be manhood or godhood with you?" said Hu the Mighty.

"Lord Hu," he answered, "there is Rhianon Ren ferch Hefeydd, and she a mortal still among the Dimetians."

"Not so," said the Mighty One; "she is immortal already. The door of the Wyddfa has never been shut against her."

"Lord Hu," said Manawyddan, "there are Pendaran Dyfed and the men of my teulu."

"It will be granted to you," said the Mighty One, "to go on dragon wings into Dyfed, and to behold there all you desire to behold; and thereafter to lead the men of your teulu, gay, triumphant, singing, to the gates of this mountain; and to bring them in here to share in your immortality."

Delight flashed into the heart of Manawyddan such as he had never dreamed of before. "I shall behold the Land," thought he; "I have won this for the men I love." With proud eyes he looked forth on the company of the Gods — and was made aware of an absence from their midst, and beneath their brightness a desolation on account of it; and most of all he was made aware of the peril it would be for the Cymry.

"Lord Hu," he said; "I behold not among this concourse Plenydd Splendid, nor Alawn Alawon with the Harp of harps."

"For what reason are you concerned with them?" said Hu. "Are not the Immortals potent in their own wars?"

"Harp and breastplate are lost," said Manawyddan. "Owing to the deed of a Cymro they were stolen."

The Gods were silent.

"Lord Hu," he said, "white the world for the Island of the Mighty, were Bran wearing the crown of London, and the door unopened through which sorrow came."

The Gods were silent.

"But the door *was* opened," he said. "The Wonderful Head is buried beneath the White Hill in London; sorrow has come into the

Island of the Mighty, and the harp and the breastplate are stolen."

The Gods were silent.

"What was lost on account of the deed of a mortal," said he, "a mortal, and not a God, will have the power to regain."

The Gods were silent.

"Lord Hu," said Manawyddan, "I will take mortality, if it please you to grant it to me."

With that the world was overcome, so far as he knew, with a great white radiance of flame and song that burst forth, and waned away, and died in darkness and silence. But in the Wyddfa, Hu Benadur Byd turned towards Gwydion, and the Gods saw with delight what it was the Mighty One held forth in his hand.

"Take you again the wand of your godhood, Lord Brother," said he. "The Gods can still place reliance on the Cymry."

IV. The Hazelnuts of Long Nourishment

DAYLIGHT shone in through the mouth of the cave, and Manawyddan awoke, and rose on his arm. "Dear," thought he, "marvelous dreams I have dreamed indeed? Then he pondered, searching mind and memory. "But there is no remembering them," said he.

He remembered nothing as to the Spinning-Woman of Arfon, nor as to the Yellow Calfskin Mat, nor the three Persecuting Foemen, nor of the Wyddfa and the Gods there, nor of the choice Hu Gadarn had given him, nor how he had chosen.

He looked back at the day before, and remembered his companion, and the storm, and their coming to ——. But where was it they had come? He could not tell. It was not this cave, he thought, in which now he had awaked. But there, he had been dreaming wonders, and who knew where the dreaming had begun?

"No use to sit here wondering," thought he. "Now to go forward, at last, towards Arberth in Dyfed."

He rose up and went out under the sky and looked forth; and saw the host of mountains, the shining lake, the valleys. "Arfon it is," said he; "naught else is like it, in this world." Then he turned to look at the slope whereon he stood, and back and up toward the peak. "Dear!" said he, "I am on the Wyddfa!" And then, "I have slept in the Cave of the Wyddfa!" So for awhile he was silent, in delight and wonder, worshipping heaven.

Need of food came on him. A hazel tree grew at the cave-mouth on his right; and he plucked ripe nuts from it, and cracking one, ate it. With its passing his lips, all hunger was gone from him; and that was causing him to wonder again, and to think. He had heard tell of the Hazelnuts of Long Nourishment, that grew on the White Wyddfa; and how none might discover the tree that bore them much less pluck nuts from it and eat them, unless he had attained his Bardhood sleeping in the Cave of the Wyddfa. If any man slept in that cave, in the morning he would be dead, or mad, or a Bard in his glory. Manawyddan knew this; and it was putting a kind of awe on him. He was a Bard of the Gorsedd of Ynys Prydain, now.

"And now," thought he, "to set out for Arberth in Dyfed." But first he would fill his wallet with the nuts; as it was the right and perquisite of a bard to do. Down into the valley then, and to swim in the lake under the sun and clear sky; the words turning themselves in his mind, *To set out for Arberth in Dyfed.* There he had been born; there he had reigned; thence, for his failure under trial, he had been exiled by the Law of the Gods; there he had longed to be, these score of years and more. He wondered why, then, he was in no haste to start — found no joy in the prospect? He knew not what should hinder his return; but surmised there would be something.

Considering that she would not be far off he gave a call that she knew to Blodwen his mare who answered it soon with her presence, and he was stroking the white nose of her and smoothing her neck within a score of breaths after his calling. Likewise she was communicating to him, this way and that, her experiences and the deep ponderings of her mind. "You gave me your cloak when you left me," thought she, "according to the nobility of your nature; but this is what befell: within two minutes of your leaving me, the one that rode with you came back, and led the two of us into the stable that is the best in this world, and fed us with oats of heaven in a golden manger."

He mounted then, and rode southward; but not too quickly, because some problem struggling for release was enchained below his mind; but he could find no name for it, nor divine its nature. Only he feared that some peril threatened the Kindred of the Cymry; as if he had heard something, and forgotten it. Suddenly a wonder of delight broke on his hearing, and he drew rein. "Evil upon me unless I know that music!" he cried, shading his eyes as he searched the valley southward. The like of a little dancing star hung low and white far off in the mid-morning: it was Aden Lanach the Beautiful singing: sight and hearing he was blessed with, of the first of the Faery Birds of Rhianon.

"Well, she will guide me henceforth," said he; "whether to Arberth or elsewhere." She circled about him, ecstatically carolling her joy; then made low flights southward, lighting often between, that he might follow her easily. "To Arberth it will be, then," thought he, and followed her cheerfully; but soon his mind was only sure of its unrest again, and its assurance that there would be much before he could come into his own land.

Mysteriously she sang, and sweetly, day in and day out; till he came one evening into Cantref Iscoed, where the Teifi flows into the sea. The sun was going down over Ireland, and soft roses bloomed in the sky as he rode along the cliffs and came over against the Island in the Sea, Ynys 'n y Mor, north of the estuary of the river. There Aden Lanach flew out from the land, and circled round the island three times; and then disappeared: he could not tell where or how. "Evil upon me," said he, "unless that island troubles me — unless I go there in the morning, and see."

But now, first, he would ride on a little, to the cliffs above the gleaming sands of the Teifi. He did; and looked out to the sandhills of Dyfed that shone against the darkening hillsides beyond. Sorrow filled his throat, that for all his longing he would not yet be crossing to the land he loved.

Agleam lay the broad waters below him, hued like daffodil leaves and blossoms, like primrose blooms and the bells of the foxglove; up the valley on his left they were a dim-growing sheen of silver in the midst of the purple and darkly-shining gloom. Beyond that glistening flood, white Teifi the bard-loved, he saw Pen Cemais in its glory towering high above the foam, a proud promontory facing towards Ireland; and eastward from Pen Cemais, his own hills. He would not go forward, up the river to where the ferry plies; although longing filled his heart and throat.

Ah, Dimetian land, what wonder he should have longed for you? Magical land, what wonder? Better to his hearing than any music would be your ousels singing at dawn amidst the bloom of the orchards of Arberth; or the carol of your missel thrush in May in the hawthorns of the upland gardens. Sweet, beyond song to him, even the chatter of marketwomen in the little lime-washed towns; or the high, clear voices of the Dimetian children at play in the twilight in summer. Sweeter than anything in the world the voice of Rhianon in the palace at Arberth — melodious with the wisdom and compassion of the world.

But he would not go forward at that time.

Far into the night he remained there, looking out over the faintly gleaming waters; remembering the delight and beauty of Dyfed, the lovely sound of the Cymraeg on the lips of the Dimetians. "I will rest here until dawn," said he. "In the morning I will make trial of what may be on the Island in the Sea yonder."

And with that, the First Branch of it Ends.

Here is the Second Branch of it, called
THE SERVICE OF PLENYDD SPLENDID, AND THE WARS OF MANAWYDDAN AGAINST TATHAL TWYLL GOLEU

I. The Enchantments of Ewinwen Daughter of the Sea-Wave; and the Counter-Enchantrnents of the Stories of the Island of the Mighty

THE ISLAND in the sea at the mouth of the Teifi stands up like a camel's back out of the blue waters northward from the river-mouth and the black rocks of Gwbert; a little passage of lolling waves between it and the shore of Iscoed. In the whole of it there is no hidden place: every part of it can be seen from Mwnt northward or from Pen Cemais southward beyond the bay; therefore it was a wonder to Manawyddan there could be anything on it to draw him from his course. But he knew that there only would he meet with the cause of his disquiet, whatever it might be.

He rose at dawn, and without a glance southward, rode at once back toward the island, and soon came above the strait. There once more he gave Blodwen her freedom, to graze upon the green wealth of Wales. "But be you within call, here or hereabouts," he warned her.

Below on the rocks he found a coracle drawn up and ready to his hand. Not a wave was on the sea at that time; only a lazy lolling, a dreamy wash and crisping on the rocks. "Here I can launch," said he, coming to a yard-wide inlet between flat rocks low-lying. He did so; and no sooner was he seated than the coracle moved forward of itself, without propulsion of paddle; making, clearly and with strange determined speed, towards the one landing place in the island. "It is obedient," thought Manawyddan: "going where I desire it to go." "Yes, obedient," thought the coracle, "obedient to Ewinwen ferch yr Eigion my mistress, and to Tathal Cheat-the-Light her lord."

He landed, and ascended to the top of the island; wondering why he had been impelled to come there. For some good reason, he never doubted. From that highest point, when he came to it, the whole place was to be seen; nothing was hidden but what might be between the cliff-top and the breaking of the waves below. But as far as he could see, there were only the turf and the fern, the gorse and the heather, the sheep grazing, the sea-crows flying.

Nothing else on the little eastern slope, or the long northern, or the western slope seaward, or the southern that faced towards Pen Cemais and Dyfed. "Better to go to land again, and ride forward," he told himself, "nothing is here." But he did not believe what he said.

Then it chanced that he looked up from that southern slope, and across the bay and the estuary; and beyond; and — he had not set eyes on the green hills of Cemais, the Dimetian hills, and had not set eyes on the grim blue-silver coast of Dyfed southwestward an instant, when a whirling wind blew by and the sun was shattered, and the world about him grew dim and changed, and slowly another world and sky and sun took their place.

It was a garden in a valley, the loveliest in the world; and a population bluebell-slender, daffodil-beautiful, wandering in it, and at their games and diversions. They came about him when he appeared, all graceful, gracious and friendly; and greeted him with birdlike voices, begging him to come with them to the palace yonder; "for Ewinwen ferch yr Eigion is expecting you," said they, "and desiring your presence like the youth of the year desires the sun." So he went up with them; and much in his mind beside the greetings he received and gave. "A marvel," thought he, "if here is not what I came to the island to find; and a marvel if here are not enchantments and perils, and the need for caution above all things."

They came into the hall, and those that were with him cried out, "He is come, Ewinwen Sea-Queen! The Son of the Boundless is come!"

"That is well," said she, coming forward in her beauty and glory. "The knife is in the meat and the mead is in the horn, and never was a welcome in the world like the welcome that is waiting this King from the Island of the Mighty."

Thus she spoke, advancing to meet him, filled with admiration. Cordial also was his mien in greeting her again.

"Friendly is the welcome, and kindly," said he. "Better be it with you than it is with me, in heaven's name."

There is no saying that he did not marvel within himself at the splendor of the hall and the feasting prepared in it: there was nothing like it in the Island of the Mighty in those days; and he had forgotten the preparations for feasting he had seen in the Wyddfa Mountain. But whatever else was in his mind, it was the need for circumspection that was most in it. "There are and have been, feasts and feasts," thought he; "but not well to partake of some of them." He felt danger flow towards him from Ewinwen and from her people; and constructed his plan in his mind. "Entertainment will be needed," he thought; "but not I will be the one entertained." He considered it further. "Yes, entertainment, and brilliant entertainment, as I foresee it," he thought, "brilliant exercise of the mind."

But Ewinwen, the more she saw him, the more she was filled with admiration for him. "A great prince among men," she told herself; and remembered a thousand others of old time, that now wore stone-guise in some far region beneath the sea because her subtleties had been beyond their penetration. There too she hoped to have Manawyddan; and never had hoped anything with such intensity. "Compared with this Prince of the Cymry, poor and mean was the noblest and best of them," thought she.

She led him to a throne on the dais beside her own. The food-vessels were of gold and ruby, of amber and sapphire and malachite; fumes arose from them potent to subdue the senses of man. But Manawyddan distrusted the food above all things; nor would he that any should be offered him; considering it as dangerous to refuse it as to accept. "But there are the stories of the Island of the Mighty," he thought to himself; "few that know them would consider they were without enchantments and powers of their own."

He turned towards Ewinwen before her mouth could open to address him, and began.

"Hirerwm and Hiratrwm themselves would have come by satisfaction here," said he, "although they never came by it elsewhere in their lives. Hunger would have quitted them here, and that before the first of the tables was cleared."

"Hirerwm and Hiratrwm —" Ewinwen began.

"Hirerwm and Hiratrwm, truly," said Manawyddan. "Well known is the story of them in the Island of the Mighty; I marvel that you have not heard of it. They were men of Pengwaed in Cornwall in the days of Arthur Emperor; since the world was made, none else was ever so afflicted with hunger. Which was the hungriest, none could tell: Hirerwm was matchless, except for Hiratrwm; Hiratrwm without peer, but for Hirerwm his brother, in the Island of the Mighty or the width of the world.

"The day they went upon a visit, three bailiwicks provided for their entertainment; and they feasted until noon and drank until night; and then were near death from sheer starvation. When they went into the hail they left neither the hot nor the cold, the fat nor the lean, the sour nor the sweet, the fresh nor the salt, the boiled nor the raw; and at the end it was the same with them as if they had tasted nothing since the Crying of the Name that awoke the worlds.

"Well, well," said he; "I marvel and more than marvel that you have heard nothing of marvellous Hirerwm and Hiratrwm; so valiant they were and so renowned. Speak none of you, of your courtesy, I beseech you; lest the hwyl of this should go from me before I have told you all."

And he went forward, and told that story; using vehemence of noble gesture, and fine and flowing language more chanting than speaking; and the hundred words of its opening had not passed his teeth outward before they had forgotten their hunger and the pleasant viands that were set before them, and whatever designs and enchantments they may have had in mind. As for Ewinwen herself, all she retained thought for was the hunger of those two brothers in the story; nor need that cause marvelling:. Taliesin Benbardd could not so have set forth a story; barely could Gwydion ab Don.

As he told it, Manawyddan himself was astounded. "Not like this," thought he, "I used to tell stories of old." But the truth was, that as he had refused to hear Gwydion on the Wyddfa, he had acquired Gwydion's magic. It was there and then he had received initiation into the subtle craft, esoteric story-telling; though he remembered nothing of receiving it.

So they were overwhelmed with the glory of Arthur; they were terrified with the devouring eagerness of Hirerwm and Hiratrwm. All without understatement he told it; all without a word of exaggeration; minutely according to truth; there ought to be no accusing him. At midnight he was one word from the end. A wailing cry rang out; the light died; the food withered into toadstools and beechmast, the splendid food-vessels into broken shells and the dried leaves of last autumn. As the light died, he saw change come on all the princes and ladies and on Ewinwen herself; but might not see what the change was. In the darkness he heard them scurrying away, with muffled barkings, mewings, and squealings.

Then he looked forth from where he stood. And there was the wholesome bay before him, and below, the mouth of the Teifi. All the waters shone dimmest silver with the starlight and the clouded moon. Beyond them was the dark looming of the Dimetian hills, with Pen Cemais towering above the sea. He could hear the splash and rattle of natural waters below. He was on the highest point on Ynys 'n y Mor, looking down over the whole of that small island, and over the coast, so near at hand, from which he had set forth in the morning. "No wonder I was disquieted," said he.

There he watched till gray dawn came and, presently, the sun over the Island of the Mighty. A mist had risen from the sea, covering everything away; and there came to be whisperings in the mist, and stealthy motions, and soon laughter; then suddenly the mist was blown away; and what was revealed was no longer the natural Island in the Sea, nor was he standing on the highest point of it, or on any elevation in the world; but beside the lake in the magical garden of Ewinwen, whose enchanted woods and blooms and mountains and palace all were glimmering in the timeless beauty of morning.

Down from the palace came Ewinwen and her courtiers to meet him: she the midmost jewel of all the loveliness there. She had it in her mind that she would not be disgraced again, as she had been yesterday: that she would have the stone-guise today on this lordly Brython, and him committed to the depths of the sea, as was fitting. The Nine Manly Games should be her means of accomplishing it. "Onlooking or partaking," she thought, "there will be opportunities." So she had given orders to her people, and made her arrangements.

But when she came up with Manawyddan, she had hard work, with his genial eloquence, to remember her designs. Copious his speech; nimble and powerful his understanding: it was difficult for her; she saw she must manage wisely.

Wise she might be; but he was wiser; and led her hither and yonder, discoursing at large; and she might scheme and plan, but she must admire. It was noon before she had him where her champions were gathered; she had meant it to be early morning. Her people made acclamations at sight of him; they understood well what she intended; and she took courage and expected success ardently, and inwardly grew proud of the excellence of her schemes.

But before ever a word could be put forth towards the furthering of these, the hwyl of great speech came upon Manawyddan, and therewith he was spaciously recounting to them the names and perculiarities of many of the heroes of old and the men of the Emperor Arthur. There were Celi and Cud and Gilla Coes Hydd, against whom no four-footed beast could hope to run the distance of an acre; when he had touched on these lightly, he came to Sol and Gwadyn Ossol and Gwadyn Odyeith; and "virtue would depart from the best of you," said he, "unless you heard about those men. Sol could stand all day upon one foot; and it would ever be a cause of weariness and bafflement to his opponent."

"Ah, me," sighed Ewinwen, "my heart will break!"

"Gwadyn Ossol — if he stood upon the top of the highest mountain in the world, it would become a level plain beneath his feet."

"Unless I hear the rest of this," thought Ewinwen, "I would rather die than live!"

"Gwadyn Odyeith" — and thereupon the bardic gift came upon him: tone and melody and grandeur of speech — "Gwadyn Odyeith: the soles of his feet emitted sparks when they struck on things hard, like the heated mass when drawn out of the forge. He cleared the way for Arthur when they came to any stoppage."

Many might have ended there; but Manawyddan did not end. They gathered to listen to him; and it seemed to them they had never heard a story before. As if Sol and Gwadyn Ossol and Gwadyn Odyeith the Mighty were out before them on the field, performing their wonders, astounding the stars. They saw mountains crushed and flattened, and the rocks of chaos kicked about till night was strewn with stars.

"And I sought to put enchantment on this man," thought Ewinwen, "when there were Sol and Gwadyn Ossol and Gwadyn Odyeith!" Tears fell from her eyes. "I am come too late to the Island of the Mighty," thought she; "there are none worthy of me now." So she mourned, hearing of the deeds of Sol; so had contempt for Manawyddan, comparing him with that one. But when he came to Gwadyn Ossol she forgot even to mourn, and had heed for nothing but hearing; and when he ate his hazelnut, and passed regally from Gwadyn Ossol to Gwadyn Odyeith, and from chanting to singing, and from making it appear that the world was of colored rock and clay, to making it appear that it was of green and roseate and purple fire — she became incited, and indeed inflamed, with noble and far-reaching projects; and through all the joy of listening — and fierce, keen, absorbing joy it was — visions went flashing before her eyes, and plans formed themselves in her mind to impose enchantments on this one and that one: on Sol the Great, and on Gwadyn Ossol the Glorious, and on marvellous Gwadyn Odyeith the Down-kicker of Mountains; she forgot realities; Manawyddan himself seemed to her improbable and fictitious; her mind, impatient and ambitious, strained towards impossible achievement.

The wailing cry rang out; of the seven branches of the Story of Gwadyn Odyeith, four were still to tell; and it was like the wreck of the world for her, to pass to her own place and be without hearing them.

But Manawyddan passed up and down through the fern, and watched the sea ripple and glimmer, and the moon-glossed bay, and the silver mystery of sea-meeting Teifi, and the dark Dimetian hills beyond. "Wonderful," thought he, "were the peculiarities of the Men of Arthur; wonderful and beautiful, indeed, are the stories of the Island of the Mighty: that accomplish all this, and no word of untruth added to them — neither exaggeration nor understatement!"

That night there was wailing among the people of Ewinwen, like the peewit over the moorland remembering what she saw in the happy beginning of the world.

"Why do ye weep?" said the Sea-Queen; "is it not enough that I should be weeping? There is but one broken heart."

"Ah, Princess, the tale was unfinished!"

"Cruel ye are, cruel, to remind me of that!"

"There is more than that," said they. "We are enhungered; it is all these days since we have eaten food."

"Ah, greedy ones! Ah, base! Ye would hunger after food were the last pools of the sea drying! If ye should eat now, there would be no victory for us: this hero would go free: he would never come by reposing where so many of old repose, beautiful in stone and granite."

WITH one story and another Manawyddan beguiled them through six days; and here now is what is told of the seventh morning of his stay there:

"*Nid da lle bo gwell,*" said he, at the moment of his opening his eyes: "Not good, that which may be bettered." He was ill-content with his story-telling, as if true bardism had not been attained. "Saved myself I have; but discovered nothing and nothing attained. Story-telling is good, but song is better; today I will make trial of song."

With that he began raising the songs of Taliesin Benbardd, the best songs in the world at that time. *The Spoils of the Under World* he was singing when the mist vanished, and the natural world with them, and when Ewinwen and her people came down from the palace to greet him. Hushed they came, in awe of the singing and its glory. All know that these songs are magical, and can put compulsion on the stubborn nature of man. When he came to the fourth verse of *The Spoils of the Under World*, to *Ni obrynaf lawyr*, they must join in and take up the song with him, and go on singing. Not all at once: the stronger they were, the longer they might keep silent. He passed from that to *The Consolation of Elphin*, and at the end of that, Ewinwen herself was singing, and singing fervently. He passed to *The Battle of the Trees*:

I have been in many a shape
Before I attained a congenial form,

he sang. When he came to:

I was enchanted by Gwydion
The Purifier of Brython,

the beauty began to die away from the singers, they bowed their heads and grew dumb; all but Ewinwen, who swayed to the tune like a poplar to the breeze, and could not be silent. He passed from *The Battle of the Trees*, and came to The Cattle-pen of the Bards. Trembling took the Sea-Queen, but she might not stop singing; in white premonition of evil she sang on with him. When he came to:

I am a Druid, I am a Serpent,

the words broke from her pale lips miserably, and she might not continue, for she knew that she had lied. Whereas Manawyddan had had his initiation into Druidism in the Cave on the Wyddfa, and might sing the line and make the claim without fear or exaggeration or the shadow of falsehood. The wailing, shuddering cry rang out, though it was but noon; palace and gardens vanished, and she and her people with them; and Manawyddan stood alone on the highest place on Ynys 'n y Mor.

"But," said he, "it is doubtful if it would be safe to return to the Island of the Mighty yet."

II. The Peculiarities of the Treasures of Ewinwen ferch yr Eigion, and the Counter-Peculiarities of the Insight of Manawyddan

CONSTERNATION took Tathal Twyll Goleu; anger took him; he upbraided Ewinwen, his handmaiden, and she with little to say in her defense.

"Wherefore is stonehood unimposed on Manawyddan? He goes up and down to destroy us; and thou art here to destroy him, and destroyest him not. He may not refuse or accept anything from thee, or stone-guise is on him; yet thou offerest him nothing."

"Eloquent he is; there is no withstanding his eloquence. He set forth all the stories of the Island of the Mighty, and expounded them; and there was such flashing and flaming in the words of them, and such flow and rhythm in his voice, that there was no interrupting nor questioning him."

"Thou knowest what powers I have given thee. When he told the stories, he was thine to impose stonehood on him, and to sink him in the sea beneath Pen Nant Gofid on the confines of Hell."

"Hadst thou but heard the stories, and him telling them —

"I should have heard exaggeration from him, or understatement; the color of this man's garb had been wrongly given, or the length of his leap an inch too little or too much. Let anything be spoken inexactly, and thou hadst but to confront him with it."

Ewinwen laughed a little. "Hast thou naught else to taunt me with? I have enhanced greatly the powers thou gavest me. Had he spoken one word inexactly he would have been stone before I had confronted him."

"And now thou hast lied to him: woe is me, it is a grievous thing to lie! Thou didst say thou wast a Druid and a Serpent; whereas heaven knows thou art neither!"

"Powerful are those songs of Taliesin Benbardd," said she. "Heaven and Earth would keep time to them, were a man like he singing."

"Well, powerful or little powerful, now must he get sight of the Breastplate of Plenydd; and if when he sees it he should covet and claim it, there will be no keeping it from him but through prowess of mine own. And if my prowess will serve, heaven knows and I know not."

"Never wast thou one for prowess and valor," said Ewinwen.

"That is true," said he. "Craft and thievery become me better." Her flattery softened him. "Well, well," said he, "there is hope yet, and good hope. Come, I will enhance your powers, and you shall amend all. I will also make you thirteen treasure-houses; a marvel if amidst them all he should find the breastplate. Let him choose; for he will desire a gift tomorrow; let him see all and have what he will. If he choose aught but the breastplate, he is yours: put you the stonehood on him; it is your right. He shall have from dawn till midnight to find it; and if he find it not, impose the stonehood. Go you wisely therefore: hinder him: lead him about: offer him all things: descant upon them. They shall have peculiarities, I promise you; and lying shall be allowed you liberally."

"Yet I would you had heard the songs of Taliesin Benbardd," said Ewinwen.

BUT MANAWYDDAN, pacing the ridge of the island, saw a little star rise over the Dimetian hills in the evening, and therewith heard music the loveliest in the world. "It is the Bird Glanach again," said he. He listened while she, poised above the bay between him and Pen Cemais, sang to him; and clear, harmonious Welsh, to his hearing, everynote of her song became. "Well, well," said he; "I am to take some gift from Ewinwen tomorrow, it seems."

And here, now, is the last day Manawyddan was in Ynys 'n y Mor.

"Lord," said the Daughter of the Sea-wave, "it was for the sake of some gift or treasure that you came to this island?"

"That is true," said Manawyddan. But he had heard nothing from Aden Lanach as to what gift it should be.

"Come you now with me through my treasure-houses, and choose what you will," said Ewinwen.

"Courteous the invitation; courteously it is accepted," said he.

With that she led him into the palace, and into the first of her treasure-houses. If the whole wealth of the world were gathered, it would seem poor to what he saw there. There were swords you would have said were fresh from Pen Gannion, from their forging between the hammer and the anvil of Gofannon ab Don. The least of them, you would have said, would put terror on the champions of Chaos, were a God wielding it along the borders of space: would have put terror on them, and driven them pell-mell.

"One of these might be a good gift for any warrior from the Island of the Mighty," said Ewinwen ferch yr Eigion.

They were beautifully set with jewels: blades with the blue sharpening or the white; blades with the lightning-hued sharpening; blades like the invisible air, and with an edge, you would say, to wound the wind. But all the truth of them was made known to the eyes that had seen Hu Gadarn's ring on the Wyddfa Mountain; at one sharp glance he saw into them.

"None of these I desire," said he.

"Wherefore not?" asked Ewinwen. "They have many peculiarities."

"Peculiarities, yes," said Manawyddan; "and I will make known their nature to you. Who should unsheathe in battle a sword of this making, he would find sorrow in the sheath, and not the sword-blade. There are fallen poplar-twigs in the Island of the Mighty already."

Shields she showed him then, that seemed even better than the swords: whiter than the shield of Hu Gadarn, or adorned in gold and enamel with zigzag patterns and lozenge-work, or with incantations in the coelbren of the bards. "Good defense you would have with these," said she; "they have magical peculiarities, every one of them."

But she might not enumerate the peculiarities; he was ready with his answer. He saw through the best of them to its true nature. "I should have no need of the head of a toadstool," said he, "or of a withered elm-leaf of last Autumn."

She showed him spears then: pointed piercers, three ells in length: hafts of ashwood and silver; heads of tempered bronze and steel. "Behold you, they have peculiarities," said Ewinwen; "it were not wise to pass them by. They will fly out after their lord's foe, and pursue him from the east to the west till he be slain; and then return to the one that loosed them. Hurling never will they need."

But it seemed to Manawyddan that they would need hurling; and that the one who hurled them would be hurling a blade of foolish reed-grass; and moreover a withered one, or one broken by the cattle at the stream. "I choose none of them," said he.

Helmets there were, of great beauty; and all having the look of possessing magical endowments. "They are impenetrable by steel or bronze or spells," said Ewinwen. "The sword forged on Pen Gannion would glance away from them; they would turn the blade Gofannon wrought and Malen Ruddgoch wielded."

They seemed to his glance to be dockweed leaves and curious fungus. It was always with the third glance he saw the real nature of the treasures: the first and the second were deceived, and the fourth glance even more than the first.

"You will not choose a helmet?" said Ewinwen.

"No," said he; "on account of their peculiarities."

She brought him where there were goblets better than the Gods used on the Wyddfa: goblets of opal and amber, mysterious like moonlight on lake water in late Autumn; goblets of gold and sapphire and diamonds, twinkling like the sun on the noonday sea. But at his third glance the moonlight would wane from the opal, the sun-glow from the diamond; he would see last year's acorns and beechmast in their stead, or pebbles and clay-clods, or broken shells from the shore. Regal torques, again, would shrivel into seaweed; jewelled harness into strands of kelp.

"None of these things will be needed in the Island of the Mighty," said he; and if she questioned him, he expounded their peculiarities.

They came into the second treasure-house Tathal had prepared for her; it was ten times larger and better and richer than the first; and he had an even keener insight into the peculiantics of the treasures in it. Nothing could deceive or satisfy him; nor in the third, nor in any of the others until the twelfth, and to the end of the twelfth. That one was so lofty it was a wonder the moon might not journey under its roof and never know a roof was above her. By silver delicate stairways Ewinwen led him from marvel to marvel; by opaline galleries hung like cobweb in the air. His vision saw worthlessness under the best things she showed him. So mounting and mounting, they came at last to the thing that lighted it all: a breastplate like the sun, most beautiful, hung by a golden chain from the far off roof. "It might be the Breastplate of Plenydd itself;" thought he. He had no memory of what he had seen on the Wyddfa, nor knowledge that Plenydd's breastplate was not on Plenydd's breast. He gazed at it, and saw no worthlessness. Unrest came on him; his mind groped towards unrememberable things. Ewinwen watched him, hope growing in her. "Here was no toadstool enchanted," thought he, "no jetsam from a lonely shore." "It would be the pity of pities," she thought, "for such a man to go roaming free, a mere mortal, in the Island of the Mighty, when the immortality of stonehood might be put on him, and he preserved forever in Uffern through my ministrations." High her hopes, tremulous her bosom, at that time.

"Choose it if you will," said she. "I may not withhold it. It would be a wonderful gift for any man."

"What breastplate is it?" said Manawyddan. "Name you its peculiarities, if it please you."

"Have you heard nothing," said she, "of the peculiarities of the Breastplate of Plenydd Splendid?"

And with that all he had seen and heard on the Wyddfa stirred in him and cried to be remembered: it was as if the warning had been shouted on the borders of his mind: *Circumspection!*

"And the Breastplate of Plenydd came here?" said he.

"It came here, and it hangs yonder."

The word of the lie from her helped him to vision. "Let us go forward, in heaven's name," said he.

"You choose not the breastplate?" she asked.

"No," said he; "on account of its peculiarities."

"Rash and unwise is this, truly," said she. "Few would accuse or complain of them; many would be content with so wonderful a gift."

"I would not be content," said Manawyddan. "The peculiarity of that breastplate, as I see it, is that on the one who chose it, stonehood would be imposed immediately, and away with him into the sea or into Uffern."

In pity she sighed, and her tears came near falling; she foresaw mortal life and death for him through his stubbornness, and no attaining immortal stonehood. Woe was her, that she could not save him!

At the end of the gallery she lit a torch at the brazier, and struck the wall; whereupon a door opened, and she led him into the thirteenth treasure-house. It was dark but for the torchlight; the floor was deep in dust, and there were broken things strewn over it. There was no seeing walls around or roof above. "There is little here for you to see," said Ewinwen.

He made search till at long last his eye fell on a leaden disk at his feet; bent in the middle, chipped at the rim, and dust-covered. He touched it; and it was a marvel what stirred in him at the touch.

"Give me peace to muse on this disk," said he.

Unrest grew in his mind as he watched it: there were wonders crowding beyond the brink of his thoughts. But the nature of the disk was not known to him, nor why it should hold his mind. Yet with meditation he would discover. But Ewinwen, watching him, thought, "It is near midnight; let him stand there pondering awhile, and I shall have my wish fulfilled."

She could not bear the thought of his going forth and dying in his day. "A beautiful fate: immortal stonehood: I will confer on him." Therewith she got to her enchantments: making pacings up and down and waving her arms and breathing her spells silently. It grew cold: a coldness fit to fashion stones in. "He is deep in his musings," she thought; "he will not hear." So from silence she went to low chanting. The light died from the torch-flame; his mantle hung cold and heavy on him, stonehood infecting it from her spells. But he watched the disk, and struggled only to get knowledge of its meaning.

Though the light was gone, he could still see it: it shone dimly, like a pool in the meadow on a moonless night of stars. "Let the spells go forward," thought he. "With the seventh of them it will be revealed."

She sang five, and the cold weight grew deadly on his limbs; six, and he felt his blood congealing and the power of speech ebbing from his tongue. She began the seventh, and came to the tenth word from the end of it; when he saw motion reflected in the disk; and with that, what stonehood she had put on him already was shaken off, and speech came back to his tongue.

"The black bat among the rafters is the gift I will take from you," said he.

"Woe is me, there is no bat!" said she.

"There is a bat, and it is the gift I will take."

He put the Spell of the Three Places upon her, and therewith compulsion; and it seemed to her the glory of her days was over, and all delight laid low. White and weeping, she took herself to her magic again, and to her wavings and pacings, and chanted this:

Ah, now, come down!
She you made great with spoils of many seas,

Gone is her sovereign ease!
She that was crowned with pearls hath lost her crown;
Autumn is fallen on the Sea-Queen's Garden,
And all the moon-pale fruitage is blown down!

There was a stir among the rafters, and a throbbing of uneasy wings.

There is no choice: light here!
You that did dower me with this rich domain
Shall not go forth again!
Sorrow and night and the unknown worlds draw near;
Autumn hath fallen on the Sea-Queen's Garden,
Fallen are the blooms, and all the frondage sere!

The bat fluttered down, and spreading its wings over the disk, lighted and cowered there. Manawyddan drew his sword. "Unless you desire death without fighting," said he, "assume your natural shape, and quit the guise you are wearing!"

"Little odds to me, with fighting or without it," said the bat; and stood forth then in his natural shape. Instantly Manawyddan remembered the cottage of the Spinning-Woman of Arfon, and the first of the three that had come to the door there; he remembered even the name of that one.

"Is it you, Tathal Twyll Goleu?" said he.

"Yes it is I," said Tathal; "and transmutations and modifications are before me. Do what you will quickly."

"And you stole the Breastplate of Plenydd Brif-fardd?"

"Yes I stole it; and useful it has been to me since."

"Give you me that breastplate, that it may go back to Plenydd."

"Find it you, if you can," said Tathal. He was armed suddenly with some kind of spear, and lunged out at Manawyddan. But uselessly; and useless what else he might try or do. "Well, I am slain by you," said Tathal Twyll Goleu.

Then Manawyddan turned to Ewinwen ferch yr Eigion. "Go you back into thea sea," said he. "There is an end forever of your working harm and injury against the Cymry: you will put stonehood on none from this out through the age of ages. Go you back into your natural element the sea; and have your proper being among the foam of the waves; and desire good for those who have had evil from you; and I will desire it for you also. And all this I command you in the name of the Wood of Math in Mon, and of the Field of Tybie's Well at Llandybie, and of the Wyddfa Mountain of Hu Benadur Byd."

Thus he put the Spell of the Three Places on her again, that none could resist or rebel against in those days. The wind blew in out of the night behind her; far off the moonlight glimmered on the sea. The torch fell down from the sconce where she had set it — and down from crag to crag till it was quenched in the sea-wave. Ewinwen rose up in the air, and floated away like a cloudlet. He stood at the cave-mouth, and watched the cloudlet drift down on to the sea. Then it seemed to him he heard her voice singing; and all that was in the song was her delight in the freedom of the wrinkling sea.

"I understand little of it," said Manawyddan, pondering. "But it was well I came here: that Tathal Cheat-the-Light was an ill one to be in the Island of the Mighty. As for the breastplate, who knows? If indeed Tathal stole it, Plenydd will know how to regain it now."

Then he turned back into the cave and his eye fell on the leaden disk at his feet again.

"It seemed to have peculiarities," said he. "I will take it with me, for a memorial of this."

So he picked it up, and then sat watching at the cave-mouth till the sky and the sea grew gray. Then he picked his way by a steep path to the highest part of the island. Over the Island of the Mighty the east was beginning to glow, by that time, with a thousand tulips of dawn.

III. The Breastplate of Plenydd Sunbright, and Pletydd Sunbright Himself

MANAWYDDAN watched the sky kindle there. Far fields of tulips were opening in heaven; spiritual roses, spiritual daffodils. A wind blew out from the Island of the Mighty, laden with echoes of exultation. From silence, as the splendor pulsed and quickened, song rose and billowed over Wales; a singing host swept westward toward

Ireland. He could see their silver glint and dimness in the sky, their beauty trailing along the wind. Exultant they came, innumerable as snow flakes, until the rising over the mountains of the Master of the Dawn. A fountain of fire, of wonder, of beauty shot up and was scattered over the summit of heaven. Suddenly out of the heart of it, out of the body of the sun, a star, a flame came streaming westward.

A Star it was, a Flame, a Dragon: a regal Dragon with the glory of the sun. Nearer and nearer it flamed: blue-bright, flooding the sky with blue brightness. Lambent wings and curving form, proud neck and sky-sweeping tail: it was adorned with scales better than diamonds; sparkling, light-shedding scales hued like turquoise and sapphire, like the gentian, like the larkspur, like the blue breast of the wave.

Manawyddan stood watching it come, tilting back his head to watch. The leaden disk was in his hand, held horizontally by the edge. And there was a moment when the Dragon was poised overhead; and at that moment a flame of light broke from the disk, and rose wreathing about Manawyddan, and fountained into the sky where the Dragon flew, and played in lightnings about the Dragon.

Then that Sky Lord looked down, and saw Manawyddan with the disk in his hand; and, as if a star fell, in an instant he was down on the island, and his dragon-form gone from him, and in its place the bardic guise and glory of a God. Plenydd Brif-fardd Prydain stood there.

"What news with you, Son of the Boundless-without-Utterance? What news from the Island of the Mighty?"

"This much news, Lord Prif-fardd," said Manawyddan. "There was one Tathal Twyll Goleu here, and he boasting he had stolen a breastplate from you."

"Where is he now?" said Plenydd.

"Dear knows where he is, since I slew him," said Manawyddan. "But as for the breastplate, I am thinking it is here."

"True is that," said Plenydd. "And you would be desiring it for a spoil, since you won it."

"I would not be desiring it, heaven knows," said Manawyddan. "I would be desiring to return it to its natural lord."

Plenydd Splendid laughed. "White your world for recovering it," said he. "I am a God again now, with power to serve the Cymry as I will. As for the breastplate, keep it you until I require it of you."

And with that word he took dragon-form again, and away with him, hurtling through the sky to the Wyddfa Mountain.

"Ah, Lord Prif-fardd, you have come back," said Hu Gadarn.

"I have come back, Lord Mighty One," said Plenydd.

"And the breastplate with you?" said Hu.

"No," said Plenydd; "with Manawyddan it is, the son of the Boundless-without-Utterance. He slew Tathal Cheat-the-Light, and won it back; and it was in my mind he would need it."

"Need it he will," said Hu Gadarn, "before Alawn the Songs may return from Dinas Alawn and music be heard in the Island of the Mighty again. But it will be the same with you as if you had it; and it will be the same with the Cymry."

"Well, now," said Manawyddan, "it will be returning to Arberth in Dyfed for me, I suppose." But the breastplate was over his heart, and he was full of unrest and the beginnings of vision. "I think there will be no returning there yet," said he.

With that this branch of the story has its end. Because it makes known how he conquered Tathal Cheat-the-Light, and sent back Ewinwen, Tathal's handmaiden, to her proper home in the sea, and won back the Breastplate of Plenydd, and desired to restore it to its rightful lord — this branch has the name of

The Service of Plenydd Splendid
and the Wars of
Manawyddan against Tathal Twyll Goleu

Here is the Beginning of the
Fourth Branch of it, which is called
THE SERVICE OF ALAWN ALAWON, AND THE CONTESTS OF MANAWYDDAN AGAINST THE THIEF OF THE SEA

I. The Nine Enchantments of Gwiawn Llygad Cath the Sea-Thief

BLODWEN MARE was grazing on the moor, and the thought in her mind that it was a long time her lord had been gone from her. Then she heard music in the air, the best in the world; and lifted her head, and snuffed the morning. "Dear indeed," thought she, "it is that Aden Fwynach; soon the chieftain will be coming."

Aden Fwynach it was, the third of the Birds of Rhianon; and she was flitting low over the gorse. Before the two of them could exchange the greeting of heaven and man, Manawyddan himself came up from the shore. "Aden Fwynach —!" said he; "now there will be knowing." Knowing, he meant, whether there would be returning to Dyfed for him. He mounted and prepared to follow her. Northward she flew, and not toward Arberth in Dyfed by any means. "It is as I thought," said he; and knew there would be some labor crying out for him to do it; and made little of his longings for his home.

All that day he rode within sound of the sea, and all the next day, fording rivers where he might; and presently he went through Arfon and the mountains, and presently swam the Menai; till he came at last to the long sands of Traethmelyn in Mon. There on the dancing waves a ship of glass glittered; and Mwynach rose from her low skimming, and lighted down on the mast-head. "So there will be putting to sea," thought he: why, he knew not, nor bothered to know before he should be shown.

He dismounted, and gave Blodwen her freedom again. "There is Mon for your grazing till I come again," he told her. She watched him till he was aboard the ship; then went up to the grassland. "No rest for

75

either of us until we come to Arberth in Dyfed again," thought she. "And dear knows when that will be."

But he, as he was astride the bulwark coming into the ship, heard unusual music with Aden Fwynach; and paused there, looking up and listening. As if her notes were clean Welsh for him, he heard warnings in them, and their burden, *Circumspection!* He made question as to what circumspection it would be; and it was as if she answered him: Circumspection inwardly; guardianship over the mind, lest unwary thoughts should enter it: above all, thoughts as to the Breastplate of Plenydd, or as to Plenydd himself, or as to Gwron, and especially as to Alawn the Songs.

"Well, well," thought he: "what helped me once may help me again;" and what he fell to thinking upon was the stories of the heroes of the Island of the Mighty again, and the songs of Taliesin Benbardd, and whatever other stories and songs he might remember; so long as they had no concern with the three Primitive Bards, or with their harp, their breastplate, or their gloves.

A wind blown from the Wyddfa filled the sails of woven glass; the little waves broke and tinkled against the prow; like a swift sea-swallow the ship went forward. Soon there was no seeing Ireland southward, much less the Island of the Mighty behind. "Pleasant, after toil to move over the sea-face with an empty and an idle mind," thought Manawyddan.

But there was that Gwiawn Llygad Cath the Sea-Thief: he was sitting in his own place under the wave, watching the roof of his world for signs or tidings. He was lonely; a certain anxiety was on him: he had heard no news of Tathal Twyll Goleu, and feared ill might have befallen. Then he saw the ship of glass riding the wave-crests, and in it some prince from the Island of the Mighty. "Ah," thought he; "something is here!"

He put forth the powers of his vision, and saw the breastplate, though it was covered with cloak and tunic; and extreme covetousness filled his heart immediately. "Evil upon him!" said Gwiawn, "it is like the Breastplate of Plenydd, so far as can be seen." But he thought of the might and magic of Tathal his brother, and how assiduous he would be to defend the breastplate; and was in doubt.

"If that be indeed the breastplate," thought he, "he that wears it will have conquered Twyll Goleu: and his mind will be well strewn with the warfare."

So then he looked into Manawyddan's mind and memory. He had keen vision, and might do as much as that without stirring from the sea-depths. "Dear," said he, "it is the mind of a fool!" Trailing across it were all things remote and of ancient happening; or it would be void like the blue vacuity of the noon sky on the least cloudy day in June. And nothing was to be learned from the semblance of the breastplate itself; whose outward beaming beauty gave him no news of its inward peculiarities. "Well, well," thought Gwiawn at last; "whether that be the famous breastplate or no, it would be imprudent to leave it unstolen." He was bred in economy — richly gifted in prudence.

He laid aside his own harp, and took the Harp of Alawn instead; since nothing less would serve him if the breastplate were Plenydd's. "I shall know that when it is stolen," thought he.

The blue of the day was paling a little and silvering; the sea-breeze tinkled in the glassy sails, the little blue wave on the prow. Manawyddan sat in the stern of the ship, chin in palm and elbow on knee, and let the wind blow and the sea flow and ripple through his mind; they feeding it with their dreams and memories, and keeping from it dreams and memories of its own.

From here and from there, hiding among the wavelets or in the gleam of the sun on the sea-face, the Thief watched him and examined the breastplate; and the more he watched and examined, the more he was eager for news, and reluctant to steal rashly. Now he was under the stern of the ship, and for sliding an arm up over the bulwark, snatching what he sought, and away with him. But were Tathal slain, how should he learn of the slaying? And to have that treasure in his keeping, and always be in doubt as to its peculiarities: perhaps to put trust in it, and then it to fail him in his need, through not being the thing it seemed?

No! Art must be exercised, and the fine points of thiefcraft; and he must learn more of this man who invaded so gaily the secret places of the sea, and had the guise of a prince of the Brython and the mind, it seemed, of a wandering fool. So the Sea-Thief pondered, perplexed, passing hither and yonder beneath and about the ship; peering up from under the ripple; perplexed, and troubled by his perplexity, the like of which had never afflicted him before; and not guessing at all that it was the Breastplate of Plenydd that was confounding the perspicacity of his vision.

He let the ship pass on from him, but not far; then hid down in the hollow of the waves, and drew out a strand of drifting shoreweed, and shook it in the air: "Be you what I need now," said he. At once it was a coracle floating: light and gracefully formed, like a rose-petal between the wave and the wave. It was little, with him, to be up out of the sea and in his place in that coracle; having first drawn out another strand of the weed, and shaken it in the air, and put his commands on it; till it was the dress of a bard out of Ireland clothing him. Then with a whispering laugh he went skimming out over the sea, and fetched round, and came up to the ship from before.

"Ha, chieftain!" said he, "is there entering the ship?"

"Heaven knows there is entering it," said Manawyddan. "Lonely is the region, in my deed to heaven; better with my soul to go two than one, and three than two, and many than three. No man have I met in all these glittering sea-fields until now: neither horseman nor man afoot. Heaven knows there is entering the ship, and the kindly greeting of the god and the man to the one that enters, and a Welsh welcome to him!"

So the Thief kicked away the coracle from under his feet, and leapt over the bulwark into the prow of the ship, and sat there, facing Manawyddan, with the length of the ship between them: not too far for converse, nor too near for ease of mind. There he sat, the little gold harp in his hands, the strings of which were endowed with the Nine Spells of Music and Magic which, if they were wrought by Alawn, would be the delight and upliftment of all these worlds; but if they were wrought by the Thief, dear knows what peril they would be.

"I shall come to those spells if there is need," thought Gwiawn; "meanwhile — I am not devoid of talents." So he began telling how he came out of Ireland, driven by what fate had been laid upon him after chess; and whither the henwife had bidden him go — to what high caer upraised above the sea-face, on what island silver-pedestalled up from the sea-floor; and no saying but it was an excellent story be told.

But when he looked at Manawyddan, he saw inattention, and eyes out beyond the bulwark, following this and that in the sea; and that was the cause of inattention growing in himself also, and invention waning, so that he could think of no new adventures to relate. Also the breastplate troubled him; and Manawyddan's mind, that gave him no news as to the breastplate.

"Is it from the Island of the Mighty you come?" said Gwiawn.

Manawyddan's gaze came in from the rim of the world and slowly and mournfully fell upon the Sea-Thief. "The Island of the Mighty?" said he; "the Island of the Mighty . . . Either in this life or in my pre-existences I have heard tell of that island —"

"Have you heard tell of Tathal Cheat-the-Light?" said the Sea-Thief. "Is there news of Tathal Twyll Goleu in the Island of the Mighty?"

Manawyddan's mind, however, was well lodged in the story of Cilhwch and Olwen at that time, and it was a refuge and strong place for him. "There was Cilhwch the son of Cilydd, the son of the Prince of Celyddon," said he. "He came to Caerleon in the ancient days, to make requests of Arthur; and not of Arthur only, but of Cai, and Gwrhyr, and Greidawl Galldonyd: all the Arthurians he named, and of many of them, named their peculiarities also. I remember that he named this Tathal Twyll Goleu; but I remember not that he spoke of his peculiarities; only that in all the Island of the Mighty — Ah," he cried, "well I knew I had heard of that island, either in this life or in some pre-existence."

The Sea-Thief looked into Manawyddan's mind, and saw there nothing less foolish than his words: the dreams of the wind, the memories of the sea — wandering vagueness, limitless spaces, wave murmur, crooning confusion. "Give you heed to me, and I will tell you," said he.

Then he set forth all the story of Tathal Twyll Goleu, and how Tathal stole the Breastplate of Plenydd, when the door at Gwalas was opened. "Gwiawn Llygad Cath came in, and Tathal Twyll Goleu with him. A gray bird flew by screaming —"

A gray bird did fly by, and Manawyddan's eyes and mind were fixed on it.

"Dear indeed to you," said he, "it seemed to be a seagull; but it might have been that Tathal Cat's-Eye of whom you speak, and he laboring under enchantments laid on him by the malevolent. Wonderful things will be happening, out here in the wonderful realms of the sea."

"Dear help him better!" thought the Sea-Thief, looking into Manawyddan's mind again and finding it crowded with vague things half forgotten since the early ages of the world. "Many would steal the breastplate and begone: there is no getting satisfaction from a fool." But his former doubts were strong on him still, and so was his inquisitive disposition; and he was ever proud of his tact. Said he then, very directly:

"Make known to me, I beseech you, the peculiarities of that golden breastplate; I have not seen its equal for beauty of design."

But Manawyddan was watching the sea with dreamy intentness. "Ha!" said he, "it is there, it is there!"

"Soul," said the Thief; "it is on thy breast, and not in the sea."

But Manawyddan's mind was full of what he had seen, and might hold nothing but salmon. On salmon he discoursed at large, and particularly on the Salmon of Llyn Lliw, the Fifth Ancient of the World; that with the Eagle of Gwern Abwy, the Owl of Cwm Cawlwyd, the Stag of Rhedynfre and the Ousel of Cilgwri, brought the men of Arthur to where Mabon ab Modron was imprisoned. But he mixed for confusion's sake the Five Ancients together, so that if the whole world had been present, none could have understood him; much less could Gwiawn Llygad Cath the Sea-Thief.

"When he came there first," said he, "there was a crag in the place from the top of which he pecked at the stars in the evening: this was to sharpen his beak. Nine score fish-spears he drew out of his back, as a token of truce and alliance. Every Spring he would swim up the Severn to the gates of Gloucester; in Gloucester they found the prison of Mabon. Neither Lludd Llaw Ereint nor Greid the son of Eri had known such imprisonment. So long had he been there indeed, that the rock was worn down with the tread of his talons till it stood but a man's height from the ground. They stole him at three nights old from between his mother and the wall; none had had tidings of him since. And I affirm to you, in the name of heaven and man, that of those nine-score dreadful fish-spears, the worst was no worse with him than the pricking of a thorn. Well may you say peculiarities, in my deed; and wonderful peculiarities!"

"This is perilous wandering of the mind," said the Sea-Thief. "Whose peculiarities are you recounting, in the name of heaven?"

Manawyddan turned and looked at him with mild surprise. "That one's of whom you asked me," said he. "The Salmon of Llyn Lliw's, as would be natural. But as to that, there were peculiarities with the Eagle likewise; and with Mabon ab Modron himself. Many would be content with these; but if more were desired, there were the peculiarities of the Ousel of Cilgwri, and of the Stag of Rhedynfre, and those of the Owl of Cwm Cawlwyd. Very marvellous, I declare to you, were the deeds, and the adventures, and the peculiarities of the Owl of—"

"Tell me nothing concerning them," said the Thief. "Woe is me, inattention is this: incoherence of thought it is; vague wandering of the mind."

"Wandering, yes; and far wandering," said Manawyddan. "Well may you say wandering: to be swimming the sea beyond Mon and Ireland, and he with his home and nest at Llyn Lliw in the Severn."

Gwiawn Sea-Thief sighed. He had great powers: none of old had treated him thus; but what he would he should have. Woe was him, was he now no better than others? And still between him and the plain deed he would do was this perplexity, this reckoning up the results this way and that. Not so was he wont to be, with whom seeing was joyous pilfering, were there aught desirable in the thing seen. He hung his head low, leaning forward, with his white, lithe hands over his brow and eyes. He had no heart for conversation, but must search all his soul and memory for some refuge against fear.

But Manawyddan would give him little silence for that search, but talked on continuously about Mabon and the Five Ancients, of this and of that; all his talk sheer confusion. "Oh, heaven!" thought

Gwiawn at last, "I will make the spells for the sake of peace, before weariness ends me."

It was no pleasure to him to do it: he hated to overcome men and gain his ends by magic: it was skilful thievery that pleased him. But here was no help, so eloquent was Manawyddan. So he began the first of his Nine Spells of Music and Magic: with his fingers stroking the harpstrings, with his lips framing the song.

It was the white time towards evening, when the sea was glittering silver, before the sky should turn rose-red and gold. He sang the secrets of the deep, the lure and wonder of the lonely ocean. The dream of the little waves gliding: the langorous dreaming of the slow, blue, sunlit waves. What is in the sea's heart, who should know? But Gwiawn made clear the dreaming of the sea — of the playground of billows, the abode of tumult, the vast dominions of the far-extending sea. His singing lulled the invisible air, moving it to desires it had never known. His notes went thrilling, sighing, drifting far over the surface of the wandering sea.

The white-breasted seagulls heard; the black cormorants; the swift sea-swallows. They spread forth sliding wings over the glitter; they came in clouds about the ship, lighting on mast and bulwark, lighting on the deck and on the sea, and listening, dreaming, listening.

The herring-shoals of the green deep heard; the pilchards and the mackerel; all the finned populations that slide through the green Atlantic dimness. The creamy silver of the glittering waters quivered now with their million legions. They had no fear of sea-crow or seagull; their old time cold cogitations were forgotten; in a deep content they glistened on the sea-face, listening; and though their ancient foes were thick about them, none worked them harm.

The Sea-Thief grew sarcastic, and desired to taunt Manawyddan. "Was the tune merry enough for you?" he said. "Could you keep your feet from the desire to dance?"

"I could not," said Manawyddan. "Had I come out here in quest of loud merriment, instead of quietude and peace, the tune would have pleased me better. Yet no saying but it was skilfully played."

"I will give you quietude and peace now," said Gwiawn.

Then he began the second spell: it had nine times more sleep in it than the first. The waves heard and trembled and were hushed; they ceased to rise and curve over and ride forward; they forsook their nodding, their slow rolling, their ponderous heaving. The Wave of Fannau was quelled; the Wave of the North betook herself to listening, marvelling, dreaming. No more eastward rolled untamed the wizard Wave of Ireland. Quelled, too, was the fourth of them, indeed: quelled was the haughty, gathering, foaming, rearing, sea-riding Wave of Wales. Sleep was imposed on the motions of the sea: tame quietness on the unbridled waters.

The clouds of heaven heard, and were overcome: the clouds of sunset, aflame and abloom like tulips westward; the clouds of the east, rose-pearl and silver; and the ash-gray clouds of dusk over the sea, broken with fading gleams of topaz and amethyst and amber. The night-clouds, dark and moon-white and moon-bronzed, came drooping down from the over-arching sky. They leaned down in a reverie over the waters; oblivious of the firmament, they took slow, immeasurable pleasure in the music of the spell. From the four quarters the winds came wandering; and died with delight, and forgot their motion.

"Ah, me," sighed Manawyddan, "thou art merry; thou art turbulent; there was a dear quiet on the sea before thou didst come here."

"Many would have been content," said Gwiawn Sea-Thief; and came near loss of equanimity. But he thought of the spells that remained to him; of the desire of sleep natural to nighttime; of the friendly character of dark night to the thievers and rievers of the world. Steal the breastplate he would, lest shame of face overtake him: whether it was Plenydd's or another's, whether he could get news of that or not. He took thought of his old mastery and his skill at filching; and grew confident.

Over that soundless sea all night long the ship went forward. Like slow, soft snow the notes of Aden Fwynach came dropping from the masthead: a far, melancholy sound in them, and misgivings of perils wandering the starless darkness. No tinkle and wash of waves against the ship; no whisper of receding water; no stirring of the four winds; no light in the world.

The Sea-Thief watched Manawyddan. Midnight was better than noonday with him, when it came to the sight needed for stealing. "Now, while he sleeps," thought he; though with some shame thus to depend, like a common thief, on the natural slumber of men. To thieve in broad daylight: to filch the treasures of the vigilant: to cut a haw from the eye of a gnat or take the queen bee from the swarm without one of the bees being aware of it: to such deeds and means he was used, and might take reasonable pride in them. "But there is no neat dealing with fools," thought he; "pride has no place here." So he stole forward, soundless as a yellow leaf falling through the mist, when the autumn sun shines crimson through the forest morning.

He drew back his empty hand in time. Manawyddan was on foot, at war as it seemed with night and the world. His sword was sweeping and circling about him: a midge on the wing, drawing near, would have been cloven in two between the point and the pommel. "Trouble me not, you winds and waters!" he cried. "My mind has been inflamed with wild music: intoxication of battle has been put on me." Ghostly the shouting, in that world where no other sound was.

"It is I who will trouble him, and not the winds and waters," thought the Thief. He would steal the breastplate now, let the Cymry and the Gods oppose him!

He crouched down by the mast, and watched, arms and hands and fingers tingling for pleasurable theft. But always Manawyddan kept himself hedged about and caged in by his sword-point. "I have heard tumult played," cried he, "by a subtle harper on a subtle harp. I have heard spells impelling to warfare; therefore, trouble me not!"

"Wonderful is the nature of fools!" thought Gwiawn Sea-Thief.

It was a contest then between the sword-point and the swift, white, filching hands. Failure of old time the hands had never come by; now this biting wall confronted them, not to be approached without scathe. He leaned out over the bulwarks on the right, and reached out from that side; but the sword-point wall was there; and he leaned out over the bulwarks on the left, and reached out from that side, but the sword-point wall was there also. There was no light and nothing that the eye of man could see; and nothing the ear of man could hear, from that soundless pilferer. But there were the white hands playing out and striving, and there was the wall they could not pass. "An edge to wound the wind!" cried Manawyddan. "I shall see the ruby drops on the deck of the ship in the morning!"

"Evil on thy sword and thee, thou wilt!" thought Gwiawn; "but the blood will not be from the bodiless wind!" With that he passed, wind-light and mist-silent, to his place in the prow again.

"Soul," cried he, "what robs thee of thy peace? Sleep and let sleep, in the name of heaven!"

"Alas, have I wakened thee?" said Manawyddan. "It is thy warlike music has afflicted me with boisterous dreams. Hereafter play only slumber on thy harp at night; keep these war-tunes for the morning of battle."

"Evil upon me unless I play thee slumber now, and heavy slumber!" said the Sea-Thief.

He went to his magic again, and got the third of his spells out of the harpstrings of Alawn. Compared with it, the first spell might well have brought feet to dancing, the second stirred hearts to riotous war. From the unfathomed antres of the sea came strange, long-limbed monsters, and lolled along the moveless waters, sprawling langorous tentacles: from the making of the world, it seemed to them, they had known no true enjoyment until then. If the waves had been quelled before, and the waters northward of Ireland, now the ancient Sea herself, in all the quarters of the world, was charmed from her old inquietude; she forsook her foam-tossing along a thousand coasts, her thundering on the precipices; she quivered and lapsed into delight; she left her musing on forgotten lands that she covers; enthralment overpowered her; she was listening, marvelling, dreaming, listening.

"Soul, soul," cried Manawyddan, "evil fall upon my beard unless I raise up song to thy warlike harping!" He was on his feet, the hwyl of a hundred battle-singers swelling his soul. He made these verses, and sang them to the tune called *The Sovereignty of Britain*, or *The Welsh Ground* — the battle-song of the Crowned Kings of London in those days:

> *Rise thou, proud Dragon! O Flame of our flame,*
> *Sire of our island's first heroes, arise!*

Not till the souls of us falter and tame
   Wane thou, O Shining One, forth from our skies!
Yea, not till greed lures our standards afar,
   And lies and vain boasting are heard in the land,
Till hatred or bitterness call us to war,
   Cease thou to shine where our battle-ranks stand!
Then, when we fail, be thou hidden from our eyes!
Stain not thy fame for the framers of lies!

The music of the spell went fading from Gwiawn Sea-Thief's mind; at "framers of lies" he had forgotten it quite. He went forward with his playing, but could get no tune out of the harp but *The Welsh Ground*: strike he what notes and chords he might, the harp answered with *The Sovereignty of Britain*. In despite of his will, and his desires, and his hatred of the Gods and the Cymry, compulsion was on him, and he must play for Manawyddan's singing:

Rise thou, Hu Gadarn! Thy shield is our shield
   E'en while our souls, like thy shield, are unstained;
E'en while we wend forth with song to the field,
   War-courteous, our old druid virtue unwaned.
Fight not for us! Make thou valiant our foes!
   Shine in their warriors' hearts, sing through their bards!
Victory we ask not, nor fending from woes:
   Leave thou the strife to our souls and our swords!
Save for this, prayerless our battle-hymns rise:
They need not prayers, who have spoken not lies!

Rise thou, proud Dragon! O Matchless in heaven,
   Here wait thy Cymry, uncumbered with fear;
Here flash the brands to which victory was given;
   The lips that have fallen to no vain speech are here.
E'en as thou gleamest from star forth to star
   On the day when new empires in chaos are won,
Warward so gleam the long scythes on the car,
   Exultant so kindle the spears in the sun —

86

Lo there, the Dragon burns bright through the skies,
Who ne'er yet shone forth upon framers of lies!

And at that the heavens lightened, as if a meteor were trailing from end to end of them in its glory, and Manawyddan knew the passing of the Dragon, the manifestation of the Mighty One. A trembling of remembrance, a stir of faint awakenment, ran through the dreaming, enspelled world about the ship. The Thief of the Sea remembered, sighing, that there were still the Gods, and that though one might overcome the Cymry, there would be no putting nefarious spells of slumber upon the Family of Hu.

But with dawn he got back his courage, and went to his magic again, and sang the fourth spell and the fifth. Strange and beautiful lights came gliding over the sea from afar: those of the Children of Beauty who have their homes in the foam about the rocks and islands. They hung like dim or brilliant stars about the ship, caring for nothing but to heed the music and sink into dream.

Between noon and evening he made the sixth spell and the seventh; and then even the ship of glass was overpowered, and moved no more over the waters. He made the eighth while the sick white sun fainted down to the pale edge of the sea. But Manawyddan waited, and would neither dance to it nor sing any war-song.

And here was the ninth spell coming now; and the Thief afraid of nothing, doubtful of nothing: the pride of his power and his poetry on him. The haggard moon came tottering up from the east. He took himself to all his magic, his crafty illusions and deceits. His was the world, he was thinking; and the cold sea and the star-fields. He remembered the ancient night in Caer Uffern, and the immemorial thrones there that lent him favor. He set his fingers to the strings and began.

There was fear that the stars in heaven would be quenched — that sleeping they would rain down from the sky and be drowned. The song of Aden Fwynach from the mast-head wandered and faltered, sobbed a little, and drifted into silence. She fluttered down on to the deck, no better than a wounded heron or a swallow fallen among the frost-hard furrows. Enchanted she was; herself the daughter of a pure enchantment.

The Thief heeded her fall, though by good rights he should have heeded only the music. "She would be worth stealing," thought he, "were there nothing better in view." Ill went the spell, for his mind's wandering to that. He recovered it, and went forward, and stroked from the strings slowly the cold, fluting notes of death. And he saw Manawyddan watching him and hiding a laugh. "Ah, me, a fool, a fool, a fool!" he sighed. It was not easy to get back the hwyl of the spell and go forward; but he did it. Chill and lonely and sweet and wailing the long notes rose. There were stars withering and dropping: there was the rare, slow whiteness of a rain of stars.

He looked up, and saw Manawyddan watching him and laughing: no nearer sleep than at first. Then the Thief was suddenly aware how it would be if the last note were played, and Manawyddan still unsleeping. He cried out in sudden terror. He forgot his spell; he knew at last the sickening nature of defeat. But it seemed to him that he might save the bird Aden Fwynach out of that disaster, and return to his own place with at least something stolen. He leapt forward to seize her, and thrust out his arm; whereupon Manawyddan thrust out his arm too, and caught the Thief by the wrist of the hand that would have taken Aden Fwynach. But might not hold him as long as the lightning flashes or the eyelid falls over the eye.

A laugh; a motion — a kind of sliding or melting of that which Manawyddan grasped: and Gwiawn Llygad Cath the Sea-Thief was far out on the smooth surface of the sea.

Then Aden Fwynach the Beautiful woke, and rose like a living jewel through the air, and away with her over the sea southward. The ship of glass woke, and trembled and started, and bounded forward over the waters. The ancient sea woke, and drove her foaming, hosted legions against the cliffs and headlands of the world. The sprawling, long-limbed monsters woke, and sank to their secret caverns in terror of the sky they had never seen before. The clouds woke to drift through heaven; the four winds woke to drive them. The nine waves without name woke, and went wandering away toward the rim of the world. The four chief waves of the west woke: the Wave of Fannau, the Wave of Werddon, the Wave of the North, and the Wave of Wales. Away with the finned and silvery families of the sea. Away with the seagulls, the petrels and the cormorants, screaming, to their commerce in the troughs of the waves.

And Manawyddan saw that the ship was bound toward Mon; and knew that whatever he had come to do, he had not done it. Was it to catch that Gwiawn Sea-Thief? He supposed that it would have been: with those spells, Gwiawn would be an ill one to have haunting the coasts of the Island of the Mighty. He supposed that was what fate required of him: and that was what he would do, if it took him eternity.

But he saw clearly that none might do it without some equipment for the hands, against slipperiness. The spells, for some reason, he need not fear: no doubt it was the breastplate was his protection against them. But for lithe, smooth slipperiness and skill in evasion, he considered, the crowned king or archdruid of all the eels in the pools and oceans of the world would be bowing his head before Gwiawn Llygad Cath the Sea-Thief.

Here is the Third Branch of it now, namely
THE GLOVES AND THE SERVICE OF GWRON GAWR, AND GWRON GAWR HIMSELF

I. The Three Subtle Crafts of Manawyddan, and their Peculiarity of being Adorned with Blue Enamel the Color of the Sky in June

SO HE CAME to land at Traethmelyn in Mon, and it was then the gold and blue of the morning. He left the ship in the mouth of the stream, and was pacing the sands, taking thought. When he turned again, behold, no sign of the glassy beauty of the ship where he had left it; no sign of it, either, out on the sparkling blueness of the sea.

"Well, now, to find the Mare Whiteflower," thought he.

He went up to a high place among the sandhills, and looked out over the green world beyond. At the edge of the wood she was grazing; and at a call from him she came. He had a foot in the stirrup, and was for mounting, when familiar music broke out of the wood; and looking up, he saw for the comfort of his heart the blue plumage and beauty of Aden Lonach: she was the second of the Birds of Rhianon.

He stood still listening to her, a foot in the stirrup and a foot on the ground, because her notes grew articulate soon; and there was sweet lilting Welsh to be heard in them. Until noon she sang; then his mind was clear as to what he needed and what he would seek: so he mounted and followed her. "One might get the gloves," said he, "if it were to win back the harp with them. Not niggardly that family, and not unreasonable."

From briar to bramble, from dogrose tangle to hawthorn thicket, she made her flights; going on before him, filling the air with delight from her throat and bill. Nothing is known of the road she led him by, but that it was long.

From some eminence, at last, he looked down over a world of tree-tops; and far off, gleaming up from that forest, a mountain lifted its white peak into the clear sky. Over oaktops and beech-tops he saw Aden Lonach glimmering: her dove-blue and jay-wing beauty scintillant above the bronze and gold-green of the trees. It was her peculiarity to shed light: he could still see her when she rose and gave over her short flights and many lightings, and sped on like a meteor afar, and became a glittering speck against the mountain; and he could still hear her music trailing far and thin, but clear, across the leagues and waving leagues of trees. Up she rose at last, lark-like: a vanishing star towards the whiteness of the peak: then was lost. Manawyddan, watching, considered what it might mean. "There should be finding Gwron in yonder high place," said he.

Day after day he rode on by dark grove and fern-green glade: night after night he caught glimpses of the stars through the leafage: and saw no sign of the mountain at all. Then one morning a flash of silver fringed with jewel-green of ferns showed between the trunks and under the beech-boughs in front; and therewith the call and laughter, and quiet singing of waters. Soon he came out into the sunlight and on to the greensward; and presently, to the river-bank.

One might have shot an arrow to the far side of the river; beyond which there was rising ground, and forest again, but not thickset: beeches with space to grow their full quivering globes of greenness, with purple stretches between. Here was the ford at his feet: the water shallow, chattering, sunlit; silver up yonder against the dark green of the pines, whereover at last a green shoulder of the mountain was visible. He rode across, and then took an alley between the beeches, purple-floored with ling-bloom; and before the sound of the river was dead in his ears, he came where the whole mountain could be seen through a gap in the trees on his right. First there was a steep vast slope, fern-covered and dotted with boulders; beyond and above were the heights, blue and mauve-pink and mauve-purple; and topmost, far away, the white peak against the blue of heaven: the same he had seen from the other side of the forest — the same Aden Lonach had flown to. So there in the hollow he left Blodwen to her freedom: there was a soft green floor, lush-grassed, between the trees, with a spring and a pool yonder, with mint and bog-cotton, kingcups and forgetmenots: a secluded place, and pleasant to graze in.

Then he took the steep on foot; and by mid-afternoon had passed this ridge and that, and left the bracken and greenness behind, and come to the foot of the highest precipice in the universe, above which nothing was visible but the remote blueness of heaven. Here he turned, and went westward: ascending still, but with the cliff on his left hand, the grass slope on his right. There was a kind of path there.

Soon all the world of the forest was stretched out below him; he was at the eagle's altitude, looking down on the treetop-covered floor of things. When the sun was low the ascent turned inward and grew steeper; then ended suddenly, cut off by a huge bastion of outjutting cliff. At the head of the track there was a door in the precipice: enormous, as if it had been set there by the giants of old.

He made knockings on the door, but in vain; and raised good shouting, but none heard him. At the third shout, the boulders that a chariot and two horses and the axle-scythes on the wheels, and the warrior and the charioteer in the chariot might have hidden behind, started from their lodgment on the mountainside and went thundering down the slope; but it brought no man to the door.

"We will make trial of silence!" said Manawyddan. So he sat down there, looking out over the forest and facing the declining sun, and made trial of the first silence, uttering no sound: but it availed him nothing.

Then he made trial of the second silence, thinking no thought in his mind. The sun sank lower; the sky grew redder; the breeze died from stirring the fern: and nothing befell.

Then he made trial of the third silence. If the sky reddened he was unaware of it; if the sun sank he saw it not though his open eyes were fixed on it; and he did not know whether the breeze had died or whether a gale was blowing.

From within the mountain came a murmur, as it were a rumor of whispering, a ripple and quiver of indistinguishable voices out from the heart of the gray rock: as if it had been a hive, and the bees at their parliament within. A hundred little waves of inarticulate whispering flowed out to him there, broke on his hearing and became articulate and intelligible: framing themselves at last into the clean Cymraeg of Gods and men.

"Who is it comes? — The greeting of heaven and man to the one that comes! — Who is it ventures so far from the mortal world?"

"Manawyddan son of the Boundless it is that comes. Give you him news, if it please you, what place is this, and who reigns king here?"

The voices grew more distinct, gathering into one. "Ah, what place is this, what place is it? Porth Dinas Gwron is the name of the gate; Gwron Giant reigns here king. . . Not to know that this is the mountain Dinas Gwron! . . . that Gwron Giant reigns here king!"

"From the Island of the Mighty I have ridden here: from Traethmelyn in Mon, and farther, seeking the Gate of the City of Gwron."

"Worn will be the four hoofs of the mare; many the worlds the eye will have seen. It is a long way to the Island of the Mighty."

"There is this news from that island," said Manawyddan. "The Harp of Alawn the Songs is stolen: Gwiawn Llygad Cath the Sea-Thief has it."

Like a hundred harpstrings plucked at once, and the sound of them dying and wandering into silence, the murmur of voices faded into the depths of the mountain; and then like a bell struck, and the hum and song of it clear and deep, one grand voice answered him:

"Did you ride here from the Island of the Mighty to give such news as that?"

"No," said Manawyddan. "But no one will recover the harp unless he shall have the Gloves of Gwron Brif-fardd on his hands; and therefore am I come here to obtain the gloves."

"It is easy to ride from world to world: it is easy to make requests and ask boons and present petitions. No one ever obtained the gloves without doing service first."

"I have done service for Plenydd Resplendent: I have sought to do service for Alawn the Songs. Were it known to me now what the service —"

"If it were known to me what aptitudes are in you? What facilities for action? What attainments and disposition? What arts or sciences may be understood?"

"There is leading armies in battle," said Manawyddan; "there is winning victories up and down the world, at war."

"Then serve you Gwron where his need may be, if serve him you can. The main part of his armies is camped out against chaos on the borders of space. The men of his teulu are spirits of consuming fire;

the frailest and puniest of them all could easily crumble the mountains between his thumb and his little finger."

"There is making songs and singing them," said Manawyddan. "There is fashioning good harps, and getting music from their strings. With my having slept a night in the Cave of the Wyddfa, I am an Institutional Bard of the Island of Britain."

"Gwron has need of a harper, indeed: of one whose fingers on the strings can maintain the dancing of the stars."

"There is building ships and sailing them," said Manawyddan; and that with little risk of the ships being wrecked.

"Ship-builder, sea-pilot — Gwron has need of them. His flaming navies anchor in the ports of space: the lightest coracle of them all is greater in splendor than yonder sun."

Manawyddan was watching the sun go down over the forest. All the sky westward was in crimson and mournful scarlet, a pomp of squandered gold and spilt vermilion. "Ship-building such as that is beyond me, indeed," thought he.

"Other crafts are known to me," he said. "There are other aptitudes, truly. There is house-building, if that were needed. Cutting good withies by the stream and weaving them into the walls between the six pillars; plastering them with clay against the weather; lining them with skins. Or felling trees in the forest and shaping them into logs, and building of them halls for the dwellings of chieftains and kinsmen."

"An excellent art: a skill to boast on! Men with this art will be needed by Gwron. The rocks of the world are the beams and the rafters; the mountains heaped on them are the clay; the greensward and the forests the linings of skin, for the houses of the clansmen of Gwron Gawr."

"There are the Nine Huntings," said Manawyddan.

"Gwron has need of a huntsman for the Nine Huntings of Nwyfre and Abred, to ride after the demons along the shores of the Nether Deep."

"It is the Nine Huntings of the Royal Fields of Wales that I know," said Manawyddan; "and therefore I could not serve him in this. But there is husbandry, if it be needed. I can sow fields and reap them."

"Here are the sowing and the reaping required for Gwron," said the voice. "In the springtime of a universe his sowers strew star-seed up and down the nebulæ; at the harvest-time, his bodiless reapers reap the Milky Way."

"I should have little success at that," said Manawyddan. "But there is making shoes."

"Gwron might well be gratified by shoes made by a Prince of the Brython: if the shoes were of the Subtle Shoemaking, of the Esoteric Craft."

Manawyddan thought over that saying. "It might be learned," he considered. He had been making shoes at one time, when he was nameless; but there was little subtlety or esotericism in the art he had known then. "But no saying it might not be learned," thought he; and was for learning it, and for making shoes for Gwron Gawr. Not one word more could he get from the voice within the mountain.

So there he bided that night: sleeping, or watching the stars come over the cliff behind and wander away above the forest to the far rim of heaven. When the sun came up he rose, and went down the way he had come, and found Blodwen in the green hollow. A blue bird flew down, peopling the mountain morning with mysterious sweet song. He mounted and followed Aden Lonach: by moorland and forest, by meadowsweet riverbank and green fields in the valley: till he came to the Island of the Mighty again; and then at last to Caer Odornant by the rifted hill; and there Aden Lonach left him.

All the shoemakers in Britain lived at Caer Odornant at that time, or most of them. So he looked in at this house and that, to get tidings of some master of cobbling; but tidings he could not get, save that they were in council under the elm and the sycamore, and no welcome with them but for satirists. He heard that with the henwife under the hill.

"If your tongue is bitter, go to them," said she, "in the broad meadow by the bank of the river."

"Bitter or not," thought he, "I will go and make trial of it." There he went, and found them in their council. He left Blodwen, and went across the grass, and sat down among them.

"Is there any man here that understands the Subtle Shoemaking?" said he.

"Yes," said the man on his right, "I do."

"Heed him not," said the man on his left. "He knows nothing of it."

"What sayest thou, upstart?" said the first.

"That thou art given to lies and boasting," said the second; "that thou knowest not what thou claimest to know!"

"Thou liest!" said the first.

Then said a third of them, "Wherefore quarrel ye?"

"Concerning the knowledge of Subtle Shoemaking," said Manawyddan.

"Ha," said the third, "they may well quarrel; since none knows that art but I."

Said a fourth, "What art?"

"Subtle Cobblercraft, Esoteric Shoemaking," said the third.

"And *thou* claimest to understand that?" said the fourth.

"There is none in Caer Odornant that understands it but I," said the third.

"Hear him!" cried the first. "Hear this lying braggart!"

"Fools and liars, all of ye!" said a fifth. "Were I one to make known my merits, I would tell the chieftain to whom he should come!"

"Thou wouldst say it was I, if there were truth in thy mouth!" said a sixth.

Then the Archcobbler cried out from the logan stone, "Peace, all of ye! The satirists come!"

Came three men riding on mules; and all the cobblers rose and showed them respect. The first was lean and sallow, with lank hair uncombed.

"Lord Satirist," said the Archcobbler, "we have need of one to go against Ceinion Grydd in the King's Wood: make known to us the extent of thy powers."

"See you yonder bough on the sycamore?" said the satirist.

"We see it," said they.

Then he took his harp, and struck a screech out of its strings that made them shiver, and began to croak his satire against the sycamore bough. By the third line the May leaves of it became hued like

October; by the seventh they fell; at twelve lines the bough was withered.

All the cobblers applauded. The Archcobbler said:

"What reward shall we give this lordly satirist for putting that fate on the two arms of Ceinion Grydd?"

"Such and so much," they shouted; and were at last for giving him a rod of gold the length of his body and the thickness of his arm. That would serve him very well, said he; "being a modest man, and not exorbitant."

Then came the second satirist. "To every man his price," said he haughtily; "it would not serve with me."

There was a stir amongst the cobblers; they were uneasy lest they had offended such a great lord of bitter speech. "Deign to make known to us the extent of thy powers," said the Arch-cobbler.

"I will satirize the river," said the man. He was thin-faced and freckled, with his eyelids down over his eyes, and long reddish eyelashes; thin lips and red hair, and thin-nosed with pale, distended nostrils. He plucked a little malignant buzzing out of his harp, and began singing his satire. And there was the placid river: never a ripple on it unless from the waterflies shooting, or where the vole with a plop dropped from the bank and trailed across like an arrow-point: a place of dark, unhurried waters, where the pike would be lurking below, and the kingfisher watching above: deep enough for a man to swim in it and have no discomfort with kicking the bottom.

And at the third line of the satirist's singing: no more shooting with the waterfly, but death taking him; no more swimming with the frog, and no more diving; the white belly of him skyward, his days ended in their prime. With the pike, no more lurking in ambush among the roots of the reeds and the lilies. Dead were the chub and the perch, the loach, the trout and the minnow. Died the lily; withered the reed; even the kingfisher floated dead, a tumble of many-hued feathers. The water ceased its flowing; it dried away; by the third verse there was only ill-smelling mud.

"Wonderful power, in our deed!" said the cobblers. They whispered among themselves, comparing this satirist with the great Gods, and were in deep awe. "Wonderful and beautiful power!" they murmured.

"What reward for working the like of this on Ceinion?" said the Archshoemaker.

"Such and so much," said they; and were for giving him the whole of a king's galanas — gold and cattle and all.

"It will serve me well," said the satirist. "I am rated at the value of a king."

Then the third satirist spoke: he was a plump, well-fed man in flashing green, with well-oiled black hair and a smiling look. "To every man his price, good souls; I would not hold my power so cheap. You, my friend," said he to the red-eyelashed man, "will no doubt be an apprentice at satire?"

Then said he with the red eyelashes: "If I knew thy name I would satirize thee, and thou shouldst be as that water."

"Though I know not thy name I will satirize thee, and the men of Caer Odornant shall see," said the well-fed one. So he began, smiling kindly as he sang; and they all turned red and then white-checked to hear him; but the red-eyelashed could make no answer, knowing not his name.

"Thou shalt be a rat," said the well-fed; and went forward with three lines of his satire.

"Enough! enough!" squeaked the red-eyelashed; "or I will jump and bite thy throat!"

"What! thou art content with as little rathood as that?" said the well-fed. So he stopped his chanting; but the red-eyelashed had still a good look of rattishness about him, even to the twitching of his whiskers.

Grand acclamation rose, with much chattering on all sides. "What reward for putting rathood on Ceinion?" said the Archcobbler. "What will be rich enough for this lordly man?"

"Good soul," said the well-fed satirist smoothly, "consider not rewards or emolument! The master of this art will practice it for the love of it: his own skill and mastery are his reward. Let there be feasting today, and pleasant harmony between us all; and tomorrow I will do the thing merrily."

So they all went off to their feasting, chattering gaily as they went. But Manawyddan pondered on all he had heard with them. "I will find this Ceinion Grydd," said he.

So he went forward till he came to a gully under the edge of the wood, and a round, thatched cottage of stone, white-washed, in the gully, and hawthorns in bloom on all sides. In the doorway sat one making shoes; he seemed older than the Five Ancients of the World; but if it came to wonders and peculiarities, he would be the last you would choose among a hundred, very likely.

"Soul," said Manawyddan, "the greeting of the god and the man to you, pleasantly and kindly!"

"Ay, ay," said he, "and to you also!"

"Is there news of Ceinion Grydd with you?" said Manawyddan.

"Yes, sure," said he. "I am that Ceinion."

"A long time you will have been at shoemaking?" said Manawyddan.

"Seven-and-seventy ages," said the Crydd. "And now I desire rest, and shall not have it?"

"Wherefore not?"

"Lest the world become destitute of my science," said the Crydd.

"There are shoemakers," said Manawyddan.

"Yes, there are shoemakers," said the Crydd, and sighed.

"I myself desire to learn shoemaking," said Manawyddan.

"There are shoemakers in Caer Odornant," said the Crydd quickly.

"They understand not the science I desire to learn," said Manawyddan.

"No?" said the Crydd.

"I will tell you what science it is," said Manawyddan. "It is the Subtle Shoemaking, the Esoteric Cobblercraft. I divine its lineage and antecedents to be thus and thus," said he. "The man from whom I would learn will have had Gwydion ab Don for his teacher; and Gwydion learned it from Math fab Mathonwy; and he from Einigan the Giant; and he from the Son of the Three Shouts himself, in Gwnyfyd before the worlds were made.

"Shoes of this making Arthur wore, and Drych Ail Cibddar of old. Also the three Sons of Erim, and of them, most of all Sgilti Ysgawndroed. Also Sol and Gwadyn Ossol and Gwadyn Odyeith: whence their powers. Also Yscyrdaf and Yscudydd: they were two attendants upon Gwenhwyfar the Queen; their feet were swift as their thoughts when going upon a message. Also Cell and Cueli and Gilla Coes Hydd — the Chief Leaper of Ireland was he. But now the Cymry go ill-shod; and only the Gods wear shoes such as these."

"Well, well," said the Cobbler; "come you into my house here, if you will; and I will teach you what I know."

So they went into the house, and Ceinion set food and drink before him, and they were pleasant enough together; though no words from Ceinion Grydd. "What is the first thing to learn?" asked Manawyddan.

"Fuel-gathering," said the Crydd. "Go you into the woods and gather fuel."

He went, and came back in the evening with what Blodwen and he, between them, could carry of it. "That is well," said the Crydd. "We will go to rest." So they lay down on the sleeping-bench. "And I will tell you this," said Ceinion. "There was that Gilla Coes Hydd: it was I who made the shoes for him."

So Manawyddan was in the house of Ceinion Cobbler for that time, desiring to learn and learning little, so far as he knew. The first month he was gathering fuel in the forest; and with all he brought into the gully, there was no increase in the fuel-stack. The second evening, when he came in, he found a rat in a cage with Ceinion. "This fellow shall I tame," said the Crydd. He got no further conversation out of him until the end of the month; and then this much when he came in with his load: "Well, you have learnt the first branch of it;" and this much as they went to rest: "I made the shoes for Yscyrdaf and Yscudydd."

The second month Manawyddan was drawing water from the well: it was far away in the forest. Whatever be brought and poured into the cask one evening, the cask would be empty when he came to it next. At the end of the month Ceinion spoke to him again. "You have learnt the second branch," he said; "many would be seven lives learning it." When they went to rest he grew talkative again; forgetting his taciturnity for a moment.

"Thou didst speak of Sol and Gwadyn Ossol and Gwadyn Odyeith," said he.

"Yes did I," said Manawyddan.

"It was I who made the shoes for them," said the Crydd; "such shoes as they were."

Three more months passed, and this and that for Manawyddan to do; and leather and last and awl never coming under his hands the while. At the end of each month the Crydd would grow loquacious again, and commend him for having learnt a new branch of it; and one month he added to his commendation:

"Arthur and Drych Ail Cibddar — were they famed for swiftness of old?"

"Famed they were," said Manawyddan. "And highly famed."

At the end of the next month the Crydd said, "Ah ha! I know wherefore Arthur and Drych Ail Cibddar were famed for swiftness!"

"Yes?" said Manawyddan; but got no more from Ceinion then. But at the end of the fifth month he said:

"They were famed for swiftness, because I made the shoes for them."

At the end of the sixth month, when Manawyddan came in in the evening, the Crydd asked him:

"What art was it you desired to learn, in your deed to heaven and man?"

"Subtle Shoemaking," said Manawyddan.

"Tomorrow I will teach you," said the Crydd, "what I learnt from Gwydion ab Don, and he from Math fab Mathonwy, and he from Einigan the Giant, and he from Menw the son of the Three Shouts in Gwynfyd before the worlds were made."

When another month had passed, Manawyddan had mastered the seven branches of it, and set the Crydd free to rest where he would in the sun. "You will not need this fellow further," said Ceinion, pointing to the rat in the cage.

"No," said Manawyddan.

"Since he is tame, he shall go free," said the Crydd; and opened the door of the cage. The rat came forth, and leapt down to the ground.

"Well, well," said the well-fed satirist: "tame you may say, in my deed! You, Lord Crydd, I came to satirize, and the three words of the rat-making satire were not out of my lips before rathood had befallen me!"

Nothing further is known of this satirist.

Then Manawyddan took himself to making shoes, and they were the best in the universe. He would make none but with leather of Spain or even Africa, after its magical steeping in a caldron for over a hundred years. The commonest nails he would nail them with were of gold of Arabia; and he would face and pattern the leather with gold and with blue enamel, bluer than the seas of mid July. He made three pairs for practice, and for training mind and hand and eye; searching within, to discover all there might be in his craft; and lest that should escape him which might have escaped Ceinion Grydd also. "There may be more to know," he said at last, "but not while still a mortal."

Then he enhanced his knowledge with deep meditation; and enhanced his poems, and his voice in singing them; and took himself to the best of his art. "Now," said he, "I will make shoes."

He made three more pairs; and the best of satirists would find little to say against them, and that little would be lies. The noblest of encomiasts would despair of coming up with the truth in praising them. Manawyddan looked at them when they were made, and enumerated their peculiarities according to his perception of them. "The one that wears either of these," said he, "will not slip nor stumble, much less will he fall. The rolling stone will become stable beneath his feet; the quagmire will uphold him well. And he will have another peculiarity: like the level road to him will be the unscaled precipice."

One pair he sent to Pryderi, his son, in Dyfed; one pair he sent to Teyrnion Twrf Fliant, in Gwent; and one pair he gave to the henwife under the hill, that every trace of the Subtle Shoemaking might not be lost from Caer Odornant. Then he made a pair of shoes that were ten times better than those he had last made; and set out with them for the Gates of Dinas Gwron.

Long he was on the journey. It was nightfall when he came to the foot of the mountain; at dawn he took the path upward, and climbed through fern and rock. At noon he came to the door in the precipice. "Will I make trial of shouting or silence?" thought he; but before he could decide, lo, a stir and humming in the mountain; the myriad voices.

"Who comes? Who waits without? Who travels so far from the world of men?"

"It is I, Manawyddan the Shoemaker, from Caer Odornant in the Island of the Mighty. Manawyddan Grydd it is, and he bearing with him the shoes he has made for Gwron Gawr."

"Shoes?" said the Great Voice within. "What would shoes be to Gwron Giant, even shoes of the Subtle Making? If it had been a shield you had brought, of the Esoteric Shieldmaking —"

Not another word could Manawyddan get from within there, although he waited until it was evening. "I will go and make the shield, whatever," said he. But the shoes he had made for Gwron, none but Gwron should have, thought he; and left them on the doorstep outside the door when he went down.

In the hollow he found Blodwen grazing, and the bird Llonach singing to her; he mounted, and followed Aden Lonach into the Island of the Mighty: a long time the journey took them; and at last to Henfordd in Loegria. It was where the shieldmakers of the island lived at that time.

He enquired of the henwife by the river, and she told him, "They are all at feast in the house of the Archshieldmaker," said she. "Go you to them there, and if your tongue is bitter it will be the better for you."

"Wherefore are they at feast, and why should the tongue of him that comes to them be bitter?" said Manawyddan.

"They can get no satisfaction in the world nor in dreams because of Tarianwr Tadwy in the grove on the hillside," said she. "And now they say satirists have come, and one of them will put cold death on him with satires; and he will take no gold for putting it."

Manawyddan would waste no time with the shieldmakers, but rode at once to the grove on the hillside. There was a round house of clay and wattles in the grove, and about it a garden of flowers, with three skeps of bees for honey.

"Tarianwr Tadwy," said he, "the greeting of the god and the man to you, pleasantly and kindly!"

He would not look from his weaving withies on the frame. "And you also — whence and wherefore come you?" said he.

"Seeking one that had practiced shieldmaking long, and the desire for rest on him, and no rest to be had."

"H'm," said the Shieldmaker.

"No rest to be had, lest his art should perish from the world," said Manawyddan.

"There are shieldmakers," said Tarianwr Tadwy.

"A haughty tribe, and a self-sufficient," said Manawyddan. "Through vainglory they will not learn his art from him."

"H'm," said the Shieldmaker.

"As for that art,"said Manawyddan, "it is Subtle Shield-making: an obscure and beautiful art, an esoteric science. He would have learned it, I judge, from Gwydion ab Don aforetime, who had it from Math fab Mathonwy his teacher. Math would have been instructed in it by Einigan Gawr in Deffrobanau, the third lost continent of the world. Einigan Gawr was taught it by Menw ab y Tairgwaedd in the Palace of Gwynfyd, between the Crying of the Name and the Going Forth of the Gwynfydolion.

"According to its rules and principles, Wynebgwrthucher was made for Arthur, and the White Shield itself for Hu."

"H'm," said Tarianwr Tadwy.

"And this art I desire to learn from you," said Manawyddan.

"H'm," said Tarianwr Tadwy; "since you have come, you have come."

So Manawyddan was there with the Tarianwr for that time, learning Subtle Shieldmaking. They say it is a harder science to learn then the other; but he had the seven branches of it in seven months. The morning after his coming there, Tarianwr Tadwy said to him:

"Go you, and set up this shield by the edge of the grove, facing towards Henfordd."

It was something to get as much as that from him: he was ever a man sparing of his speech.

Manawyddan took the shield; and as he was setting it up as his master had bidden him, saw one with red eyelashes coming up from the city; and flickering whiskers like a rat's on him. "Ha, ha — the satirist!" said he; but waited for no news then; nor did he hear any afterward; unless you would call the sweet singing news, that drifted daily into the grove after that, and was a main help to him in whatsoever task had been appointed him by the Tarianwr.

As for the tasks, they would be fetching this and carrying that; and there would be nothing to show for them when they were done. Beyond the appointing of them for him each morning, he got no words at all from the Tarianwr for three months. Then at last that one put away his aloofness, and looked up at Manawyddan, and nodded. At the end of five months he grew garrulous — a rare thing with him. "The name of Wynebgwrthucher was on your lips?" said he.

"Yes it was on them," said Manawyddan.

"Loquacious you were, in my deed," said the Shieldmaker.

At the end of the sixth month he chuckled in his throat and said, "It was I who made it, whatever."

"Made what?" said Manawyddan; but could get no answer from him, nor any satisfaction till he remembered it was Arthur's shield they were talking about, the renowned Wynebgwrthucher.

So seven months passed, all but two days; then the Shield-maker grew talkative again. "What art was it you desired to learn?" said he.

"Subtle Shieldmaking," said Manawyddan.

The Tarianwr opened his lips again the next evening, and not before. "Come now," said he; "I hate this garrulous loquacity; tomorrow I will teach you Subtle Shieldmaking, and begone where I may have Peace."

So he taught him, and went; and Manawyddan took himself earnestly to making shields. Six he made for practice; and was more careful with them than he had been with the shoes. He made the frames of strong withies, and over every withy sang its spell. He covered them with leather of Spain, or Africa, after its soaking two hundred years in waters of magic. He adorned them, according to his learning, with gold of Arabia in enchanted patterns and with blue enamel better than sky-hued. He looked at them when they were finished, and knew that their like had not been in the Island of the Mighty since Wynebgwrthucher's time. "So much for these," said he. "Tomorrow I will begin shieldmaking."

He journeyed to the banks of the Hafren, and gathered withies there unequalled in the world; and he gathered them between dawn and noon on the day of the summer solstice, chanting the songs of Taliesin Benbardd the while. He wove them to frames with the best of his skill, and covered the frames with leather from the extremes of Africa, after its ten thousand years in the vats of magic. He took blue enamel better than sapphire, and Welsh gold, the best in the world: and these he used for adornment. Three shields he made that way; and then enumerated their peculiarities, according as he divined what they would be.

"Whoever uses them," he said, "will find them good protection for head and heart, trunk and limbs, soul and form, mind and imagination. In battle, no blade will come within a hand's breadth of him; but will turn at that, as if granite and not air opposed it. Whatever the sharpening of the sword, it shall not avail: the blue sharpening shall be blunted; the white broken, the lightning-hued shall turn aside; even the wind-wounder shall get no satisfaction. And dear knows they will have many other peculiarities besides these."

What he had done with the three pairs of shoes, he did with the three shields also: one went to Gwent, to Teyrnion Twrf Fliant; one he sent into Dyfed to Pryderi fab Pwyll; one he set up in Henfordd to be an example and a rebuke to the shieldmakers. When he had done so he said, "But I have not yet made a shield."

He spent three days in meditation, and then went to the best of his art, and to the best of his poem-chanting; and made a shield. "Well, well," said he; "I wish it were a better one. Yet no saying but that it has peculiarities, and remarkable peculiarities." The year and the day since he came to Henfordd were up by that time; so he would not stay to make another shield. "Wynebgwrthucher might be envious of it — that is true," said he.

He rode forward with it towards the Gates of Dinas Gwron; but first, before he came out of the grove, released the red-eyelashed satirist from the cage of withies and the blackbird-guise he had been enduring. "No more satirizing for me," said that one; and indeed, according to the bards, he was better at panegyrics from that out than at anything else he might turn his mind to.

At Porth Dinas Gwron there was no news for him, other than the news he had had before: none might see Gwron without doing service first. "Service I have done: I have made the shield," said he.

"The shield — the shield? What shield, in the name of heaven and man? How should shields be needed with Gwron, when the moon might roll in the hollow of his own shield, when he goes forth armed along the brink of space? Now had it been a sword you had brought —"

The great voice in the hill died away there, and not a word more could he get from it. "Well, well," thought Manawyddan; "a sword Gwron shall have of me, and it shall be of the Subtle Making."

He went his way, leaving the shield where he had left the shoes: for that which he had made for Gwron Giant, none else should have from him. In time he came to the Island of the Mighty again; and now Aden Lonach brought him to Rhydychen: it was the great place for swordmaking in those days.

To one and another he gave the greeting of heaven and man, and enquired of them where were the Swordmakers of Rhydychen.

"They are gone out to war," said they.

"Against whom are they gone, in your deed?"

"Dear," said they, "against the Celfyddwr Clod Cleddyfau, as their custom is." And dear knew where the Celfyddwr was, they told him; only the swordmakers should have no quiet in their minds because of him. Satirists they had tried, in plenty; but could get no satisfaction that way. So with every war season they went out and hunted for him, putting challenges against him on the four winds of heaven; and always coming back very victorious, with news of having destroyed him thoroughly. But still they would be troubled, and soon a rumor of him would be out again; and they would change their minds about the destruction, and consider that he was laughing at them; and go forth to war with him again the next war-season. "It is because he makes swords not according to the rules of the craft," they said, "and laughs to scorn the Swordmakers of Rhydychen."

Manawyddan went about till he came to the poorest house in the city. "Go not there," said the people; "he is not wise, you see; none deal with him; his name is unknown, and unknown his lineage." In the house, an old man was singing, and a ludicrous cracked quavering voice on him; but with merriment in it, and often chucklings and laughter. "Well," thought Manawyddan, "since none knows who he is, it would be better to make trial of him." So he went in, and gave the one he found there the greetings of the god and the man affably. "Wherefore are you merry?" said he.

"The swordmakers are gone to war," said the old man; "and I am old and grasshopper-like, and cannot go."

Manawyddan thought over that a little, and said, "For what reason should you go, or desire to go?"

The old man rolled his body about laughing. "Hai, hai, hai!" said he, "he asketh for what reason! He knoweth not how disappointed the swordmakers will be!"

Said Manawyddan quickly, at that: "I desire to learn sword-making."

"Many in Rhydychen would teach you," said the other.

"I desire to learn from the Celfyddwr Clod Cleddyfau," said Manawyddan.

The old man laughed a little, lifting his face roofward as he laughed, and rolling his body. "You had better take food and drink," he said; and set viands before him, such as they were. Manawyddan, since he must keep his hazelnuts for when he might need them, ate and drank, and pondered.

"Soul," said he at last; "I desire to learn swordmaking from the Celfyddwr Clod Cleddyfau."

"The swordmakers seek him and find him not," said the old man. "It would be hard to come by news of him."

"Yes," said Manawyddan; and fell to his pondering again, and to watching his companion; and he to his polishing an old swordblade, and to snatches of curious song.

"You yourself could give me news of him," said Manawyddan.

"News of whom?" asked the old man.

"Of the Celfyddwr Clod Cleddyfau," said Manawyddan. "I desire to learn swordmaking from him."

"Well, well, well!" said the old man in amazement. And then, suddenly and gravely, "Go you out and fish in the river."

"Where are the rod and the line for it?" asked Manawyddan.

"They are there,", said the oldman, pointing to the corner; and Manawyddan took them and went out.

When the sun was going down he caught three trout, and brought them to the old man in Rhydychen; who bade him eat them for his supper, and be content. He did so; and after that they went to rest.

In the morning Manawyddan asked him again, "Is it known to you where I shall find the Celfyddwr Clod Cleddyfau?"

"The Celfyddwr Clod Cleddyfau?" said the old man; doubtfully, as if he had never heard the name before. "The Celfyddwr Clod Cleddyfau?" Then his face lit up with intelligence. "Go you hunting on the hills," said he; "and it will be better."

So that day Manawyddan was hunting on the hills, and caught nothing but an old lean rabbit, with its left ear bitten off; although there were few better huntsmen than he. The third morning he asked again, "Is it known to you where I shall get tidings of the Celfyddwr Clod Cleddyfau?"

"The Celfyddwr Clod Cleddyfau?" said the old man, absently; and then: "The swordmakers have come back," he said briskly. "Go you to Cadfan Gloff in the marketplace, and apprentice yourself to him."

Manawyddan went, and apprenticed himself; and in a month had learned some skill in making swords with the white sharpening. "Go now," said Cadfan; "thou hast learned it all." So he came back to the old man, and brought with him a sword he had made.

The old man laughed furtively. "Yes," said he; "it is a good sword; many would be content."

"I am not content," said Manawyddan.

"Go you then to Cian Gof by the fountain; ask no question, but apprentice yourself to him."

Manawyddan went; and in two months had learned all that Cian could teach him: it was, to make swords that would take the blue sharpening and be glad of it. He came back with one of them. "Yes, yes," said the old man; "few would desire better."

"In my deed to the Eternal," said Manawyddan, "I desire better."

"Go you then to Cilydd Braich Haiarn; ask no question, but apprentice yourself."

He went; and in four months had learned all that Cilydd Iron-Arm knew; and came back with a sword beautifully hued like the lightning.

"If you desire better than this —" said the old man.

"I desire much better," said Manawyddan. "It would not wound the wind."

"Go you then to the Archswordmaker; perhaps he can teach you. He went; and at the end of four months the Archswordmaker said to him, "What more do you seek to know?"

"Subtle Swordmaking," said Manawyddan. "The Esoteric Craft: the making of Wind-wounders."

"None know it, either among the Gods or the Cymry," said the Archswordmaker.

But Manawyddan thought, "There will be one who knows it among the Gods: Gofannon ab Don; and there will be one who knows it among the Cymry: the Celfyddwr Clod Cleddyfau."

"Ha, you come back?" said the old man. "What now do you desire?"

"I will tell you," said Manawyddan. "I desire to learn swordmaking from the Celfyddwr Clod Cleddyfau: Subtle Swordmaking: the Esoteric Craft. Judge you by its lineage and antecedents whether anyone less than he will know it. He grows old, and has practiced it long; he desires rest and shall not have it, because the swordmakers are haughty and vainglorious, and will not come to him to learn. He learned his art from Gofannon ab Don; and Gofannon had it from Math fab Mathonwy; and Math from Einigan Giant; and Einigan from the Son of the Three Shouts himself; and at that time the Gwynfydolion had not gone forth from Bliss.

"Further, I will tell you of the peculiarities of this art. A sword made according to it will take the four sharpenings at pleasure: without touch of the grindstone it will wound the wind and cause blood to flow. It will be tougher than whatever is toughest, and yet more supple than the leathern thong. And it will have another peculiarity: the bare blade of it will be better than moonlight, of a night when no moon may be shining. He who wields it will be victorious; a wound from it no physician will ever heal. Great will be its beauty, and its adornment with jewels, and its inlayment with gold and with blue enamel. It will be better than Gles or Glessic or Gleisad, the swords of Bwlch and Cyfwlch and Sefwlch, the three sons of Cleddyf Cyfwlch, the three grandsons of Cleddy Difwlch — though those three swords were three griding gashers. The sword of Gwrnach was of this making; and Caledfwlch Lovely the sword of Arthur. Occult, remote, peculiar is the art; and until I shall have learned it I foresee no peace."

"Since as much as that is known to you," said the Celfyddwr Clod Cleddyfau, "come you into the forge and I will teach you Subtle Swordmaking."

So that night he taught him, and in the morning went free.

Then Manawyddan made seven swords for practice, all of them beautiful Wind-wounders. They would lay low, at a stroke, the oak of nine hundred winters; they would sweep through the mountain granite and make nothing of its hard solidity; they would think little of shaving the beard from the gnat in mid air. Since there was no fault to be found with them, he considered he had mastered it, so far as a mortal might. "Well, now," said he, "I will quit this playing and make swords."

So he made three and sent them where he had sent the shoes and the shields; and then made the sword that he would take to Gwron. It was a blade to scorn the grindstone, and to take the hue of its sharpening from the will of its lord: did he desire the white, it would be white, and would be gifted with the white peculiarities; did he desire blue, it would be blue, and let the mountain granite fear it! Or if he desired the lightning-colored sharpening on it, lightning-hued it would be, and it would flash forth and flame suddenly, and lo, the gnat that was proud of her beard would be beardless, the mote on the sunbeam would be cloven in two, and the one fragment of it neither greater nor less than the other.

All down the blade were jacinths and sapphires: it twinkled in the moonlight: it lit up the world when there was no moon. More it seemed a bright gap in the air, a hard, keen, immortal invisibility, than any weapon of bronze or steel. He endowed it with all the grand peculiarities; above all, by virtue of its making, it had the edge to wound the wind, and cause blood to flow from the bodiless wind, more swiftly than the dropping of dew from the reed or grass-blade when the dew of June is at its heaviest.

He went forth with it to the Celfyddwr Clod Cleddyfau, where that one was musing in the sun. "Soul," said he, "is this a sword of the Subtle Making — an Esoteric Brand as it were — a fit gift to be given to Gwron Gawr himself?"

"I will tell you the truth," said the Celfyddwr, "without lies or concealment, understatement or exaggeration. If Gwron Giant desires a better sword than this, he must go to the Smithies of Pen Gannion for it, and humble himself before Gofannon ab Don, to get a sword forged by the Immortals; and even if he got it, it is doubtful whether it would be better than this."

By that time the year and a day he had been at Rhydychen were over; and Aden Lonach came to him, and he saddled Blodwen and followed her.

II. The Making Trial of the Equipment of Manawddan, against its Inadequacy for Battle with Dragons

UNKNOWN to him the way Aden Lonach took that time, and whether it would lead to Dinas Gwron or not. He came not to the green forest, but by a thousand mountains, the wildest in the world, and through many rock-strewn valleys that she filled with her singing, and by rush-rimmed tarns in hollows not so far from the stars. Here she would light, and there, biding his slower coming; nor was there eagle or falcon in the sky that beheld her low flights and blueness with desire to work her harm.

So he came at last to a pass, its end far in front, between two peaks like horns on the forehead of the world; and there Llonach left him, with one clap of her turquoise wings losing herself in heaven. From noon to dusk he rode forward; the floor of the valley to his left and far below, all ponds and jewel-green places and marshland pleasant for the wild duck and the grebe and the bittern, and nowhere to be seen the dwelling-places of men.

By the time the floor of the valley had risen to the level of the road and he was within a mile of the top of the pass, the sun hung low between the two peaks; and he wondered would he get down into the valley beyond while still there was daylight. Came a cry from the left and behind him:

"Ha, Chieftain!"

Manawyddan drew rein and turned. A grave and princely man came hurrying towards him by a track through the heather. Manawyddan gave him the greeting of heaven and man.

"Soul," he answered, "unless you desire to encounter the unconquerable, go not forward into the valley beyond there."

But Aden Lonach had flown out over the valley, and there become lost to sight: so it was there Manawyddan was to go. "Of your courtesy, expound this to me," said he.

"I will," said the Chieftain. "Come you with me into the hall for the night, and I shall make it clear to you."

"A hundred thanks to you, and more than a hundred," said Manawyddan; and went with him through the heather; and came presently to a pine grove under the southern peak; and hidden in the grove, the long, low, stonebuilt house of a chieftain; only it was a long time lacking its decent whitening with lime, and he heard no clucking of fowls as he came up to it, and no barking of dogs in welcome.

They stabled Blodwen as they passed through: there were the best of oats for her, and hay in the manger, and everything befitting her dignity. All about the house, between it and the pines, were red rhododendrons in bloom, shining in the grayness of the dusk — every bloom with the glory of a God in it.

They went into the hall, and there came three serving men and set meat and mead before them, *da a digon* as they say, "good and enough." The first of them was one-eyed; the second one-eared; as for the third, he was lame of the right leg and one-handed. "They are all that are left to me," said the Chieftain.

Said Manawyddan: "Give me news, it it please you, as to that unconquerable one in the valley."

"Here it is," said the other. "Whoever goes down there will never return without having done battle with the Dragon of the Seven Conflicts. The man that opposed a thousand warlike chieftains at dawn, and made piles of their armor in the evening, would yet come by his defeat with that battle-stubborn, untamed, world-compelling dragon; and if his defeat, his death."

"Dear!" thought Manawyddan, "pleasant enough that news to me! A long time I have been at peace."

They fell to conversation and the narration of stories: and hard it would be to come by the better of either of them at those two arts. Manawyddan set forth the story of Einigan Giant, when he was king in Deffrobanau in the third age of the world.

"I never heard it better told, or told with such bardic skill and science," said the Chieftain.

Then he himself took his turn, and related the deeds of Hu Gadarn in the Summer Country, before he led the Cymry into Clos Ferddin. In the first branch of it he was even better than Manawyddan had been; but in the second he lost the thread of it, and stumbled over his consonances and assonances; and in the third his hwyl failed him quite and he could go no further. "Discourteous is this: shame overtakes me!" said he. "I am preoccupied with that fierce, resistance-quelling dragon."

"Indeed, splendidly was the story told," said Manawyddan. "Hardly with the bards of the Island of the Mighty have I heard it better."

"Better you should have heard it now, in my deed," said the Chieftain, "but for this preoccupation and anxiety on me. It pities me that so courteous a Prince of the Brython should come by his defeat and his death in the morning."

"On my road the valley lies," said Manawyddan, laughing. "It will be a crowning delight to me to encounter that Winged Splendor of which you spoke."

"If it is conflict you desire, I myself can provide it," said the Chieftain. "Here are swords: here is skill; and here, heaven knows, the wish to be kindly and hospitable."

"Kindly and hospitable is the offer," said Manawyddan. "Yet it is the Dragon of the Seven Conflicts I desire to fight, and no other fighting would satisfy me."

"Yet go you not unequipped or ill-equipped," said the Chieftain. "The pity of your life it would be to meet that dragon with a sword unequal to the venture."

Manawyddan's two swords were on the wall, where the Chieftain had hung them at their coming in: his own sword and the Sword he had made for Gwron. He rose now, and took down his own sword, which was not of the Subtle Making. "A good Dimetian blade and pommel," said he: "there will be few better."

"That is true," said the Chieftain. "But wiser you, if you consent to make trial of it."

"I consent, and a hundred thanks to you," said Manawyddan. So the Chieftain took from the wall a sword of his own, and at the first sight of it, Manawyddan knew what would be. For it was a brand of the Subtle Making, forged by the Celfyddwr Clod Cleddyfau, if not by Gofannon ab Don himself. He could tell by its beauty, its suppleness like a leathern thong; its adornment of gold tracery and of enamel brighter than the beauty of the noon skies in June. They prepared to fight; and began to fight; and fought.

Furious the attack; skilled and resolute the defense: the swords making play as if the whole hall had been filled with the untamable lightning of heaven. Before the tenth blow had been struck by the two of them, the sword of the Chieftain flashed out, rippling and singing through the torchlit air; and flamed against the sword of Manawyddan, and destroyed it: in such a way that the one half of the blade from point to pommel flew out to the right and the other half to the left; and only the hilt remained in his hand.

"In my deed to heaven, a beautiful brand!" cried Manawyddan. "A marvellous, great, griding gasher truly! An inflicter of wounds equal in its sole self to the three swords of the three Sons of Cleddyf Cyfwlch of old!"

"Your desire for conflict will be satisfied, perhaps?" said the Chieftain.

"It is not satisfied," said Manawyddan. "Whetted and made keen it is."

"With what sword will you oppose the dragon?" asked the Chieftain.

Manawyddan looked over to the wall, where hung the Sword he had made for Gwron. "Unless it is equal to coming through this warfare," thought he, "I will go back to swordmaking until I shall have learnt it properly." So he went over and took it down. "With this one," said he.

So they made trial of it as before: preparing to fight, and beginning to fight, and fighting. And fighting you might call it, without exaggeration. Much more arduous it was than the one before: with better war-shouts, more skilled, impetuous leaping and driving and sweeping and thrusting and cutting and parrying. Here is the twentieth stroke of that battle: Manawyddan swept out with the Sword he had made for Gwron, and it flashed and flickered through the air, curling and marvellously rippling; and took the sword of the Chieftain, edge against point, and made two halves of the blade of it, and rooted them out from the hilt so that they flew out to left and right, making lightnings in the torchlight.

"Blood would flow from the invisible body of the wind on account of it!" cried the Chieftain. "It is a piercing gap in the air, better than diamonds: the peer of Caledfwlch the sword of Arthur! Many would be content with such splendid conflict without throwing away his life opposing the dragon."

"I am not content," said Manawyddan.

They went to their conversation again, and presently to their chanting of poems. The poems of Taliesin Benbardd they chanted, as was fitting. The Chieftain gave *The Battle of the Trees*, and Manawyddan *The Spoils of Annwn*; and neither had heard better chanting in his life than that he heard now from his companion. Then the Chieftain gave *The Cattle-pen of the Bards*, but it was not so good as the *Cad Godeu* had been. Then Manawyddan gave *The Consolation of Elphin*; and though he gave it better than he had given the *Preiddieu Annwn*, he could see that it gave no pleasure, and indeed was quite unheeded by his companion.

From the seas, from the mountains,
From the waves of the rivers,
Comes a God bearing good gifts

he chanted.

"In my deed to heaven and man, I am anxious about that," said the Chieftain, shaking his head and sighing deeply.

"Over what are you anxious?" said Manawyddan.

"About the Dragon of the Seven Conflicts," he answered. "Not with good gifts but with fierce blows and opposition will that winged Sky-traverser come. Evil upon me if I desire that you should come by your death."

"With good gifts it is I who will come to him," said Manawyddan. "There is the sword."

"Yes, there is the sword," said the Chieftain; "and there is no accusing it, truly. But whoever goes against the Dragon of the Conflicts must be equal in defense and attack: in skill and in equipment."

"My shield is a good one," said Manawyddan.

"If the sword could defeat it, so could the dragon," said the Chieftain. "It would be better to make trial of it."

"Yes," said Manawyddan. "Sword against shield, it would be better the trial should be made."

So the Chieftain took the Sword forged for Gwron, and Manawyddan his own Dimetian shield. He had made no Subtle Equipment for himself: either at Henfordd or at Rhydychen or at Caer Odornant. But this was the best work of the Dimetian shieldmakers; and though there was little studding of gold on it — to say Welsh gold, and no tracery of blue enamel, he had borne it victoriously through many battles and known no need of peculiarities in it.

So, the one shieldless and the other swordless, they began the trial. Three blows, and the shield achieved taking the flat of the sword, and was not discomfited. But at the fourth, the edge took the shield-rim, and curled and tore through leather and withies, and made nothing of iron nails, but swept in narrowing circles inwards till the whole shield fell down in one long strip about Manawyddan's feet: one moment it had been a shield, and then that flash of the sword, and it was gone; and a marvel that Manawyddan himself was unbleeding.

"Without if or were-it-not," said the Chieftain, "it would have been the pity of your life, and furthermore the loss of it, to have gone against the dragon shielded like that."

"Shieldless I must go, whatever; and in the sword trust," said Manawyddan.

"Not shieldless shall you go," said the Chieftain. "It is the hour of gift-giving: none goes out from the hail here giftless. Choose you a shield from the shields on the wall, to be your gift."

"Courteous the custom; kindly and opportune this carrying out of it," said Manawyddan. "Yonder is the shield I will choose."

So the Chieftain reached it down, and gave it to him. It came of the Subtle Shieldmaking: the Tarianwr Tadwy would have made it, or else Gwydion ab Don. The leather on it was leather of the extremes of Africa the Great, after its magical steeping for ten thousand years. The nails in it were neither of iron nor of gold of Arabia, but of Welsh gold, peerless in the world. Above all, there were patterns and designs on it, magical tracery of lozenge work and zigzags, all in enamel more exquisite in hue than turquoise or sapphire, speedwell or gentian, or the sea in proud July, or the zenith of heaven on the day in June when the sky is at its bluest and brightest.

"Now to make trial of it," said the Chieftain.

So trial they made, as before. Manawyddan took the shield, and the other the Sword forged for Gwron, and thirteen griding, sweeping, warlike blows they struck and parried that way. Wind-wounding blows they were; and all with the edge of the sword on the face of the shield, to destroy it, if destruction might be. Then they looked at the weapons. The face of the shield was without scratch or blemish; the edge of the sword without dint or raggedness: both were as flawless as at first.

"The anxiety is gone from me," said the Chieftain. "If there is any opposing the Dragon of the Seven Conffi cts, it will be with sword and shield such as these."

Thereupon they went to their songs and stories again, and presently to rest.

In the cold of the dawn they rose up; in the youth of the day, Manawyddan went forward. "Leave you Blodwen White Flower here in the stable," said the Chieftain. "There will be no room for her in yonder valley, when the Dragon of the Conflicts is making war." So it was on foot he went.

He was on the road between the two peaks when he heard the Chieftain calling to him, and turned. There was that one running after him: anxiety on him again, it could be seen.

"Soul," said Manawyddan, "for what reason is the anxiety now?"

"Anxiety yes," said the Chieftain; "you may well say anxiety! Preying on my mind it is. It is the pity of my life that you should go and encounter that dragon, after all the kindness I have had with you, so ill-equipped as you are. Unknown to you are his fierce skill and his lordly valor, the swiftness of his blows and the suddenness of his motions."

"The sword and the shield are good equipment," said Manawyddan.

"They would never be enough, without shoes equal to them in peculiarities," said the Chieftain. "Even the lithe and swift and sure-footed would come by disaster were he not well-shod. Let trial be made of the shoes you have, in the name of man!"

"Yes, yes," said Manawyddan.

The trial they would make was to run a race from where they stood to the top of the peak on their left: an exalted course, a precipitous ascent, a pleasant prospect for the two of them. They threw down mantles and weapons in the heather, and prepared to run, and ran.

There were few better runners than Manawyddan in those days in the Island of the Mighty. Lithe, swift and surefooted he was: it had been said of him that he might run against Yscyrdaf and Yscudydd themselves and come by no shame. But compared with the one running against him now he was slow and awkward and heavy, weak in his feet, and prone to stumbling. At the head of the peak the Chieftain waited for him, and waited long.

"It was good running," said that one, sadly. "Woe is me: last night cheerfully we sang together; tonight I shall sing my lamentations alone. I shall make poems in your honor tonight; I shall mourn for you in well-wrought verse."

"It was bad running," said Manawyddan.

"The running was good," said the Chieftain; "it was the shoes that were bad. Come you now," said he; "forgo pride, and accept from me shoes of good making, that I may not sing poems lamenting your death."

"Yes will I accept them, and give a hundred thanks for them," said Manawyddan.

"Wear you these, then," said the Chieftain, taking shoes out of his wallet, "and we will make trial of them."

Manawyddan put them on, and they prepared to make the trial. It would be running from where they stood on the south peak down to the road, and up to the head of the north peak beyond. "Down and up, for the sake of thoroughness," said the Chieftain; "for the shoes must be equal at both."

So then they ran; and at the first bound into the air, Manawyddan knew he was well shod; one with those shoes wherever they might light. Beneath them the soft moss of the quagmire became firm and stable; the leaping stone sat motionless till they had passed. Like the wind and the waterfall he bounded forward. He leapt from crag to crag, and hardly were his feet aware of the ground. If descent was good, ascent when he came to it was better: like the level road to him was the unscaled precipice. The mountain goat of Eryri would envy him; the wind in the pass would hail him companion. He came to the far peak as the Chieftain came to the road; and lightly leapt down the mountain side again, and met him before the road was passed.

Then he looked at the shoes he was wearing, and wondered he had taken no note of them before — with the nails of them exquisite Welsh gold, and all that adornment of blue enamel on them. It would have been Ceinion Grydd made them, or Gwydion ab Don himself. Said he:

"An exalted gift is this. Magic flows from them into the footsoles."

"It is true," said the Chieftain. "The Immortal Races have heard a sound of them; they are the peers of the sword and the shield; if there is any accusing them, it will not be by the Gods or the Cymry. You with this equipment, I shall be without anxiety: if you obtain no advantage against the dragon, I shall not loathe my food and drink; if you come by death at his talons, I shall not pine away with knowledge of having connived at it.

"Therefore go you forth gaily, and success attend you, according to the merit of your life and pre-existences."

III. The Dragon of the Seven Conflicts, and the Glory of Gwron Brif-fardd Prydain

FROM THE TOP of the pass Manawyddan looked down into the valley in front of him. It was a deep hollow, mountain-rimmed all round. On this side, overshadowed now, were steepish green slopes, bracken and grass-grown; on the side opposite, lit up with the morning sun, were vast precipices, pine-forests and soaring crags; and nowhere, he divined, would there be a way down into the valley, except the path at his feet.

Below, the valley floor was mostly a wide water, half agleam and half overshadowed, in the midst of which was an island with a few oaks on it, and an open green space, and by the shore, rocks and boulders. Thither he would go: if there were to be fighting, that would be the best place in the valley for it, or indeed the only place.

So gaily he came down the mountain side, raising blithe battlesongs; and every pleasurable anticipation was in his mind. For now he had been shown the way, and the wings of blue Aden Lonach had brought him where the strength of his soul and limbs would be called forth, as he guessed. But where was the Dragon of the Seven Conflicts? There was no sign of that lordly sky-wanderer anywhere.

The water, when he came to it, was still and deep, and had a coracle on its shore to take him across to where he would be. On the island he made search among the trees and boulders; but found none to oppose him. Then he examined the mountain sides afar, the walls of the valley. And there he saw the eagle descending to his eyrie among the crags; and there the gray hare scudding afar on the mountain side; there an old, lean fox stealing from his hiding place among the fern, and here the play of moorfowl among the reeds and on the quiet water: here a sunlit and there a shadowy silence; the dewdrop glistening on the harebell, the sun-glow high up on the tops of the pines.

Discourteous, it seemed to him, to take his pleasure there in the Dragon's sacred valley, and not to apprise the Dragon of his coming and his desire for conflict. So then he raised his battle-shout toward the north, and nothing came of it. And he raised it toward the south, and no one answered. And he raised it toward the east, and it died into silence. And he raised it toward the west, and it rolled and echoed among the crags. "The sky contains him," thought he.

So then he threw back his head, and shouted it into the empyrean: *Y Ddraig Goch a ddyry — Gychwyn!* — and with the vehemence of that magical shout, and the stir it sent ringing through the peace of the morning, conceived he would get satisfaction.

And satisfaction he got, without if or were-it-not. For as he watched the center of heaven he saw a brightness glow there, as if it had been the Star of Morning wandered forth undiminished into the domain of day. It waxed in size and brightness and beauty. Sun-colored wings flamed out from it on this side and on that. A golden, flame-bright dragon came curving and sweeping through the air. He was the glory of the wide skies: the brilliance of the sun shone through him. Pale as the primrose by the stream, as the cowslip in the mountain-field: yellow as the bloom of the broom in the valley: mellow-golden as the heart of the daffodil or the bowl of the kingcup in the marshland: all the loveliness of the sunbright morning was fulfilled in him. In his fore-talons was a sweeping sword — the blade of it a long, hard gap in the air, a flame of invisible sapphire.

Said Manawyddan, "The greeting of the god and the man to you, Lord Beautiful Cleaver of the Nwyfre!"

Said the Dragon, "The greeting of the man and the dragon to you, Lord Son of the Boundless-without-Utterance! For what reason have you come here — for fighting or for peace? It will be better for you to go back to the Island of the Mighty at once, having exchanged this friendly greeting with me."

"Lord Winged One," said Manawyddan, "let more than greetings be exchanged!"

"More than greeting would be fighting," said the Dragon.

"Of your courtesy and your kindness, fighting let it be," said Manawyddan.

122

"Here is the fighting it will be," said the Dragon. "You will remember longingly all the battles and torments of your years, and they will seem to you like quiet sleep and dreaming in comparison with it."

"Lord Splendor of Heaven," said Manawyddan, "for the sake of such fighting as that I came here."

With that they raised their war-shouts and the fighting began; and no saying it was less than the best. All the valley was full of the Dragon: of the beating of his wings, the driving and sweeping of his tail. Flashing pure, resplendent light were the dazzling eyes of him; scarring the universe, wounding the wind, cleaving the mountains, was his perilous sword. More many than the hailstones on a roof in the wildest storm in January were the blows falling on the shield of Manawyddan. And then he leaping out again, and running against the Dragon, and achieving wounding him with the Sword forged for Gwron, and compelling him to take refuge in the air. Up and down, hither and yonder, they made fierce conflict until noon; and hither and yonder, up and down, impetuous warfare until nightfall. All the battles he had fought formerly seemed like restful dreams to Manawyddan. By soul and sword, by shield and shoes, he kept the life in him; but as for success and advantage, they were more with the Dragon than with him.

The sun went down, and the Dragon leapt up and caught the fiery splendor on his wings flung out northward and southward.

"Go you now in peace, Manawyddan *bach*," said he. "Courteously you have dealt with me: not overcoming, nor yet overcome. Many would be satisfied with this: they would not stay here till the cold of the dawn."

The beauty and splendor of the Dragon thrilled through the soul of Manawyddan. "Lord Majesty of Heaven," said he, "it was for the sake of fighting I came here, though it may seem to you it was for peace."

"Well, well," said the Dragon, "for me there will be a caldron of cure in the heavens; tomorrow, I shall not come slothful and unskilled, as I came this morning. However peaceful it has been here today, there will be good fighting tomorrow."

With that, a quivering of wings, a glow in the upper air — and away with that Lord of Flaming Beauty into the fortress of the winds, the abode of starlight, the unmeasured darkening vastness of the sky.

Then knowledge of his wounds came on Manawyddan, and weariness greater than ever he had known. He lay down where he was, and deemed that life would be gone from him before day dawned. Night passed over him, full of sorrow and evil dreams. But as the stars of the constellation Caer Arianrod were setting, he woke, and heard seven companies of the Children of the Air above the mountains, and knew they were singing hymns in praise of the Dragon. Then he crawled down to the lake, and drank, and bathed his wounds; and after that was sleeping quietly until dawn.

He woke when half the western mountains were sunlit, but the lake lay all in shadow. He had no will to stir, but lay looking up into the sky, remembering little. Then in the midst of the morning sky a wonderful star shone; and waxed until it was a Dragon of Beauty coming down to the world. "Now shall I be slain," thought he, "if that Sky-wanderer is for slaying men." Then he remembered that there had been fighting there the day before, and that he had had part in it; and that from the fighting came his wounds and weariness.

But the Dragon came down and floated above the mountains and Manawyddan saw the golden fire and beauty coursing and throbbing through wings and body and tail; and the sight was new life and vigor for him; remembrance also, and keen inspiration of spirit.

"Today there was to be fighting here, and fighting there shall be," said he; and with that, to his feet with him, and to raising he dragon war-shout of the Cymry, and to very proud anticipations.

Therewith the Dragon came down; and they gave each other noble and courteous greetings, lauding each other's strength and valor and magnanimity. Proudly the Dragon beheld the hero that had come against him: proudly Manawyddan looked on the beauty of that Winged Master of the upper air.

"Yesterday was for amusement and pleasurable diversion," said the Dragon; "today will be for measuring strength against strength. Go you now, secure in my friendship, if it please you: it would be the pity of my life if you should come by harm."

"Lord Dragon," said Manawyddan, "it was for the sake of enjoyable conflict I came here, if there were anyone with the kind courtesy to grant it to me."

At that they went forward; and indeed, conflict it was, and better than conflict. By noon the boughs were broken from the oak trees; by nightfall, the trunks were snapped off or torn up by the roots, to serve one or the other of the combatants for weapons. In the joy and glory of it, Manawyddan remembered what had been there the day before, and "in my deed," thought he, "it was no better than sleep beneath a beech tree on the hottest noon in August, when no winged thing may be troubling." With soul and sword, shield and swift-leaping shoes, he kept death away from him; but if he gained any advantage against the Dragon, the Dragon gained ten times more against him.

At sunset the wings quivered forth again, and from the air above his head the Dragon greeted him.

"Pleasant is the time I have had with you, Lord Son of the Boundless-without-Utterance! And now that our friendship is well-established, go you in peace; bide not here until dawn, lest evil overtake you!"

"I will bide here, Lord Dragon, until there has been fighting between us."

"Well, well," said the Dragon, "fighting there will be, tomorrow; even though today there may have been quiet peace."

As the first night, so the second; and as the second morning, so the third. At dawn, Manawyddan was nearer death than ever he had been; but when he saw the Dragon, he leapt up stronger than before. With prouder, statelier, more admirable courtesy, they greeted each other, and either lauded the one that was to oppose him. Stronger and more beautiful seemed the Wanderer of the Nwyfre; more regal and warlike, the Prince of the South. With louder and more joyful vehemence they raised their war-shouts; and with keener anticipations they began their war.

And if there had been fighting the first day, and hard fighting the second, this day there was hard, fierce and furious fighting, and dreadful strife, and tumultuous conflict. By noon not a boulder in the island but had been plucked up by one or the other, and hurled out at his opponent; the island itself was trodden flat, and level with the lake. By nightfall the mountains were running with a thousand torrents and waterfalls, where the lake had been thrown up by the wings and tail of the Dragon, or by the splashing of hurled boulders and tree-trunks. In the evening the Dragon sprang into the air again, and was gone.

After that there were three nights of sorrow and three days of fighting: each day making the warfare of the day before seem a far off, delicate dream of peace. But always the love and friendship grew between the Dragon and Manawyddan. On the sixth night there were thirteen companies of the Children of the Firmament in the sky above the valley, and Manawyddan heard them singing this hymn in praise of the Dragon:

> *Seven times and seven score times on high*
> *All hail the golden wings unfurled —*
> *The Druid of the Circled Sky —*
> *The Flame-bright Dragon of the World!*
>
> *Ho, Regents of the Planets seven,*
> *And warrior-hearted Sons of Men,*
> *The world's hope's Dragon burns through heaven —*
> *Evil shall have no peace again!*
>
> *He laughs the footless winds to scorn —*
> *His wings the star-strewn ether cleave;*
> *He scales the amber crags of morn —*
> *Drinks at the dew-cool springs of eve.*
>
> *Flaming he wendeth down the skies —*
> *Gives light where lightning legions are;*
> *Stars of imperial omen rise*
> *Where he leaps forth from star to star.*
>
> *Through the dim asterisms rings his song;*
> *Compassion lords it o'er his breast.*

The Dragon triumphs over wrong;
Grief dies before his shining crest.

Ah, seven times seven score times on high
All hail the spiritual wings unfurled —
The lone Archdruid of the Sky —
The lambent Dragon of the world!

"Lord Son of the Boundless," said the Dragon, when he flamed down out of blue heaven in the morning, and when his beauty had thrilled Manawyddan's soul to great heights and depths of godhood, and when they had exchanged many proud courtesies — each lauding and wondering at, and taking delight in the worth and magnanimity of the other, "go you hence in peace this morning, lest harm there may be no preventing should befall you."

"Lord Glory of the Dawn," said Manawyddan, "take back this request, of your hospitable kindness. My soul is eager for fighting, after all these years of peace."

"I take it back," said the Dragon. "Today at last you shall have fighting."

They went to it; and all that had gone before seemed quiet and peaceful in its comparison. The Dragon put away sloth and playfulness, and let it be seen whether he was good or not good at war. Some starry greatness overtook Manawyddan; he was aware that he had never put forth his strength until then. From Gelli Wic in Cornwall to Pen Blathaon in the North, the noise of their warfare rang like song; and from the Island of Ireland to Greece in the East. From dawn to mid morning, back and forth with them, filled with the joy of battle. From mid morning to noon, so impetuous was Manawyddan, he became the equal of that beautiful Dragon, and more than the equal, and drove him back as much as half the length of his golden right wing. Noon to midway between noon and evening, and the Dragon was the equal of Manawyddan, and Manawyddan of the Dragon: they stood still at midmost of the island, and dealt each other thunderous, astounding blows, swifter than the woodpecker's beak on the oak-trunk. And from that until dusk, the Dragon surpassing Manawyddan, and winning success on success, and advantage after advantage, and implacably driving him round the island; glorious, unappeasable, with wings flaming up to the heavens, and with war-shouts resounding from thence to the sun.

Three times he had driven him round; the sun was low and the valley all in shadow. "I have experienced good fighting at last," thought Manawyddan. Swifter and swifter, that winged Sky Prince came against him, and impetuously drove him, and flamed above him proudly, and thundered blows on him. "It will be the last of my battles," thought Manawyddan; "the last and the best." The Sword forged for Gwron grew almost too heavy to hold; the shield became an oppression. His eyes lost their clear vision. "Pleasant death when it comes in such a splendor of fighting," thought he.

Then he remembered the Harp of Alawn that was lost, and the Gloves of Gwron that must regain it: and song dead in the Island of the Mighty, and all virtue forgone, unless the harp should be recovered. And how proud the men of that island were of old, with what warlike glory to support their pride; and not less kindly and courteous than proud. The flame-bright indomitable nature of the Cymry was recalled to him, that time and circumstance and misfortune were not wont to overcome. Thereupon he leapt back from the assault of the Dragon, and drew three breaths, and banished his mortality. and forgot it.

And looked up, and took note of the glory of the Dragon, and let the splendor of the Dragon flame through him, heart and mind, limbs and imagination. "A marvel if I perish now," thought he. He dropped sword and shield, and leapt forth magnificently against the Dragon, and flung arms about that lordly Wanderer of Heaven, and clasped him between the rising of the neck and the sprouting of the wings.

Lightly the Dragon rose, and shook his frame, tossing and curving; and beat his golden pinions twice; and Manawyddan fell. But the peculiarity of the shoes he was wearing was that he might not fall except on his feet, and falling must bound, up again, and bounding up must clasp the Dragon better than before. And the Dragon, writhing and straining and curvetting in the air, shook him again to the ground. And not the wink of an eyelid between his touching the ground with his shoe-soles and his bounding up again and clasping the Dragon nine times more firmly than ever.

Round and round the valley flew the Dragon; beating his pinions; head and neck outstretched and held low; rippling and straining and curving. But there was no loosening Manawyddan's hold that time. Then he rose up into the air, and flamed and streamed forth and hurtled through the evening sky, and presently was a cause of astonishment among the pale constellations; and rearing and plunging, sped among the nebulæ, and leapt forth from one star to another; and dropped in a moment from moonrise to sunset. But Manawyddan held, and there was no loosening his hold.

Then it seemed to him that, speeding through the abysm, the Dragon sought the World of Flames, and disported in the hollows of the flames; diving through the roaring, intertwining, interwreathing crests and billows. And dropped down to earth again, in a moment from the Harp of Arthur to the Island of the Mighty; then away with him bodily into the sea, and to play and sport in the fathomless reaches of the sea, and in caverns where monsters from the making of the world were slumbering.

And then through the very heart of the earth itself: through the core of the solid mountains, nothing hindering him. And out then into the dusk in the valley, with the first stars shining out above; and three times round the valley, slowly, drawing inward, and crying low and melodiously through the twilight. Then lighted down slowly on the island in the lake; wings outspread, and the golden head of him fallen along the ground.

"I have given you fighting, Lord Son of the Boundless: are you not content now?" said the Dragon.

"No," said Manawyddan.

"Destroying my life will you be?" said the Dragon.

"No," said Manawyddan. "Not born to be destroyed you were."

"Then let me go back to my house in the sky," said the Dragon.

"There will be a caldron of cure for me there; I will restore myself, and come back here tomorrow and give you fighting you shall not complain of."

"No," said Manawyddan; "not till I get what I seek from you or the refusal of it. Ah, Lord Winged One, do not deceive me any longer! Gwron Brif-fardd, Gwron Gawr, did not my soul bow down in delight to you the moment I saw you in the air?"

Standing before him, at that, in the tall glory of a god, was Gwron Brif-fardd Prydain — Gwron Giant himself, the Heartener of Heroes, shining duskily golden in the dusk and quiet of the valley. He had the stature of the meadow poplar; his body was of golden and ruddy fire with luminous shadows violet and purple; of blue flame was the mantle of his bardhood. His hair was light-giving, rayed out flaming halo-wise about his head, yellow like the daffodil that puts glory on March. Many stars seemed caught in his eyes. Unseen warlike harps round him filled the evening with the comfort of song. Not on this world his feet rested, but in the dusk of the middle air.

The stature of him waned; the flame-form took human likeness; he came down, until it was a man that stood before Manawyddan; but still radiance shone from him.

"It is the gloves you desire," said he; "and now I am permitted to give you them: there will be no gainsaying it with Hu the Mighty, after all the fighting I have had with you."

He took the gloves from his hands, and gave them to Manawyddan. "And as for the sword and the shield and the shoes, keep you them likewise," said he. "They were endowed with good peculiarities when you made them; and they are endowed with better ones now. And you shall find this throughout the age of ages, and true shall it be," said Gwron Gawr: "serving one of us is serving all of us; and serving the Gods is serving the Cymry; and only he is enriched who wins wealth for Gods and men. And white be your world from this out, Lord Brother!"

With the word he took the guise of the Golden Dragon again, and away with him soaring and sailing into the far-extending beauty and silence of the sky.

With the fading of his wings in that night-blue darkness, and
his vanishing at last, the Third Branch of the
Book of the Three Dragons has its end:
by reason of what is told in it,
it has the name of

The Gloves and the Service of Gwron, and
Gwron Gawr Himself

Here is the Rest of the
Fourth Branch of it, namely
THE SERVICE OF ALAWN ALAWON, AND THE CONTESTS OF MANAWYDDAN AGAINST THE THIEF OF THE SEA

II. The Three Singers and the Dragon-Boat

MANAWYDDAN lay down where he was, and slept away his weariness. Bird song woke him in the morning; and it was Mwynach, not Llonach, that was singing. Whether it was she with her singing restored it, or the presence or Gwron's beauty in the twilight of the evening before, that valley was restored, and as if only peace had been in it, and quietude, since the Crying of the Name. He himself, too, woke free from wounds; and he had the Gloves of Gwron on his hands.

He rose and followed Aden Fwynach; not by the way he had come: not to the Chieftain's house in the pass, where he had left Blodwen his mare: on foot he went now, and by strange passages and secret ravines, into a land of mountains, the vastest and wildest in the universe: dazzling mountains whose snows fell the winter the world was made, and the stars forever flame-white and large above them. Sometimes from the peaks there would be giants watching him: still as slumber; beautiful as noon; silent as stone.

Through those mute gigantic passes, Aden Fwynach led him — shining amethystine by day against the ghostly opal of the mountains; by night shaking out violet splendor from her wings. For day and night he would be travelling at that time: it was easy for him, after his warfare with the Dragon Gwron; and he still had a hundred hazelnuts in his wallet; every one of them a day's provision for him. At last he came beyond even those mountains; and to the confines of the world: and there Aden Fwynach left him.

It was a desolate place he came to: a low coast the winds howled over; with the dead sea-marshes behind, and in front the gray sea, with high white-rimmed waves rolling landward ever; a low gray sky above, and melancholy rain blown over coast and waters. He would have to

132

cross that waste of sea, he considered; for the thing he was to do now was waiting for him not in this world. He wrapped his cloak about him and paced the dreary shingle. There was no sign of boat on the wave or of bird on the wing, or of the movement of live creatures anywhere.

When the darkness of night had grown so that no eye in the universe might pierce it, he heard footsteps coming down towards the sea. He picked his way towards the ones that were coming; the shoes on his feet were such that he had little need of sight. He cried a greeting to the travellers: but it was unheard or unheeded. He could tell nothing concerning them: how many they were, or whether men or women; there was no murmur of speech from them.

At the brink of the tide he came among them where they had come at last to a stand. He felt the incoming wave wash at his feet and withdraw; and with that a long, low call broke from them, which became a wailing dirge; and he could tell that they were women, and there were three of them; but their language was not the Cymraeg, to be understood by gods and men.

When they had sung twenty verses, a sound came over the sea like the swish of huge, slow wings; then a grating on the shingle, like the sound of a keel driven in to shore. He heard them go forward, not ceasing their song; and went forward after them, and into a ship; but what like of ship it might be there was no guessing in that darkness. But he felt it turn and spring out seaward; and that it was more like a living thing than a ship built of timber.

And then came the sound of the wings again; and went on in time with the singing.

All night long he waited, and would not move until the dawn. In spite of the great wind and the billows, the ship moved on smoothly; and there was neither creaking of oarsnor movement of oarsmen, nor yet the straining of masts and boom of wind in sails. At last the blackness wavered into gray, and sea and ship slowly grew visible. From where he stood by the stern he saw the prow — that it rose and curved over like the proud neck of a dragon, with the upspringing of a wing on each side where the shoulders would be; and that these wings quivered, and swept backward and forth; and he saw the head turn a little, as glancing this way and that.

He saw, too, the three that were singing. One of them was at the prow and one at either dragon-wing. They were taller than mortal, and had ageless beauty on their faces, and ageless sorrow. Their eyes were on remote and other worlds; when he greeted them, it seemed as if he were too poor a thing for them to see.

And now he went forward and took note of the sea they were traversing: a gray infinity ghostlily visible, that seemed full of lunatic mutterings, and something malignant and ominous in the laughter and gibbering of the waves. Out yonder, gray phantoms rose and fled: tossing of arms, streaming of wild hair, appearings and vanishings. And always the rain raced over the waters, as if it had been raining there since before the world was made.

To and fro he paced, considering and watching; now to stand awhile at the prow looking forward; now at the stern looking back. A startled cry in the dirge the three were singing brought him suddenly from such backward gazing, to behold in front the crags of the highest headland in the world, its summit lost in perpetual rain, its base in the rage of the foam. On it there was no sheep grazing, nor rabbit sporting, nor goat climbing, nor weasel bloodthirstily creeping; neither grass-blade nor brake-frond, crab-tree nor sloe-bush, nettle nor thistle, sea-pink nor samphire: no natural or living thing in the world. Against it forever, the wind was shrieking, the rain driving, the wave booming and whitening. There were measureless precipices overhanging the sea, and where elsewhere the cormorant would be perched or the seagull floating in mid air, here bodiless specters were wailing.

"It will be Pen Nant Gofid on the confines of hell," thought Manawyddan.

And Pen Nant Gofid it was; and on the confines of hell it was.

The ship drew landward, and for a long while coasted the headland, making towards the point. It thought little of the fury of the seas, but lifted itself like a living dragon on its wings and rode high above the foam-crests. Jagged pinnacles of rock on all sides would rise out of the sea as the whirling waters were sucked away from them, and be covered again swiftly with the flinging of the foam. All the while, the three mournful queens were singing, their song clearly audible above the roaring of the sea.

They came at last to the end of the headland; and Manawyddan, scanning the dreadful cliff, saw, when the whipping sleet fell away, a brazen door studded with vast nails of iron and made fast with nine bolts as thick as an oak-bole of a hundred winters; and straight the knowledge came to him that it was through that door he was to go. The Sword he had forged for Gwron stirred in its scabbard: the Shoes of the Subtle Making grew impatient on his feet, the desire for leaping throbbed in them. "Have you your way then!" said he; and let the Sword forth, and went where the Shoes desired to go: out along the left and landward wing of the Dragon Boat, and from its far end, leaping and bounding over a gulf of fearful sea.

Then with his left hand he clutched at the cliff; and since the left Glove of Gwron was on the hand, there was no denying or repelling the grasp of it. With the Sword forged for Gwron he swept at the nine tremendous bolts, and because it was that sword that assaulted them, they could not resist the stroke, but fell asunder trembling, their magical life gone from them. With his well-shod feet he found foothold: like the level plain for the shoes on his feet was the abrupt and slippery precipice.

The door swung wide to his right and above him; and he drew himself up lightly, and passed through before the wave ran in or the door swung to. "Now," said he, "here is another door opened, to make recompense for the door that was opened at Gwalas."

III. The Land of Gwiawn Sea-Thief, and the Tumult Manawyddan Raised There

HE KNEW that the world was left behind him, and that he stood on the brink of Uffern, in the abode of the hellions, in a quiet and deadly peace. Behind him was the door, in front, a dark passage through the rock. In a glow of expectation he followed this until he came out on a barren hillside and looked down over the valley, in a wan light like that of the closing of a day in October when rain is in the vale and rainy mists over the mountain.

Down below he could dimly see what seemed to be motionless conflict, frozen battle without sound: a plain covered with this as far as to the foot of the mountains beyond. Here was something that might concern him; he hurried down to get news was it reality he saw, or a deceit of the vision. Reality indeed he found it: a far extending reality, to bring mourning to the hearts of the joyous.

There were armies enchanted into granite at the moment when the fray was fiercest. The war-cars were motionless in mid-career, with the ivy twined about the wheel-scythes and the axles. Over the hoofs of the prancing war-steeds lichen had grown: over their fore-hoofs held high in the air. Spears were poised that never would be hurled; swords uplifted that would never fall or wound. Throats were framed for the utterance of war-shouts that had been waiting their utterance ten thousand years. Motionlessness had seized the arrow at the moment of its escape from the bow. Chargers, wide-nostrilled, straining at the bit, had suddenly been stricken into stone. The dying had become stone before the life had fled from them; the wounded had been made granite between their wounding and their fall. All who were there were gigantic: the rain trickled from their harmless limbs and beat against their eyeballs that had been deprived of sight. The silence that weighed down upon them was more terrible than any sound.

"It will be the work of spells," thought Manawyddan. "It will be the doing of Gwiawn Sea-Thief of the Nine Enchantments, evil on the beard of him!"

It pitied him that the heroes of old should so have fallen under an evil spell. By their raiment and their torques of gold and by their aspect of warlike nobility he perceived that they had been Cymry from the Island of the Mighty, pillars of conflict in their day, hospitable and generous princes, lovers of story and song. Then he became aware how the silence of Uffern oppressed them, and that he must break that silence into fragments and never let them adhere together or congeal into soundlessness again. "The War-shout of the Dragon is needed to begin things," thought he.

With that he raised it up, and so loudly that their slumbers were shaken a little, stone though they were who slumbered. He raised it again as he went forward amongst them; and the axles of the chariots creaked, and the ears of the war-horses trembled. He raised it a third time, and the Thief of the Sea heard him.

Heard him from seventeen worlds away in Middle Uffern, and thought, "Here is peril; here is that which I must attend to." He made haste through the resistless air of Uffern, and before the seventh raising of the Dragon Shout, was in hiding among the mountains that rimmed the plain, and saw Manawyddan approaching. There was an aspect of power with Manawyddan that seemed hostile to him; and the Thief was bewildered a little, not knowing what would befall.

"Without if or were-it-not," said he, "all my strength will be needed here; this is a territory unhabituated to invasion. Spells must be raised, and good spells."

He put his hand to the Harp of Alawn the Songs, and considered what spell he should raise on it. "For there well may be thieving to be done here," said he; taking note what splendor shone from the priceless things with Manawyddan. "Treasures not to be despised, in my deed to this Uffern! A glory on either hand of him, and a marvellous glory on the breast; the like of the sun on the right arm, and in the right hand the likeness of lightning; two crescent moons in their beauty on the feet." Thus he spoke of the Gloves of Gwron on Manawyddan's two hands, and of the Breastplate of Plenydd Splendid on his breast; and of the Shield and the Sword and the Shoes of the Subtle Making that were with him. "Dear indeed," sighed Gwiawn Cat's-Eye, "it never happened to me before to be without knowledge of the nature and peculiarities of precious things, and to be bewildered by them in this way!"

Manawyddan, crossing the plain, and picking his way among the warriors turned to stone, was full of pity for them. He thought of the Island of the Mighty from which they had been miserably exiled; and of how gaily and courageously they had invaded hell. He thought of the blackbird at song in the Dimetian woodlands, of the Gwentland nightingales, with music worshipping heaven; and of these petrified in Uffern, and hearing no note ever that those birds sang. So he made sweet pennillion about the blackbird and the nightingale, and sang them; till one listening would have seen moonlight and mystery in the glades of the yew-forest, or the May sunlight on the oak-leaves that quivered at the trill and ripple of the blackbird's anthem. Dumb heads turned slowly towards him; eyes yet half-granite watched him in confused wonder as he strode forward and sang.

"Sweet the bardism here!" said the Sea-Thief. "Pleasant the consonance, melodious the assonance of the singing. A peril to me is this, I shouldn't wonder! Better," thought he, "to raise spells against it quickly;" and yet he was loath to put a stop on singing so enjoyable; and slow were the spells in coming to his lips, and slow his fingers in moving to the strings.

Manawyddan, striding forward, saw the barren hills so desolate in front of him, and the dreariness of the fine, eternal rain of Uffern; and he thought of the golden gorse abloom where the south-west wind wanders over quiet mountains, and of the bees' murmur among the gorse-bloom of Wales; and made delicate pennillion of these things, and sang them in such a way that you would have thought, there in abominable Uffern, that it was on the slopes of Moel Hebog you were, or dear knows, perhaps on Eryri. Before the fingers of the Thief were well on the harpstrings to counteract him, he must stay and listen to this miraculous Welsh singing again, and be wistfully envious, on account of it, of the beauty of Wales. And the stone warriors trembled, and a motion of life quivered in their limbs and a little haze of thought in their minds; they remembered that there was adorable beauty somewhere, and the Cymraeg spoken among its mountains: they half perceived the shame that had been imposed on them.

So Manawyddan sang his three pennillion of the Gorse in Bloom; and that was as many as he had made of them. By the time he had ended them, the Thief, sighing with sorrow that they were ended, remembered his peril, and cast off his weakness; and the first note of the spell rose from the Harp of Alawn, and the first word of it from the Thief's lips.

It came stealing down over the plain: cold, sweet, desolating music, freezing back the minds and limbs of the warriors into stone. "Ah," said Manawyddan, "whatever power is in Uffern has its center in that music! Here is guidance for a searcher, and good guidance."

At a bound he leapt up onto the back of one of the stone war-horses, and stood up there, with all the keenness of his eyes making search of the plain and the hills in front of him; and because of the desire in his heart to see things, the Breastplate of Plenydd awoke on his breast, and shone out, illumining gray Uffern as if the sun were shining there. Illumining every inch of the ground there: illumining presently a gap in the hills, and a throne upon a granite pinnacle in the gap, and Gwiawn Sea-Thief on the throne, the harp at his breast and the spell flowing from his mouth and his fingers on the harpstrings.

Then a desire for speed in the heart of Manawyddan woke the Shoes of Subtle Making on his feet, and, "Speed shall you have, and more than speed: speed and surety, in the name of man!" said they. And with the word they took to putting forth speed: astonishing speed. They leapt from granite horse-head to stone warrior's shoulder; if they rested on the uplifted sword-blade, it was propulsion of them forth to wherever next they might desire to alight. So swiftly Manawyddan ran, owing to their faithfulness and extraordinary abilities, crossing the plain and nearing the mountains where the Sea-Thief was; and as he ran, he raised up a clamor of shouting against the spell the Sea-Thief sang.

"Ha, Gwiawn Llygad Cath, Gwiawn Forleidr!" cried he; "attend you to the living, and trouble no more with these enspelled ones! *Cadw'n pawb*, is thiefcraft forsaken and forgotten with you? Sad it is when the faculties grow dim, and he who delighted in skilful thieving has no more skill to filch or steal!"

He ran swiftly, and shouted vehemently as he ran; it might well have bewildered any man to behold and hear him.

"Here are shoes," he cried, "of the Esoteric Shoemaking — the wonderful craft the Gods admire — and they are without peers for excellence in the four quarters of the world. Were a Thief here, that might lay claim to the name without affronting truth and modesty, I declare to you that he would endeavor to steal them, and persevere in his endeavor until he succeeded: he would not sit there idly harping, and hoping heaven or hell might favor him!"

Gwiawn Sea-Thief sighed at that: he suspected there might be truth in it; for aught he knew there might be powerful truth in it; his fingers faltered on the strings; the spell was impaired with him.

"Hyperbolically thou callest thyself Sea-Thief!" shouted Manawyddan; "boastful is thy claim to be the Archfilcher of the World!" Bardic hwyl took him: and unrivalled eloquence: and he began to make known the peculiarities of the shoes. He covered three leagues of the plain as he forthtold them, filling Uffern with boisterous noise. "Woeful is this: a sluggardly lack of enterprise," cried he; "it will be punished during the remainder of thy days. Thou wilt pine away, regretting the adornment of blue enamel on shoes no longer to be stolen!"

Gwiawn's heart was set on making the spell, lest the stone warriors should quite awake, and lest Manawyddan himself should be on him, with hostile intent no doubt. But it was difficult for him, hearing the praises of the shoes, and eagerness to steal them growing on his mind. He saw them flash and twinkle whitely as Manawyddan ran; and was in such division of mind that his lips quitted the utterance of magic, though half the spell was still unsung. He made hasty plans for stealing the shoes, considering that he would be shamed if they were left unstolen; and, in his perturbation, rejected the plans when they were made; and saw not that Manawyddan had crossed the plain, and entered the gap in the hills, and was at the foot of the pinnacle on which he, Gwiawn, sat enthroned; and at ten bounds had surmounted the pinnacle, and drawn the Sword that was forged for Gwron, and lifted it high in the air, and —

But then the Thief saw; and between the beginning of the descent of the sword and the inflicting of wounds, away with his plans and desires, and away with himself also, in the guise of mist and unreality and an unstable form.

Manawyddan, sheathing the sword, followed him. "Only the gloves will serve here," said he. As swift as wind the Sea-Thief floated; and as swift as he floated, Manawyddan ran. Through a winding passage and dark caverns in the mountain they sped — and came out at last on a mountain side, under the sky of Uffern (such sky as it is), and looked out over a valley huger and more desolate than the Valley of the Granite Warriors. It was a ghostly and dreary wild, the grayness of October twilight filling it. Inaccessible mountains girdled it round; no rain fell in it. But afar under the crags dim shapes like specters rose and were driven on the wind, and fell away soon and were lost. There was no sign of Gwiawn Sea-Thief anywhere.

Manawyddan went down, and forward across the plain; and came presently among fallen giants; and saw that they had been kings in the Island of the Mighty at one time. The sight of them pitied him more than that of the Stone Warriors had done. In the deep dust they lay; there was no breath in their bodies, yet the color of life was on them: he saw that they were not honorably dead. And on their faces was contentment and loathsome satisfaction.

A moon rose above the mountains in front, and shed grim light upon their pallor, their limbs thrown broadcast, the eyelids fallen over their eyes, the curves of their nostrils and the heavy curves of their mouths. He picked his way, dreading to touch or brush against them. A wind came by him lightly, and blew the dust over the plain; and he saw the right arm of one of those sleepers crumble under the wind, and as dust blown away; but still, on the face, that aspect of ignoble and supercilious bliss. Even the breath caused by his passing made them crumble; but only their limbs and bodies: their faces lay there still alive and terrible in their sensual, white delicacy. He would not raise the Dragon War-shout; he would neither cry aloud nor sing, for fear of wasting away those enchanted sleepers; but went silent and picking his way, as swiftly as he might; for, searching with his vision from the midst of the plain, he saw Gwiawn presently, seated on the peak of the mountain in front of him, and the Harp of Alawn at his breast.

Gwiawn saw him; and saw also that where Manawyddan had passed the crumbling of the sleeping princes ceased; even that the limbs which had crumbled into dust were made whole again. He sensed some magic with Manawyddan, that would restore their forms to the sleepers, and with their forms, sentience and motion; and all this troubled him greatly.

"I ought to be raising a spell against him," thought he; "a spell against him and against the wakening of those sleepers."

So he collected his mind diligently, that he might make the second dreadful spell of Uffern and the Deep, with its peculiarity of being especially dangerous to Crowned Kings like Manawyddan. But before a finger of him could get to the harpstrings or the first word of the spell from his heart to his throat and lips, Manawyddan, down on the plain, lifted his shield above his head, and caught the ghastly moonlight on it, and flashed that upward for Gwiawn to take thought on; but he would shout nothing for fear of the crumbling. He knew nothing, himself; of the wholesome effect Gwiawn had seen his coming had on the crumblers.

Gwiawn saw the shield flash, and was grieved. "Woe is me!" said he; "there is a shield with him, of the Subtle Making, with esoteric beauties and peculiarities!"

His conscience began to trouble him sorely, thinking how shamed he would be if the shield were left unstolen. The more it flashed light at him, the more he was troubled. Thinking he was, that there would not have been the like of it in the world since the days of Wynebgwrthucher the Glorious, the shield of Arthur. And alas, he had never attained stealing Wynebgwrthucher; and whispers had gone abroad to his discredit over that.

Manawyddan came on, taking the crags and precipices; and soon Gwiawn saw that there must be spell-raising quickly. So he strove to put the Shield that was made for Gwron out of his mind, and to turn wholly to the spell again. He struck three notes out of the beautiful harpstrings, and got three words of his singing out of his lips. But there was that shield: the moon above was shamed by it. It asserted itself; one might say that it boasted; it allowed nothing in all that wide valley to be considered but itself; it manifested peculiarities of the Subtle Shieldmaking that Manawyddan himself had never heard of until then. Gwiawn Forleidr could do nothing but enumerate in his mind its most evident glories. "Unwise the man who neglected stealing it: imprudent he who filched it not from its lord when he might." But still he hesitated, and was ready with no plan and feared old age might be overtaking him, and the decay of his faculties. "My mind and my fingers were quicker of old," he sighed; and then, starting up, "Evil upon me, he draws near: there will be no safety but in the spell."

So he began his singing again, and his stroking the harpstrings smoothly, delicately, subtly. From rock to pinnacle Manawyddan came bounding, holding on high the Shield made for Gwron. "Come you, I will be your help," whispered the shield; and flashed lightnings up at the peak and at the Sea-Thief. For all Gwiawn Cat's-Eye gazed up at the moon, the flashings broke upon his vision and beckoned it downward towards what was far brighter than the moon. Tears dropped from his eyes then, to see the beauty of the still unstolen shield. He thought of the golden nails arranged like the winter constellations, of the enamel bluer than the skies of June. "Ah, me, ah, me!" he sighed; "were there a thief of skill and industry here, he would steal it, as the Son of the Boundless said."

So in great agony of mind he took to his framing plans again; and framing and rejecting them he was when Manawyddan bounded up on to the peak, and the Thief woke from his bewilderment, and took mist-form again, and fled over a wilderness of myriad mountains that lay in front.

"Come you, trust us and we will serve you!" whispered the Shoes of the Subtle Shoemaking to their lord Manawyddan at that; and trust them he did; and they fled with him after the Sea-Thief. He saw vast chasms beneath him, and stayed not to consider, but leapt forth; from peak to peak over the howling darkness and the wind he went, like a dragon launched through space; and ever far before him was the little cloud that was Gwiawn. Upward and upward: aerial riding: dragonlike soaring and leaping: he came at last to the topmost peak of all those mountains; and looked down to a valley floor the depth of the world beneath him; and midway between him and it, shone the grim moon that lighted it. In the midst of it, in a circle, were what seemed to be the bones of giants or demons; and into the midst of this circle he saw the cloud that was Gwiawn Sea-Thief sink.

Leaping and running, he came down presently into the plain; and journeyed across it a week at the swiftest the shoes could take him, and then saw that what had seemed from above to be the bones of the giants were the vast stones of a Gorsedd Circle on a great mound there; and in the center of it he saw Gwiawn Sea-Thief on the logan stone, and heard the terror of the spell he was making there.

"There will be sleepers in this Gorsedd Circle," said Manawyddan; "and they will be no more wakeful for hearing the spell."

Sleepers there were, as he was to find: Druids, Bards and Ovates, each order in its own circle: dear knows how this fate had been put on them.

"War and tumult come never into the Gorsedd," thought Manawyddan; "but it might be salutary to bring them there now." The more he thought, the surer he was of it. "Salutary it will be, and more than salutary," said he; "whatever penalties may be imposed."

"In your deed it will be salutary!" whispered the Sword forged for Gwron; "let me out of the sheath and you shall know!"

"Trust you in us and in the shoes!" whispered the Shield of the Subtle Making. "Trust you in the sword and in me!"

"Bear you tremendous war into the Gorsedd!" said the shoes on his feet. "Come you where we will carry you, and you shall see!"

So he gave them their way, and drew the sword from its sheath, and clashed it against the Shield, and made lightnings with the two of them, and shouted on high the War-shout of the Dragon, *Y Ddraig Goch a ddyry — Gychwyn!,* and leapt warlike into the Circle of the Ovates.

He saw the Ovates in their green robes, each at his vast stone in the circle: they were gigantic, and motionless like the dead; the stones they leaned against kept them upright; their heads hung back or over their breasts or shoulders; the skin on their faces was yellow and drawn tight; the lank hair falling in strands, black over the yellow; they were eyeless, and with thin lips drawn back and long teeth glittering. But he knew that they were enspelled and not dead; and ran forward eagerly towards the Circle of the Bards.

The stones of that circle were, it might have been, a league from, and within, the Circle of the Ovates; not one stone in all the Gorsedd but was higher than Cadair Idris piled on Pumlumon. From the logan stone in the inmost circle came constantly the insidious music of the spell the Thief was raising there; and "I must break this," said Manawyddan. So he began his shouting of taunts again; and it was his shouting against the Thief's singing for the souls of the sleepers.

"Ah, Thief of the Sea and Uffern!" he cried; "quit idleness and folly; quit cowardice; betake yourself to your proper thieving! Are you so rich there is nothing for you to covet, or to desire, or to appropriate against the wishes of its true owner? Is your ancient calling forgotten, to which you were an honor of old?"

And still the cold music came down to him; and he was ashamed that men of the Three Orders, even though enchanted and unhearing, should be where such spells were made. "It must be stopped, lest all virtue perish," thought he. "He may have overcome his craving for the shoes and the shield; yet with the sword one might still play upon his proclivities."

So he drew the sword from its sheath, and "Come you," it whispered, "I will make the lightnings!" So straightway it began as he flourished it to flash and burn and gleam in the dusk; kindling in Uffern unwonted glories; and as it did so, he published news of it and of its peculiarities to the four quarters of Uffern with exceedingly loud shouting, thus:

"In the name of heaven and man," he cried, "is Caledfwlch Lovely with you? Have you the famous sword of Arthur Emperor? Or have you purloined the brand of Gwrnach Gawr, that Cai had from him of old? Very subtle was Cai: he put the blue sharpening on the sword; and slew Gwrnach with it. But behold, here is a sword with the sharpening of the hue of the lightning of heaven! What! Have you all Pen Gannion at your disposal, that you despise Swords of the Esoteric Making? Have you fallen into meager, eventless honesty?

"Riches were this sword for its owner, even were he King of the Islands of Corsica, or Chief Justiciary of Greece in the East. It will take the blue sharpening at will, and pass from that to the lightning-hued; and all without coming within ten hedges of the grindstone!"

He went on enumerating its peculiarities as he ran, distracting the Sea-Thief woefully. "Were it desired that a gnat should be shaved," he shouted, "it would shave her as she hovered over the stream beneath the willows, and would leave no unevenness or bristles on her chin; and she would not dream that her beard had been tampered with. It will divide the mote as it floats upon the sunbeam, so that neither half should be jealous of the other's superiority. Moreover, none of these feats will get boasting from it; none will drive or waft it from the even temper and balance of its mind. Is there no temptation on you to filch it skilfully? Come, I will make known its peculiarities better: it will take, and has taken now, the sharpening of the hue of the bodiless air, and therewith wound the wind, and cause blood to flow, faster than the fall of the dewdrop from the blade of reed-grass in the morning, when the dew of June is at its heaviest!"

And therewith he swept out with the sword, and behold, the blood was dropping from the wind where he wounded it: dropping as fast as he had said it would — plain there for Gwiawn to see.

He saw it; and could do no more with his spell-raising. His whole nature ached with covetousness. Never in his life had he purloined a Wind-wounder from any man. Nothing would do but that he should steal it. He made and forsook plans anxiously; because of Manawyddan he was perturbed, and the calm power of thought deserted him.

Manawyddan came running through the Circle of the Ovates, the Sword forged for Gwron performing miracles of scintillation as he came, because of which there began to be among the Ovates a far off dreaming about the Island of the Mighty and things ancient and heroic, and the beauty they had seen of old, and the wisdom appropriate to their order; it was like a mist forming along the rim of the sea, or the silvering of cloud-edges above the eastern mountains when the moon is near her rising, or a presage on the winds of February that the crocus and the daffodil will soon be in bloom. This the Sea-Thief knew, but could not get to his spell to hinder it, because there was the sword to be stolen, and Manawyddan was drawing near.

Drawing near: and in the Circle of the Bards now. He saw their blue robes mouldering; he saw their faces ghastly with death. They were gigantic: the stones they stood by were as high as the Wyddfa piled on Cadair Idris and Pumlumon; they themselves were in stature loftier than Pumlumon. He would not stay to look at them; but made his way ever towards the Circle of the Druids and the logan stone in the midst; the treasures he carried with him sparkling in the dark air; the vitality of him shocking the deadness of Uffern.

"Woe is me!" thought Gwiawn Sea-Thief; "he is too near; I must make spells and hinder him, lest evil befall."

So he quitted his plan-forming, and went to framing the Fourth Spell of Uffern, potent against bards especially.

"I must counter that," thought Manawyddan: "I, too, am a bard. I must arouse his propensities," thought he. The sword would no longer arouse them, it seemed; nor yet would the shield nor the shoes. "But here is that which will," thought he. So he took to his shout-raising again, to publish news of what he wore on his breast.

"Gwiawn Llygad Cath Forleidr!" he cried; "I marvel intensely that this blindness should have fallen on you! Alas, that you should be overtaken with this pusillanimous honesty, so repugnant to the nature of thieves!"

"Bitterly you insult me!" groaned Gwiawn. "Wherefore is this, in heaven's name?"

"Wherefore is it?" cried Manawyddan; "wherefore? Have you heard no tidings of the Breastplate of Plenydd Brif-fardd? What should he lack who had thieved it — were the Harp of Alawn with him also? He would have full power over the Island of the Mighty: he would make little of the Cymry and the Gods. I marvel that you know not this."

"I know it," sighed Gwiawn. "I merit not your reproaches."

"Here is that, then, which you do not know," said Manawyddan. "The breastplate is here, and might easily be stolen were there a Thief here."

Gwiawn left his spell-making. "You have it?" he cried; "in your deed you have it?" Let all the victims of Uffern be freed if they might he cared for nothing but for stealing the breast-plate. Joy drove fear from his mind: with feverish joy he devised his plans.

Manawyddan, shouting and running, passed the Circle of Druids at last, and into the Cylch Gwyngil in the midst of the Gorsedd. He saw the druids each at his vast stone: gigantic skeletons with the rags of their white robes upon them: fleshless faces looming up into the sky. "Life shall be restored to them," thought he, "before I go out from Uffern." Whether with the coming of the breastplate into their circle, or with the shouting of Manawyddan, life did steal in a measure into the Cylch Gwyngil, and a far off tremor of dream into the minds of the druids; and this the Thief failed not to perceive presently, and grew anxious over the waning of his powers.

"They will be remembering the Face of the Sun and the Eye of Light," thought he; "dear knows they will be remembering the Island of the Mighty soon! Escape from me they will, if this goes on."

Something must be done, he considered. "There would be no peril from yonder brawler could I get to the end of a spell."

So he drove the breastplate from his mind, and in its place there put the Fifth Spell of Dangerous Uffern: it was potent above all against druids.

Manawyddan by that time was half way across the Cylch Gwyngil between the Circle of the Druids and the logan stone. He saw that desire for the breastplate had departed from Gwiawn Sea-Thief's mind. "Further temptations must be raised," thought he. "It is the nature of that one to desire to thieve, if suitable temptations be offered him."

"Gwiawn Llygad Cath!" he cried. "Ah, Gwiawn Llygad Cath! You were a Thief aforetime, they tell me; but now your glory is departed. You have grown sluggardly; mediocrity has overcome you; and honesty, to shame your lineage and your name!"

"What now?" cried Gwiawn, breaking the true hwyl of his song, and the tears dropping from his eyes with the bitterness of the insult.

"What now?" cried Manawyddan. "What now, in the name of man! The best treasure in the world now if there were a reputable Thief to steal it!"

"Peace upon you!" cried Gwiawn; "fear you nothing for me! Mine will be the breastplate presently, if you will but let me finish the spell!"

"Finish you it, finish you it!" cried Manawyddan. "But who spoke of the breastplate? Leave you the breastplate to thieves without renown or ambition, and take a proper pride in your calling! Two treasures are with me here, and the poorer of them worth thirteen times the value of the breastplate!"

"Unkind and discourteous is this!" cried the Thief. "Better would it become thee to name the treasures, and to quit this vulgar noise and tantalization."

"Take courage," cried Manawyddan; "take courage, and divine for thyself what these treasures are. The breastplate will protect its lord against spells; but thou hast no need of protection. But with these two

148

treasures that are on my hands, what glory were thine! The whole world would be astonished at thy thiefcraft; thou wouldst regain thy self-respect; and thereafter pilfer at thy will both from the Gods and the Cymry. For the thing snatched at would be caught by thee; and the thing caught would be held. It would be a trifle for thee to enchant mankind; and no knowing whether the Gods could withstand thee!"

"The Gloves of Gwron Gawr!" shouted Gwiawn. His mind was enfevered by that, and beturmoiled endlessly: he had no peace nor quiet, between his desire to finish the spell and his intense desire to filch the gloves.

"Yes the Gloves of Gwron!" cried Manawyddan. "Well mayest thou say the Gloves of Gwron! Virtue dies out of the world," he cried, "or thou wouldst not contemptibly neglect thy opportunity to steal them!"

"Heaven knows I desire them, and neglect no opportunity to acquire possessions," sighed the Thief. But he fell to harping again, seeing Manawyddan so near. But the power of the Fifth Spell had been broken by that time. He began the Sixth; but could not finish it for thinking of the Gloves of Gwron. He began the Seventh, but drifted away from it to ponder theft. At the third *englyn* of the Eighth he saw the gloves on Manawyddan's hands, and could think of nothing for coveting them. Manawyddan was but seven spear lengths from the logan stone when the Thief began the Ninth Spell: if he should come by finishing it there would be no waking any sleeper in Uffern till the end and head of the age of ages. Manawyddan drew the left glove from his hand, and flung it out to the left of the logan stone.

Gwiawn's eyes followed it through the air and marked where it fell. "O all-enriching heaven!" he cried, "how should this be forgone?" No sound of the Ninth Spell after that. Up with him, and a leap toward the glove. He took it up, and away with him; not leaving the harp behind.

"Treasures flow to me!" he cried; "fear not that I shall lack the rest of them!"

No apprehension was on him at that time; only keenest joy. He felt that he was twice the thief he had been. Out from the Cylch Gwyngil he ran, and out from the Gorsedd Circle presently; and

Manawyddan following him at the best speed the shoes could make for him. The men of the Three Orders dimly wakened behind them: so far as that into the vague nonentity of their peace, faint foreshadowings of dreams intruded.

Out they sped over the plain: the Thief putting distance slowly between himself and Manawyddan. They came to the beginning of that great wilderness of mountains, and climbed the slope as vast as the world almost; and there, because of the peculiarities of his shoes, Manawyddan gained on the Thief. Leaping then, with both of them, from mountain top to mountain top; and ever a valley between the Thief and Manawyddan. Then down into the Valley of the Crumbling Kings; and there Manawyddan achieved flinging out his shield to the right of Gwiawn's course. Gwiawn swerved and pursued the shield, that rolled upon its rim away from him, bouncing and leaping, back toward the mountains and Manawyddan. So Manawyddan gained upon him; inwardly commending the shield for its wisdom and loyalty. But soon the Thief caught the shield, and picked it up as he ran. "Two treasures have I won," said he; "wrongly thou didst accuse me of losing my skill."

At the end of that plain and valley, Manawyddan was five spear lengths behind the Sea-Thief; and the Sea-Thief was gaining on him again, for the best the shoes could do.

Then they fled and followed through vast ravines and gulleys; between gaunt cliffs and dark waters. There, when the chance came, Manawyddan swung his sword on high, and flung it out to the left of the Thief. Gwiawn glanced back, and considered it might be safe to thieve it. So he swerved again, and ran along the mereside, and struggled to wrench it out of the rock it had pierced; and after awhile succeeded, and ran on laughing; but Manawyddan gained well on him that time. Said the shield to the sword, "Shall we resist Gwiawn Cat's Eye?" "Not yet," said the sword; "lest Gwiawn be deprived of his advantage, and our lord displeased."

They came out at last into the Valley of the Frozen Battle; and the Thief would not pass straight through it, for fear the sleepers were sleeping too lightly, and they might be wakened by the noise of their passing. So he turned to his right, and skirted the valley under the hills; and neither of them was gaining on the other.

They drew towards the place where was the sea-door beyond the passage through the hillside; and there Manawyddan saw that the Thief would be passing out into the sea, and no pursuing him farther.

He took thought as he ran; and kicked the left shoe from his foot so that it fell out well to the left of the Thief and away from the rise of the hill. Gwiawn looked back to see whether there would be safety in getting it; and it seemed to him there would not, and he went forward. But there was his nature to take into account, and his extreme delight in thievery. "Ah, heaven!" thought he, "if that shoe should remain unacquired!"

He looked back again, and saw his peril, and darted forward. He strove to overcome his covetousness: he did grand battle against himself. But to filch and purloin, and to take pleasure in doing so, was the essence of his being. "Were it unstolen," thought he, "life would be unbearable because of the humiliation. "*Gwell angau na chywilydd,*" said he; "better death than shame."

He turned, and doubled, and dodged, and picked up the shoe; and Manawyddan gained on him while he did so; and while he kicked off his own left shoe, and put on the shoe he had stolen instead; and neck and neck they were ascending the hill and making towards the sea-door.

But now all the advantage was with Gwiawn Sea-Thief Manawyddan being one-shoed; and when the Thief came to the passage through the rock, Manawyddan was a spear's length behind him, or even more. "Intolerable," said the left shoe then, "to be apart from my brother, and on such a foot as this!" The next stone it came to, it kicked out and set rolling, and stubbed the Thief's toe on it, and turned over the Thief's ankle, and caused him to stumble grievously: and Manawyddan gained on the Thief.

"Ha, I grow impatient of this!" said the sword; and came forward, and knocked against Gwiawn's shins, and got between his legs, half tripping him: and Manawyddan gained on the Thief.

At the sea-door was the Thief, and in act to open it. "My lord will desire restraint from me no longer," said the shield; "to be borne by an upstart, and drowned in the sea!" Down it slid from Gwiawn's left shoulder, and bumped hither and yonder making confusion; and because of that Manawyddan, though limping by that time, gained on the Thief again.

The door was in the midst of its being opened; the smell of the sea was blowing in. Grievous, to Manawyddan, was his being without the left shoe: it was a cause of stumbling to him, and of falling out forward. And as he fell:

"Remember you me!" cried the right glove of Gwron Gawr from his right hand that wore it; "remember me, and my perquisites and peculiarities!"

Gwiawn Llygad Cath was in his leaping seaward, half way between the sea-door and the sea. And Manawyddan remembered the glove, as it had urged him to; and grasped out with it: many would have said foolishly if they had seen him.

"Now come you back with me into Uffern," said he; and rose up, and brought the Sea-Thief back with him on to the hillside overlooking the frozen battle.

"I told you these were the Gloves of Gwron," said he.

IV. The Harping of Alawn Alawon, and Alawn Alawon Himself

"SLAY ME NOT," said the Sea-Thief. "You shall have the treasures."

So he returned to Manawyddan the glove, the shield, the sword and the shoe. "I am grown wonderfully honest," he sighed; "it is a pity that you have brought me to this!" But he took courage, seeing that he was not slain. "I shall steal them again," thought he.

"There is still the harp," said Manawyddan.

"What?" said the Thief.

"There is still the harp," said Manawyddan.

"Woe is me, the wickedness of man! Not from you I had the harp; rob me not unjustly; steal not the harp from me by violence, lest evil be spoken of thee!"

"No," said Manawyddan; "there is another spell you shall play on it before I take it from you."

"There is virtue to consider," said the Thief. "Incite me not to unlawful spell-making."

"It is the Spell against Filching and Cheatery," said Manawyddan. "Come you! the Spell for Changing the Nature of the Thievish I must have from you: the Spell to Endow the Dishonest with Honesty. It shall not harm your moral nature."

"I know not that spell," said the Thief.

"Well, well, now," said Manawyddan, "it might be death for you not to play it."

"Death?" said the Thief. "To play it would be worse than death. It would be pining away till the end of my days: existence without laughter, life grown delightless. Shame it would be; humiliation forever; miserable mourning for faculties lost. Ask not this in the name of heaven!" said he. *"Mil gwell angau na chywilydd!"*

But Manawyddan had the Spell of Spells with him, that the Gods use to put compulsion on the hellions when they least desire to be compelled. "Were you hearing, at any time, of the Three Places in Wales?" said he.

"Evil on Wales and all the places in it and out of it!" said Gwiawn. "Is beautiful art to be lost from the world? What thief has thou heard of that was more skilful than I?"

"The first of them is a Wood, and Math fab Mathonwy with power in it," said Manawyddan.

"If there, were a hundred woods I would not play a spell so dreadful," said the Sea-Thief. "Where would thiefcraft be, were I turned honest?"

"The second is a field, and Tydain lord of it," said Manawyddan. "Very wise is Tad Awen, the lord of that field; and it is my desire that you should play the spell of your own free will, and without compulsion."

"Evil on him and all his fields!" said Gwiawn. "Ruin you desire for me, and shocking loss for all these worlds."

"The third is the Wyddfa Mountain," said Manawyddan. "Listen you now: By the Wood, the Field, and the —"

The Thief cringed down, white and panting. "Hush!" said he, "lay it not upon me! Lay not that spell upon me! Ah, fearful is that spell!"

"Then play you Honesty to the Thievish, I beseech you!" said Manawyddan.

"Yes, yes!" said he; "keep you silent, and yes will I play it — Wait now —"

He began fingering the harpstrings, and fingering them ill because of his trembling. But if his fingers did it ill, the harpstrings did it better, and it was Honesty to the Thievish he got from them. One by one he rid himself of his ancient proclivities, till there was no skill left in him. From being the Archfilcher of the Universe he became quite honest.

"Take you the harp," said he. "I stole it aforetime; take it you now; there is no more joy in life."

He thought of lonely places under the sea, and longed for them; of chasms ten leagues deep among the mountains of Uffern, where no one would come to mock at him. None were there but demons older than time, that gazed all night at the moon and were too weary to be malicious. He would have quiet to pine away and die there; he hoped death might be near.

"Tell you me what harp it is," said Manawyddan. "I desire news as to that from you."

"It is the Harp of Alawn the Songs," said Gwiawn. "A door was opened at Caer Walas in Penfro; and I went in and stole it. Ah, me, a beautiful exercise of thiefcraft it was! I was skilful then; I had my powers!"

"Come you!" said Manawyddan; "there is more you shall play on the harp, again. Take you courage: there must be further spells."

Gwiawn looked up at him, and then down at the frozen battle on the plain. Misgivings filled him. "It is not to waken yonder men?" said he.

"To waken them it is," said Manawyddan.

Gwiawn gazed at him appalled. It seemed to him that never before had he understood the Cymry — what depths of folly were in them. "Look you," said he, "there is wisdom to consider. Go you hence: easily can I carry you across the sea. Leave hell in quiet where it is: it can do no harm to the Cymry, now I am lost to it."

But it seemed to the Son of the Boundless that he had come there to conquer hell; and that there was much for him to do there yet. "Soul," he said, "play you Waking to the Warriors."

"Seven score thousand they are sleeping in their stone," said Gwiawn. "Waking, they will all hanker for revenge."

"There will be no revenge for them," said Manawyddan. "Play you the Waking, if it please you."

"There will be revenge," said Gwiawn: "tempestuous, heedless, dreadful revenge. And they will discriminate little between you and me when they take it."

"Well, well," said Manawyddan; "there is a spell for waking them: there is a spell for everything. Play you the spell; it is what I demand of you."

Gwiawn remembered the Three Places in Wales, and feared what might happen. He took up the harp sadly, and began to play; and it was nothing but Waking the Warriors he could get from it, so honest his fingers were grown. As he played it, they went down.

The moon shone grimly over the warriors of stone. The harp began its murmur and speaking, glad of the work it was to do. The notes flowed down into the frozen battle, and hurried among the stone men: a whisper, a quiver, a curious laughter; a sudden excitement, and a breathless busying; expectation; haste. Then the harp-notes rose, leapt up, a fountain of cold, sweet sound; and cried mysteriously over the plain and skyward; and cried and thrilled piercingly; and would not be silenced.

Then there was motion down there among the stones, and life surging through the field of death. The men of stone swayed presently; their limbs strained to embody life: they were set in motion, and life flowed into them with the keen sound. Every atom of the granite was shaken by the sound that rose and rose, higher and deeper and faster: a high wind of harping; a clamor of harping beating like hail over the plain. Higher and faster and deeper the music came: higher and faster and deeper. On the backs and sides of the horses, muscles rippled beneath the skin. Manes were shaken; there came to be tugging and champing of bits. Frozen brains quivered and grew eager; blood coursed in veins; mind dawned after a fashion; memory came surging from the depths. The last note of the harping died; and the war-shout so long withheld from utterance broke from seven-score thousand throats.

All this they saw as they went down into the plain, drawing nearer always to the battle that no longer was frozen. Living warfare rolled and roared there now. Scarlet banners took the wind; wheels of chariots screamed. There were war-cries and groaning, wounding and slaying; hurling of thirsty spears; helmets cloven where swords fell. Hell was loud with war noise, where an evil silence so long had been.

"Peace must be imposed here," said Manawyddan.

Said Gwiawn Llygad Cath: "There is little sagacity in my tongue now: truth must I tell, woe is me!"

"Tell you it without concealment," said Manawyddan.

"Here it is for you," said the Thief; "truth without concealment or prevarication; to this am I come! Not I can bring those fighters to peace. There is no spell for it: the harp is useless."

"Give me the harp," said Manawyddan. "I will make trial of it, whatever."

So then he began playing. Head bent over the harp, he strode on, making what music he could; and Gwiawn, following him, wondered what would come, and did not desire it, whatever it might be. For, good it could not be, he considered.

A lull came on the warfare. The harpnotes stole into the minds of the fighters, whispering, *Wait now — hush!* Swords dropped; the butts of spears came to the ground. Then one of the warriors turned, and saw Manawyddan; and watched him closely, not understanding things. Then he saw Gwiawn Llygad Cath following the one that harped. "Ah, ha!" he cried, "it is the one that put stonehood on us of old time."

That cry went through all the host. They remembered what had befallen anciently; they remembered the Island of the Mighty and all their losses. Manawyddan came on, harping; and every note he played reminded them of the Island of the Mighty. There they stood, heads bowed down, and many with their hands over their eyes; bitterly thinking of their losses and of the Island of the Mighty. Then they remembered the one that had put these losses on them; and it was told among them that that one was advancing toward them across the plain, following the one that harped.

Soon one of them drove forward in his chariot, and cried to Manawyddan that the man who came behind him was Gwiawn Sea-Thief; and that he was to be destroyed and obliterated for his misdoings. "For he set this disgrace upon us, and stonehood here in Uffern," said he.

"I gave warning how it would be," said Gwiawn to Manawyddan. "It will be hard for you to answer them."

But Manawyddan strode on, harping and harping; and Gwiawn would neither turn nor flee, but for safety's sake followed him. It was maddening to the host in front to see him come thus; and a murmur rose, and then a roar; and they swept forward to make an end of it.

"Woe is me," said Gwiawn; "I was never good at fighting! Give me the harp; let me play Thievishness to the Honest, and I will steal their anger and save your life."

"Fighting will be none," said Manawyddan; "I shall impose peace on them yet."

He strode on; and for all he sought to play peace at them, war was the best they heard with him: loud war-music it seemed to them, inciting them to valor.

"Play peace! Play peace!" cried Gwiawn. "For the sake of man, play peace!"

"Peace it is," said Manawyddan "peace and pity. Stop you! I shall quiet them yet."

But peace it seemed not to be, to any ears but his own.

"Ah, that I were a gifted thief!" sighed Gwiawn. "I would steal the harp, and play delightful peace at them; and save this Son of the Boundless as well as myself."

A hundred chariots drove down on them; and Manawyddan played and played. The horses backed, reared up, and swerved aside: the music turned them. Chariots on chariots strove at them from either side; the host was divided — the music sundered it. Better than swords was that harping: a nobler defense than spears or shields. It drove them back; it parted them: where they pressed on, there were they pushed back. They were mighty giants, and they strove to come at him; and with keen sound, and no weapon, he drove them asunder and pushed them back.

It was pity and peace he played them; although it seemed to them to be rage and hatred. He went through the host of them; leaving them as he passed with nothing to say. He went out on to the plain beyond them, the Sea-Thief following him, and left them listening in wonder. When he came to the foot of the mountains he felt the music waning under his fingers; later, the harp sobbed and all sound died from it. "Let me rest now, for I am weary," it whispered. And then they heard a tumult in the valley behind them, and the host there waking to pursue them.

Presently they came into the valley of the Crumbling Kings; and there Manawyddan began tuning the harp again: the sight of those that were under enchantment there reminding him that he would need it. As he tuned he heard a murmur from the strings, and listened:

"I have done what few harps could do," it whispered; "and in a region hard to make music in. Tuning will not be enough."

So Manawyddan took thought what more than tuning he could do for it. "Is it the Spell of Spells you desire said over you?" he answered. "Is it the Three Places you are for hearing of?"

"The Three Places it is," whispered the harp.

So Manawyddan spoke that spell to the harp; and it sighed happily. "Behold, it is new life to me to hear that," it said. "I shall sing again, for all I have suffered."

They came within a bowshot of the Crumbling Kings where they lay; and Manawyddan turned to Gwiawn Llygad Cath.

"Take you the harp," said he, "and play Awakenment to the Kings!"

Gwiawn stopped, and gazed at him wildly. "Is it lies I hear from you?" said he. "Is it lies and idle speech — and you a king from the Island of the Mighty?"

"No, no," said Manawyddan.

"Unwise he who will never learn," said Gwiawn. "We had better go back to yonder valley: those warriors that you wakened are harmless enough."

Manawyddan laughed pleasantly. "Soul," said he, "play you the Awakenment, and we will go forward."

Gwiawn sighed, and the tears fell from his eyes. "If I were as I once was," said be, "I would steal the harp and save you. I would play seven times deeper slumber to the kings. Evil on this honesty! It makes a man worthless in perilous times."

But honest he had become, and there was no help for him. He took the harp and played the Awakenment; and dreaded what should come. For he knew what those kings had been, and what manner of sleep he had put on them.

Playing, they advanced; until they came to the head of some little eminence, and could look down on the kings where they lay. Manawyddan saw the crumbling limbs refashioned and grown firm; he saw a stir among the sleepers, and their rising here and there upon their elbows and turning their faces towards the music. As for Gwiawn Llygad Cath, because of fear, he bent down over the harp as he played it, and would not look at the kings.

The lurid moon shone down on these, and wakened in the rubies and flashed in the emeralds of their crowns. There was something that reminded them of the Island of the Mighty in what they heard: something that had the whole sadness of earth in it. The place where they lay seemed fair to them, but the Island of the Mighty seemed disastrous. They thought of their ancient losses and strivings when they reigned in it, and were ill content to lose the luxury of their dreams. They watched Manawyddan and Gwiawn come on, and were filled with detestation of them.

"The spell is finished, and they are awake," said Gwiawn Llygad Cath.

"They make no opposition," said Manawyddan.

"They will," said Gwiawn, "and I tremble at it."

"Tremble not, but give me the harp, and I will play peace and pity to them," said Manawyddan.

So he took the harp and began to play.

And pity and peace he played: but for their ears and Gwiawn's it was wild warfare and incitement to hatred. A moaning went on the wind: it was the grief and anger of the kings. They would not stir unless they must; but the music was a torment to them, with its wild, wilful defiance and its sound of the winds of the Island of the Mighty, its music as of all the waters of Wales. They would not stir because they had stirred enough of old. Woe was them! It was rest they desired, and the luxury of lawless dreams.

They would not stir — but stir they must: the limbs that had been dust, at the propulsion of that music refused to be still. It played on them and shook their minds into life; and shook to life all the hatred that was in them; all the depths of evil. The moon and their anger lit their lurid rubies and caused the frost of their pearls and opals to sparkle and shine.

And Manawyddan came on against them, and the Harp of Beauty played its part. He did not know what manner of opposition it would be; but knew that it would be loathsome and sickening. Red the moon shone down: stern and keen the music that rose and battled with the silence of desolate hell. Against the music the kings opposed their silence and the glitter of their eyes and rubies in the dimness.

They came at last to the rim of that prostrate multitude, and saw what the opposition was to be. "Hateful is this!" cried Gwiawn Llygad Cath. Snakes crawled out from the mouths and eyes and raiment of the kings; white and faded, like the skin of a leper. They rose in the air, soundless and wingless, but fanged horribly; from all sides myriads of them came against Manawyddan and Gwiawn. There was no protection against them but from the harp.

Manawyddan played and played on it; and all he had a mind to play was pity and peace, and the wholesome music of the Island of the Mighty. But the notes as he played them became as it were wind-wounding swords and shields of the Subtle Making: the serpents fell dead in clouds and hosts as they came near the harping. But they were myriads; and myriads coming anew.

Warily Gwiawn Llygad Cath came on after his lord; and could not keep from bewailing his honesty. He would have stolen from the serpents both their hideousness and the danger in their fangs. The air thickened with them continually; the harp itself grew weary of the contest — so sternly Manawyddan played.

"Weary not!" he whispered; and played the Three Places in Wales; and the strings took courage again. He did his best with the harp, advancing always. The music rose, soared, burned, trilled and lightened; it leapt up and grew tremendous; it frightened Uffern; it woke in all the quarters of hell. The recumbent kings writhed under it; it was for them the Island of the Mighty, a very sore affliction. Splendid was the harping: Alawn the Songs, hearing it from afar, was prouder of his harp than ever he had been. The snakes withered under it, and fell in clouds dead to the ground. "No shame to be conquered by such a man as this," thought Gwiawn Llygad Cath.

So they passed presently beyond where the Crumbling Kings lay; and soon by a secret path, well known to Gwiawn Llygad Cath, through and over the mountains, and out on to the Gorsedd Plain. The harpstrings were weak and limp again; but as he went he comforted them with the Spell of the Three Places in Wales.

Said Gwiawn Llygad Cath, "Come you now! get to what you desire. If it is on the logan stone you would be, go there; but be careful lest you put awakenment on the men of the Three Orders in their circles."

"Wherefore on the logan stone? said Manawyddan.

"It is the midmost place in Uffern," said Gwiawn. "It is there you will come by your desire, if you can get to it."

"We will go there," said Manawyddan. "But first play you Awakenment to the Three Orders."

"If I must, I must," said Gwiawn. "But if I were as I once was, I would steal their powers from them first; and it would be the better for you and for me."

So he played Awakenment; and as he played they went forward. He finished it, and still there was no sign from the Gorsedd Circle.

"Lord," said Gwiawn, "take you the harp, and do your best with it. There will be frightful opposition here: these druids were worse than the kings."

They went forward a long way; and there was only silence against them, and the moon glaring down over the gaunt, gigantic stones of the Gorsedd. Manawyddan took thought what he should play; and it seemed to him the best would be *The Going Forth of the Gwynfydolion.* He played it till all Uffern was loud with the grand Hai Atton of the Host that went forth in the beginning: a triumph of proud music, proud hope, proud resolve to take Infinity by storm. Then he played

The Fall into Abred and *Dark Inchoation*; till all Uffern was filled with sobbing. Then he played *What Shall Be, and Is Not Yet* — the rise of the Gwynfydolion: their casting off the slough of Abred; their mounting on high in their spiritual war-cars, and their thundering on the gates of Ceugant: their triumphant going-in at the end of time.

In the midst of it suddenly black night came over them, and the world was gone: there was no moon; no plain was visible, nor far mountain; no Gorsedd Circle of vast stones.

"Ah, dangerous this opposition," said Gwiawn Cat's-Eye. "Far more powerful, these druids, than any of the men of the valleys we passed!"

"Who were they of old?" asked Manawyddan; "and what gave you power to bring them to this?"

"They were masters of magic in the Summer Country, and they sought to use their magic against the Gods and the Cymry; and therefore I had the power."

They went forward through that darkness, walking warily; and Manawyddan harped and harped, and the harpstrings of Alawn did what they could. They knew there was need for them to do it; and although grown weary, put forth their strength and their will. The notes increased; leapt from them and lightened: whirled forth as faint and then burning light-flakes against the darkness till they had made a twilight of their own, and there was dim seeing. And then —

There was utter emptiness around Manawyddan and the Thief, below and above; and the path they trod was swaying out into space like the loose anchor-thread the spider floats out on to the breeze.

"Go you circumspectly!" said Manawyddan. Picking his way, he caressed the harpstrings, and sang spells over them, and persuaded forth the notes. They fell like snowflakes in the void, and where they touched the path, congealed and made it firm; till it was like a bridge of ropes woven, made fast at either end; till it was like a fallen tree-trunk, with fair footing on it. Above and below them loud winds howled; and by the twilight the harping made, they went on.

The solid ground was beneath them again, and the darkness was gone. The moon was shining over the plain and over the gaunt stones of the Gorsedd Circle; and over mysterious movements in the Circle.

"Not till now was there danger," said Gwiawn. With the word, the world in front of them broke into a vast conflagration from the floor to the roof of Uffern. Gods and men and elemental beings heard the roar of it. The far off mountains glowed; fierce light shone down into their deepest gorges, troubling solitary demons brooding there till they whimpered over the change of their changeless world.

"Give me the harp, to play Thievishness to the Honest on it!" cried Gwiawn Llygad Cath. "Then will I steal the heat from these flames."

He was kneeling to Manawyddan, imploring him; but no sound of his voice was to be heard. But Manawyddan considered that the Harp of Alawn would be equal to conquering that hot opposition, and waved negation and uncompliance to him; and went on with his harping.

The glare was on them; the scorching heat on their faces. He bowed his head over the harp, and whispered encouragement to it; and played and played. "Drive you your might against those dreadful flames," said he.

"I am nearly dead, but I will make trial of it," said the harp. Then it took thought of Alawn its lord, and sighed to him for power; and put forth what power it had or could come by. Nothing to be heard, for a long time, but the roaring of the flame. Then slowly another sound rose against the roaring: harping — self-multiplying, tremulous, eager; harping — triumphant, soaring, heavenly; harping — to shake hell with a wonderful delight.

He played coolness against the burning: he played all the fountains and rivers in the world and Wales. He played the waters of Hafren, from their source on Pumlumon the Five-peaked to the sea; he played the little magical fountain of Tybie in the Field at Llandybie. He drove forth the cool notes: it was like faery fluting on the wind. He drove forth the cold icy notes: it was like winter coming down with the north wind out of the top of the world.

The scorching heat receded; and he went forward playing. The glow died from the far mountains; the roar of the flame died down before the triumph of the harp. He went forward, and the fire feared him; an arch parted in the flame; the fire sundered and gave way. "No, but you shall die quite!" said he; and played and played.

Then — a sudden cold; the flame vanished away; the grim moon of Uffern looked down on freezing desolation. Manawyddan and Gwiawn passed between the stones of the outermost circle, and were in the Circle of the Ovates. And these stood each at his stone: muteness on his lips, glittering hatred in his eyes; but there was the look of living flesh on them now; they were no longer like men long dead.

Manawyddan looked at the harp. Two of its strings were broken and withered. "We have done our best," said the others. "Yes, yes," said he; "there is little more to do." So he hurried forward, and Gwiawn after him, till they were nearing the next circle. It was cold and silent, and the stones towered up ghostlike, and there seemed to be plotting and a shudder in the air.

"Lord," said Gwiawn, "I distrust the bards. Play you, if true wisdom is beyond your learning."

"What is the true wisdom?" asked Manawyddan.

"To restore me to competent thiefhood, and let me steal the bards' songs before they are sung."

"There are but five strings left," said Manawyddan. "You could not get the spell you desire from them."

"No," said Gwiawn; "and we shall be destroyed, since I cannot save you." At that he looked back, and cried out again: "And the serpents come now!"

It was true: they were flying and drifting in through the stones of the Circle of the Ovates; and their eyes like fire-shot rubies for anger when they saw the ones they pursued.

"Heed them not!" said Manawyddan, and bent over the harp, playing.

Then rose a slow, low chanting from the bards in the circle before them. "Ah, me!" cried Gwiawn: "the worst peril of all: the Ninth Spell of Caer Uffern — my own chief spell of old!"

"Come you forward, and fear it not!" said Manawyddan; and whispered to the harp again, and played.

"Go you; I am enspelled!" said Gwiawn. "I would have saved you, if I had possessed my thiefhood." So there he sank to sleep; the stonehood he had imposed on so many now at last imposed on him.

"Well, if there is to be saving him or any of them, there must be hurrying forward now," thought Manawyddan. So he played the harp against the spell of the bards, and with bowed head pressed on. Enough was left in the harp to bring him through that circle; but when he had passed it, and silenced the bards in it, but three strings were left. The rest were broken and useless.

Now the last circle, that of the druids, rose before him. Between its stones he could see the Cylch Gwyngil beyond, and in the midst of that, the logan stone. He pushed on, and felt the power of the druids rise against him; but would not tax the harp as yet. Suddenly there was a cry that put out the moon: Uffern vanished; the gaunt enormous stones vanished; there was no floor of hell beneath him; he was falling through an empty dimness; there was nothing but himself and the harp; he was falling and falling, and might fall forever. He bent his head over the harp: "Is there life in you yet, my darling?" said he.

"A little," said the harp. "A very little."

"Come you now, then; for Alawn your lord's sake let us have music with you! Come you now, in the name of the Wood, the Field and the Mountain!"

He was falling and falling, and only vague emptiness about him, and no knowing when the end of the fall would come, or where. He stroked the strings, and they gave out a murmur. "Come you now, little heart dear," said he; "make you the best of your music now!"

Then came a small breath out of the strings, and a faint sobbing of tune.

"Ah, courage, little fountain of music! Courage, little heart of the music of the world!"

"Yes, yes," said the harp. "I will do my best."

Then a voice cried out, "There is no world: the Gods are dead;" and a whirlwind took Manawyddan, so that he no longer fell, but was hurled round and spun in the darkness.

"Answer you that lie, little harp!" he gasped. But small need of his requesting it. The harp in an anguish of anger would affirm the being of its lord, Alawn the Songs. It spoke out loud on the emptiness; it gave the lie to the voice that cried; music shouted proudly from the three strings of it, heroic music, affirming Alawn and his brothers. Then the atoms of existence coalesced and resolved themselves again; and Manawyddan stood in the Cylch Gwyngil in the midst of the Gorsedd Circle, having passed the druids at their stones.

But they were not conquered; he saw them approaching him from all sides; and the bards from their circle, and the ovates from theirs; and the air above their heads was thick with the white glistening of the serpents from the Valley of the Crumbling Kings; and from the plain beyond the Gorsedd Circle he heard a thunder of hoofs where the warriors that had been stone-guised followed. All these, he knew, desired vengeance on him above all things, and would have it if they might. "From the logan stone I will deal with them," thought he; and made his way thither.

But he was troubled about the harp; because now there was but one string left to it; and that worn and loose. "Will there be any more playing you, little heart?" said he.

"No," said the harp; "none will play me more: there will be no more music while this universe endures."

Then it came into Manawyddan's mind that there was something left to him yet; and he took the Gloves of Gwron from his wallet. "Will you make music for hands wearing these?" said he.

"What are they, in the name of man, before I die?" said the harp.

"The Gloves of Gwron, darling! The Gloves of Gwron Brif-fardd Alawn's brother."

"White their world!" gasped the dying harp. "Make haste: they may save me!"

So he put the gloves on his hands, and began stroking the harpstring with them. By that time he was on the logan stone.

And music came. It was very low at first, but very marvellous; and none in the Cylch Gwyngil but was astounded to hear it. He played on, and forgot all but his playing. It was very rich and noble; he could hear in it the thunder of the waves against Pen Cemais, the sweetness of the boisterous forest-traversing winds of Wales. He could hear the blackbird, he could hear the missel thrush; he could hear the nightingale of Gwentland at song. "I thought there was but one string," said he; "but there are three . . ." He played on, and always the music grew louder and better; and because of it the world grew dear and beautiful in his heart again; and he marvelled and played on. "I thought there were but three strings with it; but in my deed there are five!" said he.

And the music grew, and fountained up; and he took no heed of the druids or the bards; had no memory of the serpents; heard no thunder of the warriors. "Dear indeed," thought he, the loveliness of the music enrapturing him, "I thought there were but five strings; and there are seven."

"Am I awake, am I alive now, Manawyddan son of the Boundless?" sang the harp.

"In my deed to Alawn you are awake, my darling!" said he. "In my proud deed you are alive, and singlehanded you are conquering hell."

"Give me leave!" cried the harp; "stand you away from me; I must announce my mind in hell!"

He knew its truth: that it could not lie to him; he trusted he might leave it to its own free will. He withdrew this hand, and the music did not cease; he withdrew that hand, and the harp did not fall; he stepped back from it, and down from the logan stone, and it hung in the air there and sang. As if myriads of swift fingers played it, it sang, it cried out, it announced its mind. There was lovely music in Uffern: hell was overwhelmed with lovely music when the Harp of Alawn announced its mind.

To the proud command it gave, flames rose up from the ground about the logan stone and went circling and wreathing skyward: flames amethystine, faintly gold-tipped, shot with shimmering green. Then amidst the beauty of the flames he saw shadowy fingers twinkling and wandering over the strings. The flames licked up the gloom; they banished the moon and the night sky. Presently, noon shone beautiful above, and a flower-scented breeze went wandering through Uffern: and all from the fingers twinkling on the strings.

And then there was a human form among the flames; and the Harper of Heaven harping in Uffern, announcing the beauty and glory of the world. His body was like the sunset, and taller than the poplar in the meadow: the tall poplars of Pontamman would not reach to the height of his head. His hair was like the daffodil, with dusks deeply golden; his eyes like Llyn Gwynant in the twilight, when its smooth lake-surface begins reflecting the stars.

He was singing: and what would be the likeness of his song? What would be the likeness for the song of Alawn, when the Prince of Harmonies sang in hell? What the sun sings of a noonday in August, beaming over the beech-tops in the forests of the world; what the Gods of the Midwood sing in Autumn to set the maples mysteriously aflame. It called up daffodils from the barrenness of Uffern, and tipped their spears with yellow flame. It evoked the foxglove from the soil, and adorned him with bells of enchantment, to be lord and archdruid of all the flowers on the mountain. Beautiful the Singer with all the beauty in the world: is it a wonder his song would strew the world with beauty?

Where his harpnotes blew and wandered, they changed to flakes of gentle flame. The strain of old unease was healed: peace and delight came with the sunlight. Where the harpnotes drifted and fell a million blossoms came to bloom. Sun-hued butterflies haunted Uffern; they found it a pleasant place of flowers. Faery bees went to their industry; although aforetime there had been no honey in hell. The men that had been enchanted lost the taint of their enchantment; remembering the Island of the Mighty, they desired new birth there among men. Ah, but the song was too great for Uffern: the bounds of hell might not hold it in! It rang out through the worlds and continents and islands: Alawn rejoicing over his harp regained.

In the Island of the Mighty they heard it clearly: heather bloomed there; gorse flamed there yellow; blackbirds' bills were filled with tune. They heard it in Europe and in Africa and in the Islands of Corsica; buds at the sound of it trembled into blossom in the Island of Ireland and in Greece in the East. As for the harp, it had its way now: its lord had returned to it, and it would announce its mind. And it did: from the Top of Infinity to the Bottom of the Great Deep it proclaimed godhood to the worlds and stars.

When Alawn had made an end of his music, hell was glistening like the dewdrop on the harebell in the morning sun. Then he gave

Manawyddan the harp, bidding him take it into the Island of the Mighty and into Dyfed, and there use it as he might find need; and after that, launched wings from his shoulders, and took the guise of the purple dragon, a marvel for Uffern to see; and away with him into the wandering-place of dragons — the empyrean sky, the abode of blueness, the beautiful region of the summer stars.

When he was no longer to be seen there, Manawyddan turned and looked out over Uffern. He saw no man. The harping of Alawn had freed all those who had been under enchantment from the burden of their bodies; and they had gone forth gaily, seeking more wholesome incarnation in the Island of the Mighty or the width of the world. They, and Gwiawn Sea-Thief with them: there was no further news of him to be heard in those times.

But there came three companies of the Children of the Air to hold Uffern for the Gods; and whilst Manawyddan was going down to the sea he heard three hymns with them in praise of the Three Dragons; and here are the hymns he heard:

Where my Blue-bright Dragon rideth
Darkness never, nor wrong, bideth;
For ten times bountiful is he
To strew his gems o'er sky and sea,
And shake down beauty on the world
Till the hills are empurpled, the skies empearled.
He whispers through the woodland gloom,
And the wild white wood-anemones bloom,
The wood-anemones and bluebells,
And the rhododendron in the dells.
His laughter thrills the windy hills
Till they're aflame with gorse and heather,
It runs on the winds and the wild March weather,
And lo, the light of the daffodils!
They are Plenydd's laughter altogether.
And it's he that goes about in Wales
To make her wonderful, dear knows,
With wizard blooms and wizard tales,

Dance of the fairies, scent of the rose,
And songcraft, bardism, wandering dreams —
Gods in the mountains, Gods in the streams!

Where my Golden Dragon rideth
Never fear nor sorrow bideth:
For flamingly he passeth far
Round the world's outposts, star by star;
And where he passeth, traileth flame
That takes men's souls with thirst of glory;
He fills the earth with deeds of fame,
And the bards with noble song and story.
And oft he shineth o'er the sea,
A leaping light, a luring star:
And "There is none shall be free," saith he,
"But out on the wintry wave afar;
Forsake thy steed and scythéd car,
To raid the realm of the wind-driven wave!
Who loseth life," saith he "shall save
More than life; and who shall dare,
And go down laughing into the grave,
And meet defeat without grief or care,
I shall hold him dear and brave;
I shall grant him guerdon rare."

Ay, but his bravest and most dear —
What wars shall they wage — what prize win?
He sets them comradeless and lone,
Praiseless to live, and to die unknown;
And looseth on them hordes of fear,
And looseth on them, from within
Sorrow and shame and mordant sin;
"These shall your foeman be," he saith;
"Life on life ye shall war with these,
And know no truce in the hour of death,
And no delight at all, nor ease;
And when your toil is bitterest grown

Most shall ye be forlorn and lone;
And ye shall hear no word from me,
Nor splendor of my godhood see;
No victory shall bring you fame
Or throne or empire or renown;
Never bard shall sing your name
In a song of praise in any town;
But at the last, uncumbered, strong,
Ye shall wage for the Gods their wars on wrong,
One with that immortal band
That stands and hath stood and shall stand;
Ye shall go forth where I, too, go,
And find these mortal worlds from woe."
   These, Gwron, are thy most dear;
These that give all and siffer all,
And ask no aid when foes are near,
And fear no ruin, and heed no fall.
Thou holdest these more dear and brave
Than the kings that triumph by wold or wave!

   Where my Alawn Harper plays,
What wonder fills the nights and days!
What systems and what suns are born —
What holiness pervades the morn —
What sanctity broods in the gray
And fiery-hearted passing of day!
Blest is he through whose mind, grown dumb,
The rippling chords and glory come
Who hath no thought-motions of his own
But that deep Music from the Unknown
Which midmost space and time and things
My Alawn Harper, harping, sings
Till men and mountains, star and clod
Grow great with dreams, and the dreams are God.

With Manawyddan's hearing those three hymns, and his
pondering their meaning, the Story of his Wanderings
ends. Because it tells of his services for the
Primitive Bards, Plenydd, Gwron and Alawn
and because those three were often
appearing in the course of it
it is called the

Book of the Three Dragons

Here is the Fifth Branch of it, Called
THE CONTESTS OF AB CILCOED AGAINST THE PRINCES, AND THE WHEAT THAT GREW IN THIS VALLEY OF GORSEDD ARBERTH

I. The Battle on the Hill of Gorsedd Arberth

WITH ALL SPEED Manawyddan returned to Dyfed then; and nothing delayed him on his journey. What would he do when he came to Arberth? No one would know him for Pwyll Pen Annwn, the king that had reigned there of old; unless Rhianon the queen were there, and the few men of his teulu that might still be alive. And how could he doubt Rhianon would be there, when she had sent her Faery Birds so many times to guide him? No doubt Pryderi their son would be king there: should Manawyddan make himself known, or should he take service in Pryderi's teulu, and trust Rhianon not to betray him? So his mind went working as he rode one: both before and after he came into the land of his heart. Most of all when the day dawned on which he should come into Arberth.

He had crossed the Teifi in the evening, having rested the whole of the day before, that he might ride through Dyfed hidden by the darkness, and meet no one by the way.

And then, while the darkness was growing gray, he came through the valley of Gorsedd Arberth, and saw that famous hill on the right in front of him; and fell to remembering what had happened on it of old, and the hill of wonder that it was, and the throne of rock on the top of it, on which none might take his seat at any time without either seeing some wonder passing through the valley, or else suffering blows and violence. There he himself had sat of old, and see Rhianon riding by, when first, for his sake, she came from the Land of the Immortals into Dyfed; and there he had stationed himself again, the time when all his disaster fell upon him. It stirred and rocked his heart to see the place looming up there out of the darkness into the dawn; and it came into his mind that, evil upon him unless he went up there now, and took his seat on the throne there. The wonder which he might see, he thought, would be his guidance in the courses he should follow.

When he came to the gate he found it swung wide; and that was unusual, thought he. The world was gray and dusky now, and soon the sun would rise. For the tumult in his heart he paid little attention to things as he rode up the path to the hilltop and the throne. And there, behind the throne, he dismounted, and as if dreaming went towards the throne to take his seat on it. But there was one on the throne already; and a youth crouched down at her feet.

She rose up when Manawyddan came; and he knew her for Rhianon his wife, and she him for the one that had been Pwyll Pen Annwn her husband. As for the youth, he was Pryderi their son.

WHEN THE sun was showing a streak of red gold, the first glimmer of his disk, over the mountain rim, Rhianon said,

"Challenges must be made, dear soul, against the Son of Cilcoed; for he is out against the Cymry and the Dimetians, and hither thy son and I have come to oppose him."

"And I also, " said Manawyddan. "For he was one of the three I was to destroy."

"There will be duties for each of us while the challenges are being made, and afterwards," said Rhianon. "Here is the dutry of Manawyddan: to be seated on the throne here, and to play challenges on the Harp of Alawn between this and noon. By then the music will have drawn Llwyd ab Cilcoed on to the hilltop here; then Manawyddan shall have the Gloves of Gwron on his hands, and shall seize him."

"You knew that the harp and the gloves were with me?" said Manawyddan.

"Oh, I knew," she laughed. "and as for Pryderi, his office will be to stand before Manawyddan his father armed and equipped; and he will let no harm come to Manawyddan while the challenges are being raised. For spells will be harmless against you, dear soul, while you have the Breastplate of of Plenydd on your breast; but there may be the shooting of shafts against you, and there may be an onslaught by the hosts of Llwyd; and it will need all the skill and patience of Pryderi to keep harm from you between this and noon."

Manawyddan, proud of his son that he saw now for the first time, a young hero with the glory of his youth on him, said, "Fear nothing for Pryderi, dear soul!"

"I fear nothing for him," said she, "unless it be overeagerness and impetuosity. As for me, I will do my part of it now; I will raise bulwarks here against the onslaught of the men of Llwyd."

The circle of the hilltop was of smooth greensward; the slopes were covered with heather and bracken at that time; it was in front of the throne, some dozen strides or less from it, that the path up from the road came into the greensward. Rhianon went to the western side of the head of the path at the edge of the circle where the heather began, and made her pacings round the circle till she came to the eastern side of it; and there she turned, and went back to the place from which she had started. Nine times she made these pacings, with rhythmic wavings of her arms and with subtle chantings weaving a druid protection from the hilltop. At the ninth time a little line of flame sprang up in her footsteps, that might have been invisible to many, yet that nothing evil could pass; and there was no gap in it except where the path entered the circle.

"The gap must be left," said she, "in order that the challenges from the harpstrings may go out to Llwyd wherever he is, and trouble him, and compel him to what shall follow. Stand you here in the gap, Pryderi dear! It will be pleasant to you defending it, if defense should be needed."

They took their places as she directed them.

"Raise now the challenge music, dear soul," she said to Manawyddan. "And raise song with the harping, and it will be better."

Manawyddan touched the seven strings of the God-harp; and though he touched them ever so lightly, seven proud shouts they answered back at him, startling the morning. "I will raise a tune for warriors and heroes for this," he thought; and considered that *Merch Megan* would be the tune he desired. So then he began getting the notes of it from the harpstrings, and making verses and singing them.

At the end of the first verse the hosts of Llwyd ab Cilcoed were plain to be seen, covering away the floor of the valley and overflowing on to the hills beyond; and Llwyd himself was at the head of them. Rhianon looked out over them with calm eyes, Pryderi with impetuosity and exultation; it would be the pleasant morning of all his life, he supposed. Covering away the bracken they came; blotting out the harebell and grass-blade and the heather.

"Let there be patience and quiet consideration," said Rhianon to her son. "Advance not against them beyond the circle of the hilltop; leave not the smooth-cropped sward for the heatherland."

"Fear you nothing for me," said Pryderi. But he thought, "The delightful memory of my lifetime will be this morning's adventure."

Manawyddan went forward with his harping, and made another verse and sang it; and at that the dark host rose, moaning and filling the air of the valley. They gathered soon about the flame-circle on the hilltop, and broke there, and then surged in at the gap where Pryderi stood to withstand them. A bright sunray shoneddown on him, lighting the gold of his hair, the gold and enamel of his shield, the amazing swiftness of his sword.

At midway between dawn and noon he had forgotten all things but the delight of the fighting; yet stepped never beyond the smooth greensward, but repelled them where he stood. By noon it might be that half Llwyd's army had perished under his sword. Already they were pressing against him less valiantly; whereas he was as if he had been at rest since the Crying of the Name.

"Dear soul, beware of over-impetuosity!" cried Rhianon. But the truth is that he heard nothing. He saw Llwyd ab Cilcoed approach, and could attend to little else at that time. He swept out at Llwyd with his sword three times; and all the blows were parried. Then Llwyd swept out at Pryderi three times; and the third stroke so vigorous Pryderi was near staggering when the took it on his shield. Then Pryderi swept out at Llwyd again; and so vehement the blow, there was no escaping death from it without stepping backwards and going downwards.

Manawyddan's song rang out so that the whole host of the hellions was shaken; and the grand warlike mood came upon Pryderi – he, impetuous as a fire in a chimney. And with that, Rhianon became aware of danger threatening, and cried out warning to Pryderi. "Ah, dear soul, beware of rashness!" she cried; but what was warning to him, when he was dealing in battle with the chief foe of the Dimetians?

Llwyd gave way before him; so that, arm and sword, none could have reached him from the gap in the circle where Pryderi stood. So Pryderi set his left foot forward; one stride beyond the end of the greensward, and swept out at Llwyd from there. And Llwyd gave way before him. Up with his sword again — quivering, eager, angry with Llwyd. Forward with his right foot, and a stride of it beyond his left: two strides of him out of the circle of the greensward and into the heather.

With a cry the hosts became unreal and fled, and wasted away over the valley. "Pryderi! Pryderi!," cried Rhianon; but it was too late, even if he had heard her. There was Llwyd ab Cilcoed making speed down towards the road, and Pryderi leaping forward to pursue him. And at that, immediately awareness came upon Pryderi's horse, the Wind-driver, that flight was out before his lord; and he remembered what the duties of a horse would be. With a leap and a whinney he was at Pryderi's side, from where he had been grazing in the greensward circle behind.

Useless then Rhianon's warnings; useless Manawyddan's rising and rushing forward. Pryderi was in the saddle and away; the Wind-driver impetuously leaving the wind behind him, and Pryderi reaching out to clutch at Llwyd's shoulder before they were half way down the hill.

"Aye, aye," thought Llwyd; "a man would not escape from that Gyrru'r Gwyntoedd, but a wild boar might, were it a swift one." So he fell down from his manhood, and took wild boar guise as he fell; and doubled this way, and doubled that way, and bewildered the Wind-driver and embarrased him; and escaped through a gap in the hedge onto the road.

Blodwen Whiteflower was at Manawyddan's side before Pryderi was in the Wind-driver's saddle almost: she knowing there would be peril for her dear lord's son. "Go!' cried Rhianon; "endless peril unless you overtake him." In an instant Manawyddan was in the saddle, and

Blodwen kicking up sods into the air as she earnestly bore him in pursuit of Pryderi.

And Rhianon, from the throne on Gorsedd Arberth, saw phantasm and illusion put upon the whole of Dyfed. Where it passed over tilled fields and grassland, tilled fields and grassland became stony desert; white-walled farms and cottages were blotted out from visibility as if they had never been there. And always it spread out over the land: Llwyd the boar breathed it out around him as he fled.

Manawyddan, leaping the hedge into the road, shouted to Pryderi; and again and again as the road fled from under Blodwen's hoofs. But Pryderi answered nothing but, "Yes we shall catch him, if we make speed!" Dear knows what pride was on the swift Wind-driver. Forgetful of all wisdom he was, that day; anxious to please his lord in despite of wisdom. Blodwen could not come up with him; and he could not come up with the boar.

Out at the end of the valley, at last, the boar sped, pleased with the ruin he was working. Out after his sped Pryderi, the road fleeing and vanishing under Gyrru'r Gwyntoedd's hoofs. Out at last came Manawyddan on Blodwen; he casting one glance out to his right, hoping for a sight of Arberth his chief city; but no lime-washed Arberth was to be seen on its hill.

No Arberth; and no recognizable Dyfed. In place of the fertile valley, an open plain, sterile and desolate; and over it, low skies glooming and wind moaning and rain copiously falling; the like of a region that never had been in Dyfed nor anywhere in universal Wales. "It is the machinations of Ab Cilcoed," thought Manawyddan. "The illusion and phantasm have fallen on Dyfed."

On and on with them through this waste. "Pryderi! Pryderi!" cried Manawyddan. "Dear help the horse, there is no speed with him today!" sighed Pryderi. Speed there was with the Wind-driver; unjust, heaven knows, was the accusation. Mile after mile fled by; and Gyrru'r Gwyntoedd could not come up with the boar, nor Blodwen with Gyrru'r Gwyntoedd.

Then suddenly a vast, phantasmal caer loomed up in the midst of the plain. Rain, and tireless beat of hoofs: driving rain, and splashing where the hoofs fell. Howling of the desolate wind; silence of all voices. On towards the caer fled the boar; and the Wind-driver and Pryderi; and the Whiteflower and the Son of the Boundless-without-Utterance.

And now the Wind-driver was gaining on the boar; and by as much, the Whiteflower was gaining on the Wind-driver. Never since the Going-forth of the Gwynfydolion had such delight in hunting come on any man as came now upon Pryderi. With bright pride and young impetuosity he urged the Wind-driver forward. Over the waste the boar went pounding towards the open gate of the caer. In through the gate with the boar. Pryderi not stopping at the gate for consideration; making nothing of care of caution or the circumspect forming of plans. In through the gate with Pryderi.

Manawyddan thought, "I will go in after him; although it may be perilous. I will protect my son in yonder caer of enchantment." So he sped on after Pryderi. But when Blodwen's nose was within a hand's breadth of coming between the gateposts – laughter and wailing broke out, and the gates slammed in front of him, and the whole great fabric of the caer began quivering from the ground to the tower-tops; and from the ground to the tower-tops it wavered into unreality, and became like smoke dispersing or a trembling phantasm of the magicians. He saw it so vanish, and no sign of it left on the surface of the plain; and much less was there sign of Pryderi and the Wind-driver. And shout as he might, he could get no answer to his shouting.

Here was a pass that was beyond him: that he had neither the weapons nor the spells to deal with. The Breastplate of Plenydd itself on his breast would give him no vision of the caer, nor provide his eyes with the least tidings of Pryderi. If there was to be help for his son, it must come from Rhianon.

"Blodwen *fach*," said he, "was ever a desire in your heart to serve your lord?"

It was the same with both of them as if she put clean Welsh to her thought, and made answer, "There was, dear soul, and there is now."

Then said he, "If there is swiftness in the world, and in the power of white mares to attain it: put you forth that swiftness now, between this and Gorsedd Arberth."

In my deed to God I will," though she; and he understood her as if she had put vocal Welsh to it.

He mounted, and turned her head at that; and she kicked the world from beneath her shell-formed hoofs; and in a little while was on the top of Gorsedd Arberth. Manawyddan told Rhianon all that had befallen.

"Sorrow not on account of this," said she. "For my part I rejoice that the Breastplate of Plenydd saved you from falling with Pryderi into the power of Llwyd. For if you had also had been enspelled, I hould have been powerless in this. But now it is clear to me what must be."

"Is there news of it for me?" said Manawyddan.

"This much news," she answered. "I demand a promise from you."

"Name you the promise," said Manawyddan. "Made it is, already, whatsoever it be."

Then she said: "I must go to my son Pryderi. If there is any saving him before the worst of the enchantment falls, I will save him; but it is unlikely that there will be. No, no; it is protection under enchatnment that he will have from me; and it is you that must save the two of us hereafter.

For I must put myself under the phantasms and illusions of Llwyd ab Cilcoed for the sake of Pryderi, or there will be no saving him. Here is the promise I demand of you: that you will neither follow me nor grow impatient of waiting for me; and that you will not set foot beyond the boundaries of this valley till you hold Ab Cilcoed in your hand and power."

"Gladly I promise it," said Manawyddan. "Is it long I must wait?"

"Unknown to me is that," said she. "But I shall return; and with me Pryderi our son — when you yourself have put freedom on Dyfed. This much I can foretell for you," she added: "there must be ploughing done here first, and sowing the ploughed land, and reaping the harvest. The ploughing will not be done by mortal ploughman and mortal oxen; the reaping will be by none of the Cymry. Wait here therefore; and let there be unusual vigilance with you; and you shall not be without help from the Immortals.

"But if you should leave this Valley at any time, or seek to follow me now, the three of us would be powerless against Ab Cilcoed from that out, and this holy hill would fall into his power, and there remain until the sky falls."

"I will not fail you in this," said Manawyddan.

"Health and peace remain with you,: she said. Then she mounted her chariot, and shook out the reins; and with that, her two horses rose up in the air, and she and they and the chariot became invisible; and that was the last he saw of her at that time.

II. The Ploughing of the Valley of Gorsedd Arberth,
and that by no Mortal Ploughman

MANAWYDDAN FETCHED stones from the river, and cut turf from the sod, and built himself a cabin on the slopes of Gorsedd Arberth; and lived there while the summer was waning, and while the trees were flaring and paling, and while they were growing naked in the rain and misty weather; and while the ruddy purple tops of them were bowing and moaning under the wind.

Here is what the chief duty of him would be: to be on the throne on the hilltop at ever dawn and sunset, and getting what music he might ouf of the Harp of Alawn: sheltering the harp with his cloak if there were rain. In this way protection was maintained over the valley, and the phantasm and illusion that covered all Dyfed else, was kept away from it.

The summer was well over before he had quite finished the hazelnuts of long nourishment that he had brought from the Wyddfa; but even then it was not difficult to find means of supporting life. There was hunting on the hillsides and fishing in the river; there were mushrooms in the fields in the mornings, and the natural berries on bramble and hedgerow. Often the hunt would bring him to the tops of the mountains, this side or that, and to the verge of the enchanted regions. Would the deer fleeing from him leap forth beyond that, it would come by its vanishing away and being lost in a land peopled with demons: a desolate, unrecognizable territory where darkness brooded, and unearthly winds screamed perpetually amidst whirling snow and fog and terror. Into it Manawyddan never passed; though it might happen to him to look out over it from the mountaintops.

There seemed to be no magic left in the Harp of Alawn at that time. Peace nor ease drifted into his mind while he played it; no strain of superlative beauty, no proud shouting, arose in response to his fingers on the strings. Furthermore the chief peculiarity of Gorsedd Arberth: that no one might take his place on the throne there without seeing some marvel, or else suffering blows and violence, seemed to have waned away and become outworn. While the starry evenings of August were giving way to the evening of rain; while September was paling, and October yellowing and then flaring in the woodlands, he saw nothing marvelous either at dawn or at dusk; and often he longed even that there might be blows and violence to be combatted and endured; but there were none. "Easier to be battling through crises," thought he, "than to go forward with this empty waiting." Where were Rhianon and Pryderi? He knew nothing of their fate, beyond that he could do nothing to save them from it, at that time.

On the last morning in October he rose before dawn, as his custom was; and made his way to the hilltop, the harp in his hands. The valley was filled with the fogs of Autumn; on the yellow leaves and crimson stalk of the blackberry-thorn the drops were hanging; dank and brown the broken brake fronds and brown and bloomless the heather; chill and melancholy the air his breath made clouds in; his footsteps splashed on the sodden and slippery path. He took his place on the throne, and watched the daylight growing.

As he looked out over the fields that should have been ploughed, and that had felt no ploughshare cleave them since last year, the prophecy of Rhianon came into his mind: that there would be immortal ploughing of them before any good came to Dyfed. Considering that, it seemed to him that the best tune to be raising now would be the *Caingc Gyrrwr y Wedd Ychain*, the song the Dimetian ploughmen used for guiding and encouraging their oxen and for dedicating their labor to Hu the Mighty, who at the beginning of things, with his two Exalted Oxen, Nynnio and Peibio, ploughed that island from end to end, that mankind might have spiritual life there.

So he set himself to playing that tune, and to singing the song that goes with it; and when he had sung the first verse of it he paused in amazement, hearing lovely Welsh from lips not his own for the first time since Rhianon had left him: hearing articulate song; and a voice not human but more than human rising out of the mist in the valley below, intoning the slow, long, melodious cry of the ploughman to his oxen, that comes at the end of the tune:

Tyr'd ti!... Cwyd!... Tryr'd ti!... Cwyd!... Cwyd!

And then at last there came to be some bright liveliness in his hope, and in the harpstrings when he touched them something of their old dominance and regality, a rumor of their natural ringing shout. Without pause he played and sang the second verse of it; and at the end again, out of the slowly waning mist in the valley, the cry came majestic and melodious.

Tyr'd ti!... Cwyd!... Tryr'd ti!... Cwyd!... Cwyd!

"Here at last is the wonder proper to be seen or heard from this throne and hilltop," thought Manawyddan; for he knew the voice that sang, and that the singer could be none other than Hu Gadarn; and that before him through the vale no mortal oxen would be treading, but King Nynnic and King Peibio the Great-horned. They had been kings once, of what are now Scotland and England; but for their exorbitant pride Rhita Gawr subdued them and they were turned into the Ychain Bannau or Exalted Oxen with which Hu the Mighty ploughed the island.

The sun rose and the fog vanished; and Manawyddan, looking down over the valley, saw that he had not been mistaken: saw what it would be a main glory for any man to see, and what would be remembered by the most forgetful during ten lifetimes, or indeed more than ten. There over the fields between the road and the river passed the two Exalted Oxen: mild their slow, blue, luminous eyes; immense their far-extending horns. There they drew after them through the soil the Plough of Wonder; and there strode the Mighty

One, following the plough, the Master of the White Shield, Hu Gadarn, who was deputed to be the Emperor of the Gods and the Cymry at that time.

Manawyddan sat watching him, and let his fingers have their will with the strings, and let fingers and strings between them raise what glory they might and were sure to raise, with Hu Benadur there to inspire them.

From dawn till noon the Mighty One passed to and fro through the valley driving his exact, well-ridged, faintly-shining furrows, his spiritual furrows through the fields. Wan and fickle was the sunlight in the morning, waning at noontime into grayness; dark blue loomed the mountains where the rain swept them, beyond the lonely valley. Turbulently the river roared with the floods of Autumn; melancholy was the voice of the wind over the tops of the bending, red-purple, leafless trees. In lonely majesty aloof through the sad glory of Autumn the Ploughman of Ynys Fel drove his furrows until the waning of the day. When the early twilight was darkening, the work was finished.

Manawyddan saw him rise up from the world at the eastern end of the valley, and drive King Nynnio and King Peibio away through the dusky sky. Then he made his way down to his cabin and kindled the fire on his hearth there, and took what food he needed; and sat brooding over the fire until it was time to sleep.

III. The Sowing of the Valley of Gorsedd Arberth, and the Seed Sown, Sown by a God

THROUGH THE WINTER Manawyddan watched, but no fresh marvel appeared to him. Fog and rain and wild storms of November: many the meteors trailing through night when the wind might drive the clouds beyond the mountains and lay bare a dark blue stretch of heaven. Rain and bitter wind of December: Manawyddan on the throne at his accustomed times, and harping in spite of the tempest. Chill blast of raging January: snow on the hillsides; snow sparkling in the rare sunlight over the whole valley at noon. Thaw and rain and fickle sunshine of February: wan the quiet star of the snowdrop in secret places in the woodland. Greeness budding on the trees; the first notes reawakening bird-music. The first day of March: and already on her stalk, here and there in the valley, the yellow glory of the daffodil.

Manawyddan was on the throne at the hilltop before dawn, his cloak fluttering about his shoulders. He remembered the prophecies of Rhianon and the ploughing of the vale by Hu the Mighty; and wondered when the sowing would be, and which of the Gods would be the sower. But that was the office, commonly, of Amaethon ab Don: who passes unseen through the sky strewing spiritual seed while the sowers of the Cymry sow wheat or oats or barley, lest the crop should be poor though it might appear most rich, and the bread be food only for the bodies of men; and that wisdom and valor and truth may be nourished by the harvest.

So, late in the year as it might be, he would invoke Amaethon, singing the song of the Dimetian seed-sowers. By the time he had sung one verse of it, the sun had risen and was shining in a clear sky eastward; but over the valley in front of him hung a great cloud: mellow and golden its eastern rim with the slant beams of the sun; — indeed, it appeared to him that a wonderful mellow-golden light ws shining through the whole of its milky dimness. Soft rain began to fall from it: over the valley, and not over the hill where he was sitting. The slant beams of morning shone inmingled with the raindrops, making them seem drops of light and yellow, rich fertility. He saw the cloud pass over the valley towards Arberth or the place where Arberth had been; but at the head of the valley it turned and came back; and always the golden glow of the rain it shed went increasing, until it seemed he must again be seeing the wonder natural to Gorsedd Arberth, and might well be within a little of witnessing the passage of an Immortal through the sky.

He put fingers to the strings again, and sang the second verse of the song, as if he himself had been the sower. The wind went blustering and shouting through the valley, driving up cloud-fleeces from the sea and Ireland; high overhead the clouds were herded and driven, now and again to break in swirling and gusty showers; and now and again there would be fickle gleams of sunshine through the rain; but always from that one light-shotten cloud fell the golden drops of fertility. Manawyddan would remain there until noon, he thought, or until Amaethon might have finished his work. But at noon the sowing was still going forward; and so too at mid-afternoon, when the sky cleared and silvered a little; and at sunset, when the cloudless west was all palely gleaming and primrose-hued, and the last of the clouds had been driven from the dim sapphire of the east. Still there was that scattering of golden drops over the valley; and now the One that scattered them was visible: Amaethon ab Don striding through the heavens in his flame-form: beryl-mantled, and with hair golden like ripe wheat.

At last the sun was quite sunk behind the hills, and then the immortal sowing was finished. Then Amaethon flamed up from human into dragon guides, and streamed forth, pale green and daffodil-golden, northward through the sky.

Manawyddan went down to his cabin, and took what food he needed after his day-long fasting. "There still must be reaping," thought he; "and that by the hand of no Cymro."

IV. *The Reaping of the Valley of Gorsedd Arberth, and that by the Hand of no Cymro*

MARCH WITH its bluster of winds: green shoots on the trees; the ruddy treetops of winter taking on pale, bright greeness, – March with the beauty of daffodil blooms. April with the rainswept skies: April with the blue gaps between the racing whiteness of clouds. Delightfulness of May; and greater delightfulness of June: and ah, the bloom of the bluebell in the woodland – the foxglove on the mountain worshipping heaven! Manawyddan guarding the valley, with song and harping: that one place in Dyfed free: he keeping it free: from terror and night and the phantasm and illusion of Llwyd.

He watched the young green wheat put its little spears up through the soil; he watched the spears grow above the furrows, until what had been brown was beautifully green. He maintained his vigilance while the winds of Spring were running and rippling along the floor of the valley, making delicate green waves in the wheat; and while the green was turning golden with summer; and while the wheat was ripening;

and unitl it was ripe. "The wheat of the gods in the valley of Gorsedd Arberth," said he; "And none to reap it but the Gods."

One afternoon at that time he passed through the fields between the Gorsedd hill and the eastern end of the valley, contemplating the ripeness and beauty of the wheat. "It may well be that Amaethon will reap it tomorrow," he thought. "Today would be too soon for it; tomorrow its ripeness will be prefect."

On the throne on the hilltop he remained that evening until the great ruddy moon was rising out of the purple shadows and dimness above the hills; and made verses and sang them in praise of the beauty around him, and of Amaethon, who would come to reap the valley in the morning, he was sure. Tomorrow he would see another wonder from the throne there; he would see Amaethon reaping what Amaethon had sown; and then – Dyfed would be freed, and Rhianon and Pryderi would be restored to him.

But in the morning he veheld no wonder from the throne when he came to it: no sign of a God passing through the valley. Instead, there was a certain sadness in the air; and on himself, a remembrance of his losses.

He went down presently towards the road; and at the foot of the hill, for some reason, felt a desire to make search in the heather. Here is what he found, and it satisfied him: an ear of wheat, bright golden its hue; every grain undamaged in its place; and the ear after its being bitten off the stalk. He put if in his wallet, and went forward to the eastern fields. They were covered with tall standing straw; every ear had been cleanly bitten off at the place where the stalk joined it. Not enough was left of the grain in all those fields to save the young daughter of a harvestmouse from starvation, much less to satisfy her hunger.

Manawyddan walked on through the straw, considering the probablilities. "No God accomplished this reaping," thought he; "no God, and no Cymro. Better to examine the fields of the west," he thought.

He went there; and with musing by the way, forgot hunger, and took no food at noon. When he came to the western fields, and contemplated the tall, richly-laden wheatstalks there, and brooded on their beauty and their wealth, and on the fates that should come to them: it became clear to him that the morrow would be the day for their reaping, and that no other day in the year would do so well.

As he went forward through the wheat he heard a strange rustling and whisper in it: it seemed almost articulate, and as if the wheat-ears were at intelligible conversation — were there such a thing as to interepret it. Pleasantly the sun shone down on the golden field; pleasantly the soft wind murmured, and the wheat nodded under the wind. "Were there understanding the wheat, there would be learning things of importance," thought he. But as far as he could see, thre was none, and would be none.

But by the middle afternoon he remembered hunger, and that he had eaten nothing during the day. He turned to gather wheat-ears; but Rhianon's prophecy rose in his mind: that the hand of no Cymro should take part in the reaping. Then he thought of the ear he had picked up at the foot of Gorsedd Arberth, and that was now in his wallet. "Better that than nothing," thought he; and winnowed it between his hands, and blew away the chaff, and raised the grain to his lips, and ate it, and —

Having so assumed wheathood in some degree, and become skin to the standing wheat in the fields – what should happen but that the rustling of it under the wind became clean, melodious Welsh for him, and its conversation easily understood. Here is what he heard with the wheat:

"Tonight Llwyd will reap us: last night he was reaping the fields of the east."

"Wherefore will he reap us? Wherefore will he reap us, in the Name of God and Man?"

"Wherefore did he reap our brothers of the eastern fields.?"

One great golden ear made answer to that: it was the largest and most beautiful in the field, and its stalk the tallest:

"He reaped them mainly for the sake of the peculiarities of my kinsman, the King-Ear of the Eastern Fields."

"What were the peculiarities?" asked the wheat.

"I marvel that they should be unknown to wheat of your dignity!" said the King-Ear. "Whoever should take that regal Ear, and drop it by night in the heather at the foot of Gorsedd Arberth: if he had no power to go upon that hill before, therefrom he would obtain power to go the next night as far as to midway between the foot of the hill and the throne; and it would be a main advantage to him."

Wherefore in heaven's name will he reap us tonight? To reap us is the perquisite of our lord Amaethon, we thought."

"That is true," said the King-Ear of the Western Fields. "But upstarts are usurping the privileges of the noble, and thieving and rieving are grown common. For the sake of my peculiarities, mainly, he will reap us: they are said to be even better than the peculiarities of my kinsman of the east."

The wheat sighed under the wind. "Dear, it is the pity of our lives we shan't have news of those peculiarities," it sighed.

"News you shall have," said the King-Ear; "sorrow no longer! Whoever might attain dropping me among the heather on Gorsedd Arberth, at midway between the stile at the foot and throne at the head of it; althought that night he would have no power to go beyond the place of the dropping, the next night he would have power to go as far as to the foot of the throne; and it would be a main advantage and privilege for him."

"Dear indeed, it may well be that he will attain dropping you there," said Manawyddan,

"Hush, hush!" whispered the wheat, laughing softly over the whole field. Not another word of Welsh could he get from it, after that.

He went on as far as to the head of the valley and the edge of the phantasm and illusion; then turned, and looked out over the shining fields. He spoke out loud so that the wind might hear him and carry the message if it desired to. "It may appear to you that you are ready for harvesting now; but not until tomorrow shall you obtain it from me," said he. "Not until the sun is well in the heavens will I take the sickle in my hands and come to you. Evil on the impatient among you, that will not be content with as much as this!"

At sunset he was on the throne on Gorsedd Arberth, making known to the harp what he desired of its music. "Not protection, but the spreading of news it must be," said he; wherefore be loud and subtle and wary; and where there may be ears, penetrate you them!"

So then he played: and whatever he put into the music, the harp put ten times more into it of its own will and imagination; vehemently asserting all night long the power and rights of the Gods.

Manawyddan would remain there all night: he dismissed the desire for food and rest. When the moon had set and the world was in darkness it seemed to him that he was granted extraordinary hearing. From far in the west of the valley came a sound of rustling and faint squeaking; he heard little teeth gnawing wheat-stalks, and the fall of wheat-ears to the ground. Then came the patter of innumerable tiny feet along the road; and at last, at the foot of the hill, what might have been consultation among mice. "Llwyd ab Cilcoed and his armies," said he.

Soon he heard movement on the pathway; although it was quieter than the footsteps of the little gray mouse at midnight on the stone-flagged floor of the mill kitchen. "Will it be better to wait at the place where the ear should be dropped?" thought he; and rose from the throne to go down. But with his rising all sound ceased; and in the dark, unguided by sound, it seemed to him little good could be done. He took his place on the throne again, and instantly the hearing came back to him. He was aware when the wheat-ear was dropped in the heather; he heard the footsteps returning to the road.

When day dawned he went down and found the ear, and put it in his wallet. But when the ant arose from her nest in the fields west of the valley, she found them barren of nourishment: no food there, nor the shadow of food, nor a rumor of food to comfort her hearing. Not one stalk was bent or fallen; not one ear remained on its stalk; not one gleaned grain lay on the ground. "Evil on the place!" said she; "there is neither profit nor advantage to be found in it for the eagerly industrious!" Manawyddan would not trouble to go out there and examine the fields. It was well known to him how they would be.

At noon he went down, and through the middle fields about the foot of Gorsedd Arberth between the road and the river, and beyond as far as to the top of the hills. He saw that by next morning the wheat would be ripe there for its reaping; and he heard faint music, whispering and rustling, from every grain in its ear and from every bearded ear that shone delicately golden on its stalk.

He took the King-Ear of the Western Fields from his wallet and winnowed it in his hands, and put the grain between his lips; and as soon as he had swallowed it, once more the language of the wheat became soft, intelligible Welsh for him; and he listened to its conversation.

"Dear help us better!" said the King-Ear of the Middle Fields. "Tonight Ab Cilcoed will reap us; unless the Gods or the Son of the Boundless should reap us before. Prepare you therefore for the reaping."

"Wherefore is this ignominious fate put on us?" said the wheat. "For what reason shall we be deprived of our peaceable reaping tomorrow with the Gods or the Cymry? Is no thought to be taken for our dignity, and for our rights and well-established privileges?"

No thought is to be taken for them," said the King-Ear. "Evil are the times, I declare to you: when men without lineage usurp the rights of the noble, and thieving and rieving grow common!"

"The Son of the Boundless is here: let him be persuaded to reap us now, for the sake of Amaethon the Gods' Husbandman!"

It is unlikely that he would be persuaded," said the King-Ear. "It would be injudicious to reap us before we may be ripe; and ripe we shall not be until tonight, at the moment of midnight and moonset. And then Ab Cilcoed will come, and he will desire to reap us chiefly on account of my peculiarities; and what he desires to do he will do. And I will confide to you this," said the King-Ear: "My peculiarities are considered by the wise to exceed by far the peculiarities of either of my kinsmen, the King-Ears of the Eastern and Western Fields."

Mournfully the wheat murmured under the wind: "Ah me! There may well be pining away in store for us if we shall not have to hear news of those peculiarities!"

"News of them you shall have, and shall not be chargeable for it," said the King-Ear; "Therefore sorrow you no longer! If Llwyd attain carrying me tonight to the foot of the throne on Gorsedd Arberth, and dropping me there without being discovered, the whole of the valley will be in his power, and the hill of Gorsedd Arberth with it; and thereafter it is doubtful whether there will be any prevailing against him, either for the Gods or for the Cymry."

"In my deed to the universe," cried Manawyddan, "he may well attain carrying you to the foot of the throne; but a marvel if he should drop you there without being discovered!"

"Hush, dear! hush!" murmured the wheat, laughing; and not one word of news could he get from it further.

So he went ot the hilltops beyond, and looked out over the region of phantasm and illusion; and then turned and looked back over the wheatfields and towards Gorsedd Arberth. Standing there, he began enumerating the noble peculiarities of the wheat, according to the knowledge he divined of them: speaking out loud to put the news of them on the wind, that the wind might carry it to whom it would.

"Without if or were-it-not," said he, "this is the Wheat of Amaethon in the Valley of Gorsedd Arberth: no Cymro sowed it, and it will be reaped by no Cymro without Amaethon's permission.

"It will have this peculiarity: Whoever may achieve reaping it, and threshing the ears in the barn; and grinding the grain in the mill; and mixing the flour with water or even buttermilk; and kneading the dough in the trough; and baking the loaves in the oven, or upon the girdlestone scientifically set over the fire; and thereafter feasting on the bread without lavish greed or miserly parsimony: it will be the nourishment of power in him, and the cause of his becoming wise; and of his acquiring knowledge of the esoteric books of Tad Awen; and of his understanding Druidism both the inward and the outward parts of it.

"And he will have another peculiarity: Poetry will become the natural speech of him, and his daily utterance will be adorned with powerful consonance and mellifluous assonance; and if he but make a request of his friend he will frame it in the *cynghanedd*, so that all shall think him inspired.

"And he will have another peculiarity: Without exertion or anxiety, or raising up turmoil or putting forth force against any man, he will be enabled to exercise dominion over a third part of these islands: and that third will be the best third, and the one most beloved by the Gods and the Cymry; namely, the region between the Severn and the Western Sea.

"And beyond all this, there will be many peculiarities with the wheat, and many endowments of virtue to be obtained from it such as experience shall give further knowledge of: wherefore fortunate in my deed will be the whetter of the sickle, and the reaper of the fields, and the master of the threshing barn, and the lord of the mill, and the kneader of the dough, and the heater of the oven, and the one that may be nourished with the bread.

"But as for reaping you," he said, addressing the wheat, "let there be patience in heaven's name! Often the impatient will lose their virtues and ennobling peculiarities; therefore curb you the rash, eager impetuosity characteristic of your nature!

"Here is what I shall do for you, unless disasters befall in the night. I shall obtain permission from Amaethon in my prayers at dawn; and come here with the sickle between dawn and noon, and reap you vigorously until evening; by nightfall not a stalk shall be standing in the fields. And next day I shall carry you to the barn, and thresh you with vehemence from dawn to dusk; and bear you away in sacks to the mill, in such a manner that if so much as a single grain be left upon the threshing floor, the little gray mouse will be entitled to it, and will obtain it as a free gift, and without the setting of traps or the warning of cats to be on the alert.

"And the day after I shall grind you in the mill between sunrise and sunset, and bring away the flour in the evening to the bakehouse: and if any flour remain beneath the hopper it shall be the perquisite of the rats and vermin. And the next day I shall exercise the art of baking and dough-kneading: neither so languidly as to leave the flour unmixed nor so vigorously as to make the bread heavy; and I shall heat the girdlestone scientifically over the fire, and maintain an equable heat in the oven, and make bread of you the equal of which will hardly have been known in these islands since the days of Arthur Emperor in remote antiquity.

"And thereafter I shall eat the bread; *and it will give me power over Llwyd ab Cilcoed, very likely.*"

"Therefore be you contented, I charge you, to go forward peaceably with your ripening until midnight and moonset, and to wait for your reaping until midmorning!"

"Delightful is the fate that you foretell for us!" sighed the wheat. "Alas that it should be beyond our hope and expectation."

"Hush dears, hush!" whispered the King-Ear. "It may all befall in the end as the Son of the Boundless-without-Utterance has prophecied."

Manawyddan went back to Gorsedd Arberth, and was on the throne before sunset; but raised no music and chanted no song at that time. "Protection of the fields would be undesirable tonight," thought he. But when the moon was oversailing the heavens, and ruddy and golden above the Gorsedd hill, he took the harp to his breast. "Now," said he, "not protection of the valley, but the issuing of challenges will be required of you, *cariad bach:* the issuing of unendurable challenges, and intense incitement to thievery for them that may be of a thievish disposition.

With that he began to play; and according to the magic of the Harp of harps, and its knowledge of what would be fitting and was required of it – the music was such that no one within hearing, if he was naturally thievishly disposed, but was afflicted with an overwhelming desire, and filled with an indomitable resolve to rieve and thieve and filch and maraud and steal and purloin and acquire unjustly whatever valuable thing might be within reach, to the utmost of his power and genius, between that and the dawn of the morning.

He set down the harp beside him on the throne, and put the Gloves of Gwron on his hands, aware that it was for this night's work he had obtained them; and began his vigil.

At midnight and moonset he heard rustling and creeping in the valley below: innumerable tiny paws pattering through the intense darkness. He heard — for he was gifted with unusual hearing again – the gnawing of wheatstalks by countless sharp little teeth; he heard the ripe ears fall to the ground. He heard the whole host gather presently in the roadway below; and the creeping of a few of them up the path till they were, as he judged, midway between the stile and the throne. Then a silence and the end of the creeping; and the silence broken soon with conversation no louder than the soliloquies of the snail in his shell in midwinter, when a little fickle sunshine may call him from his sleep and dreams.

"There is the pattering of paws on pebbles to consider," said the whisperer. "There is the creaking of the grassblade bent down beneath the traveller's weight. Where are the four Slippers of Multiplied Soundlessness for my four paws, and their peculiarity that no one can hear the footfall of the wearer of them unless he can hear the ant breathe, and the oak imagine, and the dewdrop meditate on her impending fall from the reed, and the earwig recite to herself poetry beneath the fallen stone: or unless listening to the music of the Immortals hath endowed him with the superexquisite hearing of the Gods?"

Manawyddan heard them bring the slippers, and the slippers drawn over the paws; and he heard the whisperer say then:

"There is the luminosity of the wheat-ear to consider; alas that of its peculiarities some should be deleterious! Where is my wand of illusion and phantasm wherewith I may put darkness about the wheat-ear such as no eye could penetrate, except the eye that can see the more upon the moonbeam when no moon is shining, or count the hairs in the beard of the gnat as far off as from the top of Pengwaed in Cornwall to the bottom of Dinsol in North Britain, or discover by keen vision the cogitations of the pilchard that wanders through the forests of the ocean; and except the eye that with gazing on the Breastplate of Plenydd Brif-fardd has acquired the vision of the Gods that see all things?"

Manawyddan heard them bring the wand and put it in the right forepaw of the whisperer; whom then he head continue thus:

"That is well; but there is the danger of pursuit to consider, and that of being grasped at by the pursuer. Where is the Ointment of Intense Swift Slipperiness, that I may thoroughly grease my fur therewith?"

Manawyddan heard them bring the ointment, and the liberal application of it to furry body and limbs.

"Now," said the whisperer, "there is hope of success, and even certainty of it. Were anyone to pursue me he could not catch me even if he could overtake the wind at its fleetest; and if he could catch the bodiless wind, and firmly maintain his hold upon it, yet could he neither grasp nor maintain his hold on me. There will be no peril from anything, except from the Gloves of Gwron; and Gwron will not part with them of his own free will, and none could take them from him either by force or fraud. As soon, therefore, as this wheat-ear is dropped at the foot of the throne, complete will be my power over Gorsedd Arberth, and complete the ruin and subjugation of the Dimetians and of the Princes of Dyfed of the Family of Pwyll."

"Clust fab Clustfeinad would hardly have attained hearing that without careful listening," thought Manawyddan; "although he was good at hearing things."

He heard the faint, infinitesimal sound of four paws on the pathway approaching him; although the journey of the snail over the leek-leaf would be noisy in its comparison. He saw the luminosity of the King-Ear of the Middle Fields, although it was veiled with such illusion and phantasm that it would have been easier, standing at Gelli Wic in Cornwall on a drk night, to perceive the cricket beneath the myrtle-bush in the Islands of Corsica, or concealed under the wild thyme in Greece in the East. He did not move till the one with the wheat-ear was at his feet, and cautiously shifting its load from its shoulders. Forth then with his right arm, and down his hand.

The one with the wheat-ear taking flight, and its flight swifter than the summer lightning or the meteor in November coursing through heaven. A clutching with the right of Manawyddan, and the right Glove of Gwron on the hand. With the thing clutched a violent effort to escape; and its equipment for escaping when grasped better than that of the footless wave of the Atlantic of the bodiless wind of heaven or the ghost that travels in the Nwyfre. Useless his effort: entirely unavailaing to him swiftness, smallness, lithe slipperiness, agility, magical powers.

Manawyddan took the left glove from his left hand, and imprisoned the one he had captured in it, and tied up the opening of the glove. He heard quiet, dismay-hushed, bewildered scurrying, over the slopes of the hill and down through the valley. He took his place on the throne again, and waited until it was dawn.

V. The Peculiarities and Well-balanced Nature of Hirewin Frith the Chief Tabby-Cat of Dyfed, or indeed of the Island of the Mighty.

CHILL WAS the dawn when Manawyddan rose up from the throne. The east of heaven became a primrose, and then a daffodil, and then a wealth and glory of tulips flaming. A wind came wandering through the valley: sweeter its breath than that of any wind that had blown there since the fall of the phantasm and illusion. Slowly he made his way down the hillside; musing, and uttering his musings aloud.

"In my deed," said he, "although there was some success with me at midnight, there will be little tidings of value for me to bring this morning, either to Rhianon Ren my wife, or to Pryderi my son, or to the Dimetians my people, or to Blodwen my white mare. But there is one to whom I shall bear valuable tidings; and they will be the cause of grave delight with her, and of sleek complacency of spirit. Pleasant will be the tidings I shall bring to Hirewin Frith, the old gray tabby-cat beside the hearth in the kitchen."

At that he heard a miserable squeaking out of the glove. "Wherefore squeakest thou?" said he.

"Lord," said the One in the glove, "I squeak because of the mention of tabby cats. All my life, so great is my sensibility and the repugnance of my nature towards them, that if I but hear them named it is a cause of terror and squeaking with me, and even of losing the functions of my mind. Bring not these tidings to Hirewin Frith, in the name of Heaven and Man!"

"Ungenerous is this!" sighed Manawyddan, shaking his head in sadness. "Lacking in good feeling it is, and in consideration for the well-being of others. There is no nice altruism in it: I blush for shame to hear it spoken. And even though thou experiencest repugnance against tabbies, yet will Hirewin Frith experience no repugnance against thee. Rather she will drawn to thee by subtle and sympathetic affinities.

"Hearken now, and thou shalt understand her the better," he went on. "Although of lofty lineage, she is devoid of arrogance; and turns not aside in disdain from the cranny that harbors the pilferer of meal. Kindly and thorough is her nature; and moreover, equably balanced.

The broiled trout on the dish might be entrusted to her keeping, so dominant is the power of conscience in her breast. Delicately she delights in purring before the fire; in cleansing her striped fur with her tongue. Even the hunting dogs respect her: not only on account of her dignity, but also by reason of the rending sharpness of her claws.

"Further I will make this known to thee: so great are her efficiency, and her wise sagacity in the chase, and her mastery both of speed and of strategic cunning, that there has not been a rumor of vermin in the kitchen of the palace since the day she forsook kittenhood and betook herself to serious courses."

So far was this news from giving confidence to the one in the glove that he fell to squeaking even more dolorously than before, and with greater energy. Manawyddan sighed deeply. "Why, in heaven's name, is this unreasonable squeaking?" said he.

"Lord," said the other, "it is on account of my profound distrust of Hirewin Frith, as thou callest her. It is not in the nature of tabby-cats to manifest tenderness towards members of my family."

"Tenderness she will manifest," said Manawyddan. "Thou wilt be entertainment for her from noon till dusk; and afterwards she will delight in remembering thee. I will saddle the mare, and we will hurry forward to bring Hirewin the tidings. Ill would it become me, returning to Arberth, to bring neither gifts nor good news to anyone."

He saddled Blodwen, and set forward towards Arberth; but the kindliness of his words brought no alleviation of squeaking to the one in the glove. At the head of the valley the noise of it rose above the hoof-beats of Blodwen, and disturbed the current of his thoughts.

"Is there no contenting thee?" said he. "Unforgivable is the sin of ingratitude."

"There is neither joy nor peace of mind with me, on account of the tidings thou art bearing to the one I distrust."

"Distrust her not," said Manawyddan. "Exceedingly trustworthy she is; as her foremothers were before her, that were the Chief Cats of Dyfed since Hu Gedarn led the Cymry into this island."

"Even were they Chief Cats of the Island of the Mighty they would be repugnant to me and I should abhor them earnestly: both them and their descendants, and their kinsman collaterally. If thou wilt refrain from this, thou shalt have good tidings to bear to thy son Pryderi; and thou shalt give him pleasure enough, and more than pleasure."

"What tidings shall I bring to him?" said Manawyddan, drawing rein.

"Tidings of the end of the enchantment," said the other. "Tidings of the lifting of the phantasm and illusion from him."

"It is beyond the power of such a one as thou art to do that," said Manawyddan. "Be content with humility; forgo ambition; give pleasure cheerfully to the humble; lift not thine aspirations over high. To Hirewin Frith thou wilt be a pleasing diversion at first, and later, the cause of comfortable repletion of body and praiseworthy complacency of mind; but to Pryderi fab Pwyll thou wouldst be of little use or advantage. I shall bring news of thee to Hirewin, and leave Pryderi untroubled."

At that the squeaking was multiplied a thousandfold, and became more mournful than ever. "In my deed to Gods and Men, it will not be beyond my power to release Pryderi; and that thou mayest believe me, look forward along the road towards Arberth."

A sound of galloping hoofs came from in front: where, it might be a mile away, Pryderi on the Wind-driver came approaching. The storm and darkness had all gone from the land; the Vale of Arberth lay all green and lovely westward, the road winding through it; but no life moved there except such green growing things as the wind stirred, and Pryderi fab Pwyll on the Wind-driver.

"Delightful is this, truly," said Manawyddan. "Long have I desired to see Pryderi. We will go forward together and carry him the news: he was ever of a kindly disposition, and tender to the feelings of faithful animals."

He roade forward; but still there was no peace for the squeaking in the glove. "Dear help thee better!" said Manawyddan; "are pride and shame lost to thee?"

"Lord," said the one in the glove, "fulfill now thy promise, and set me free from this prison and from the fear of tabby-cats."

"Promise?" said Manawyddan; "Promise? It is incredible to me that there should be this niggardly stinting of pleasure to the sleekly

199

well-meaning. What I promised thee I shall fulfil; and what in my heart I promised to Hirewin. Come; it will be the delight of his life with Pryderi to know that there is good news for Hirewin Frith, who was ever a favorite with him. Ill would it become us to refrain from giving pleasure to at least two this morning: and Pryderi and Hirewin shall the two be."

He rode forward; and there rose from the glove such squeaking as it would be given few mice to raise, even at the best of times. "What is it now?" said he.

"Lord," said the other, "with every pace of thy going forward my anxiety concerning Hirewin Frith is multiplied. Refrain from giving her news of this, and I will cause it that there shall be no disappointment for thee; and that thou shalt cause pleasure to two this morning, besides thyself and me: namely, to Rhianon Ren thy wife as well as to Pryderi thy son."

"Alas, inordinate ambition!" sighed Manawyddan. "Alas, the vaunting tendency of the boastful, ill-regulated nature! Undoubtedly it would be beyond the power of any mouse to accomplish this!"

"Though it may be beyond the power of mice, it will not be beyond my power. Look forward along the road and thou shalt see Rhianon Ren riding hither; and the tidings thou shalt give her will be that there is no more power in the phantasm and illusion to harm either Dyfed, or her, or Pryderi."

Manawyddan looked and there, at three hundred strides beyond Pryderi came Rhianon in her chariot; her three Faery Birds circling and soaring about her head and singing as they flew. The morning was afire with the beauty it caught from her and from them.

"Well, well," said Manawyddan; "utterly delightful is this! It would be an honor to any man to receive news of a mouse such as thou art. We will go forward to meet Rhianon and Pryderi."

But even then there was no end to the squeaking. "Alas," said Manawyddan, "bitterly I am disappointed in thee! On account of thy wilful cacophony the music of the Birds of Rhianon is spoiled."

"Thou didst say it would be an honor to receive tidings of a mouse such as I am; and grave are my misgivings on account of that saying."

"Cast thy misgivings aside," said Manawyddan, "and take pleasure in the pleasure of others, as becomes thee. Thou hast caused delight, since day dawned, to Pryderi, and to Rhianon, and to me also; and it is doubtful whether thou hast caused so much delight to anyone before. And beyond all this thou art singularly fortunate: it is reserved for thee to cause even greater delight to another before the darkening of evening; and not only delight, but the purring of complete satisfaction. I marvel intensely that thou shouldst not be rejoicing at this."

"Loathsome to me is mention of purring!" said the one in the glove, "To what other is it reserved for me to give satisfaction?"

"Understandest thou not yet? Alas for thy cantankerous, disagreeable spirit! To the kindliest wearer of gray fur in Wales thou art reserved to give pleasure; and it is an honor to thee, and a main privilege," said Manawyddan. "To the sleekest and most delicately-minded of clawed ones thou shalt give it: namely, to Hirewin Frith the Chief Tabby of Dyfed."

At that the squeaking became loud, obstreperous and intolerable. "Lord," said the one in the glove; " set you me free from this prison, and release my mind from apprehension concerning tabby-cats; and you shall bring pleasure to thousands between this and noon."

"This is indeed unbecoming in one of thy dimensions," said Manawyddan. "Rarely is it given, even to the mighty, the generous and the valiant, to give pleasure to thousands between a morning and a noon: assuredly it will not be given to a mouse such as thou art."

"I declare to you that I will do it; and that without inordinate exertion or difficulty. I will give pleasure to all the Dimetians, and I will raise the illusion and the phantasm from Dyfed."

"None would believe thee unless first he saw them raised," said Manawyddan. "Unwise in a braggart, to overtax credulity."

"Set me free from the glove and I will show you," said the other.

"What sayest thou?" said Manawyddan. "Heretofore I have treated thee as a friend: in spite of thine ill-conditioned spirit I have been patient with thee. But now I am justly enangered at thy presumption. It is unbelievable that anyone would attempt miserable haggling with a chieftain of the Brython. So contemptible an offense is this that the Chief Judge of Dyfed would scorn to pass judgment for it; yet shall one be found who, out of consideration for me, will not hestitate to pass judgment."

"Woe is me on account of my fate! Who is it that will pass judgment, in heaven's name?"

"It is Hirewin Frith," said Manawyddan. "Stern and equable is her nature: not to be influenced, in passing judgment, by compunction or by sentiment, or by bribery."

The squeaking became worse than ever. "What power is with me to dissipate illusions and phantasms whilst I remain imprisoned in this loathsome glove?"

"Speak not evil of the Gloves of Gwron," said Manawyddan. "By the Wood, the Field and the Mountain, take thou the illusion and the phantasm from Dyfed!"

The one in the glove groaned. "I am defeated," said he. "Behold you Dyfed free from enchantments!"

There it was: the green, beautiful, populous land. There was white-walled Arberth on its hill, and the sounds of a city rising from it. There were the farms and cottages, wherever they had been of old. There were the countrymen and laborers in the fields. The dog awoke barking where he was herding the flock. The quiet kine awoke and became visible grazing in their pastures; the sheep awoke on the hillside and bleated with delight of the sunshine and the morning. Man, woman and child awoke everywhere, and thought they had fallen asleep a moment since over their work or their play. The lark awoke in mid air; the blackbird in the coppice; the speckled thrush in the orchard. And high over all these singers the Birds of Rhianon soared and sang. Between the sea and the Tywi and the Teifi there remained no enchantment anywhere, no sleep-producing illusion or phantasm causing unseenness on any living thing. Right glad was Manawyddan; right glad were Rhianon and Pryderi as they hastened forward to meet him.

"DEAR SOUL," said Rhianon Ren, "wherefore is there squeaking in the glove?"

"It is a mouse," said he, "that I am bringing to the palace as a gift for Hirewin Frith."

"In the name of heaven and man," said the one in the glove, "it is a disgrace to thee to speak untruth. Llwyd ab Cilcoed am I: that set free Rhianon and Pryderi, and lifted the illusion and the phantasm from Dyfed."

"As to untruth," said Manawyddan, "gravely am I compromised by it already on account of thee. Yesterday I made prophecies concerning the wheat which thou hast falsified by stealing it; and it is a cause of serious compromise for me; and I may well suffer for it in future lives. Therefore judgment must be passed on thee; and the one to pass the judgment will be Hirewin Frith: owing to her understanding of the nature of vermin, and her knowledge of their temptations and extenuations, and her nice critical ability in all points concerning them."

"Lord," said Llwyd from the glove, "speak no more of Hirewin! Already my men are bearing the wheat to the barn for you; the harvests of the middle fields and of the east and of the west. Tomorrow it shall be ground in the mill, without expense to you of time or labor. And the next day shall be for the baking: and if there is one loaf short, or half a loaf, or indeed so much as would stay the hunger of a mouse such as you think I am, my life shall be forfeit. And now put spells on me, as you did on Gwiawn Cat's-Eye my companion, and deprive me of dishonesty and the tendency to thieve."

Manawyddan answered him: "Not I put spells on Gwiawn, but he put them on himself. I require that thou also put on thyself an illusion and a phantasm that shall cause thy disappearance and that of thy host from the Island of the Mighty from this out through the age of ages, and that shall prevent thy working harm against the Cymry until the world withers and the sky falls. Otherwise even now Hirewin Frith shall pass judgment upon thee for thy misdoings; and a marvel if she execute not the judgment as soon as it may be passed."

"All this shall be," said Llwyd; "woe is me that there is no escape for me." Thereupon he put the phantasm and illusion on himself and on his host; and it became clear to Manawyddan that the glove was empty. They heard no news of him thereafter; nor was any rumor rife concerning him in the Island of the Mighty from that out.

As for the wheat of Amaethon, they found it in the barn: the whole harvest of the valley, and not enough missing to save an ant from death by hunger. Three sacks of the grain they saved for sowing the three parts of the vale of Gorsedd Arberth; with the rest they made bread that was nourishment for the whole of the Dimetians between that and the ripening of their crops; and beyond nourishment, it was the complete restoration of their virtue and mirth and valor and wisdom, and the erasement from their memory of whatever ills may have befallen them through the phantasms and illusions of Llwyd ab Cilcoed.

And from that out there was strange prosperity in Dyfed, and delight such as had never been known there before. For three years Manawyddan and Rhianon held the sovereignty in Arberth, owing to the anxiety of Pryderi to learn wisdom from them, and to perfect himself under their instruction. At the end of the three years they rose up, and went forward to the Wyddfa Mountain where the Gods were awaiting them; and gay, exultant, singing, they entered the kingdom of the Immortals.

With their entering there, and their attainment of
Dragonhood with the Sons of the Dragon,
this Branch of it ends. By reason
of what is told in it, it is called

The Contests of Ab Cilcoed against the Princes,
or The Book of the Three Operations
of Illusion and Phantasm...

Here is the Sixth Branch of the Story, Namely,
THE SOVEREIGNTY AND DEATH OF PRYDERI

I. The Causes of the Glory of the Dimetians, and the Equipment for Sovereignty of Pryderi fab Pwyll

AS IF being nourished with the wheat of Amaethon, year after year, were not enough to make the Dimetians excel every other people in the reign of Pryderi fab Pwyll, it was then that the Cow Llefrith Laethwen came up out of the waters of the Tywi, and spread delight and enlightenment wherever she might travel; and it was then that the peculiarities of Gorsedd Arberth became renowned over the world.

It was a privilege granted to many to take their place on the throne there: Pryderi knowing to whom it might be granted. Kings and chieftains came from afar, and bards and princes, to behold the wonder that might be seen there, and to hold conversation with the Immortals that they could not attain in their own lands. Never an Eve of May but Pryderi himself would be on the throne there from dawn until midnight, receiving the counsels of Hu Gadarn that Gwydion ab Don would bring to him; and fast the friendship, on account of this, between Gwydion and Pryderi: dear they were the one to the other; not as God and Man, but as sons of the one Divine Mother. Also it happened at times, and that not seldom, that when Pryderi was on Gorsed Arberth, came Rhianon Ren, serene and compassionate, or the God Manawyddan son of the Boundless, to have converse with him; and owing to these things, if there was any man in the Island of the Mighty who had good knowledge of the God-world, it was Pryderi; and this was a main cause of the excelling nobility of the Dimetians.

As for the wheat of Amaethon, news already has been given of many of its peculiarities. Three sacks of the grain would be saved after the harvesting every year; and with them the valley would be sown; the rest of it would be made into bread, one loaf of which would be feasting for a hundred kings; and they would desire no other food, on account of its diversity of delicate flavors, and of its nourishing strength in them, both of mind and limbs, of heart and of creative imagination. The Dimetians needed little food beyond this and the milk of Llefrith Laethwen.

She had that name because of her color, that was a luminous milk white; and because of the plenitude of milk with her always, and that without need of calving. Whoever might drink it, if he were wise he became wiser, and if brave, braver; and if noble of heart, the nobility would be multiplied in him. Drinking it was healing for the sick; and for the ignorant and stupid it was the gaining of intelligence; and if there were one naturally afflicted with cowardice, but desirous to be brave; or one given to lying or braggart speech, but sager in his heart for truth and modesty, the milk of Llefrith Laethwen would cause the fulfilment of his aspirations in him. It was her custom to travel the world, conferring benefits on whomsoever might desire them; but always she would be Ystrad Tywi at Calangauaf; and then the Dimetians would come to her at the town of Abercennen, and obtain all the milk from her they might need, enough and plenty. It was no wonder that in every noble quality they excelled and were superior to the rest of the world at that time.

It was while Pryderi was holding court at Dinasfawr above Abercennen, the second Calangauaf of his reign, that they brought news to him of her first coming forth out of the river; and every year, after that, power and glory and sovereignty were multiplied on him; and every year there was increase of his wisdom and magnanimity and compassion kindness; till he was the star and prop of the Dimetians, the Dragon of Dyfed, the Beacon and Hero of the Western World.

In those days white-walled Arberth exceeded London in renown; it was the gathering place of the kings of the earth: Pryderi would not forgo it to assume the Crown of London. Cantref upon cantref, and indeed whole kingdoms, had been long adding themselves to his dominions; and not one of them by conquest; but all by the will of lords and kindred; until he was holding the sovereignty of all Wales south of Gwynedd and Powys. Then the kings and druids came to him, saying,

"Sawel Benuchel is dead: is it your will to wear the Crown of London?"

"It is not," said Pryderi. "Better with me the city of my fathers." And he added, "Appoint you Sawel Benisel, if it please you."

They took counsel together, and appointed Sawel Benisel as he had advised them, and prepared to invest him with the sovereignty in London. But when he heard of it, he rose up in the council. "In my deed to heaven," said he, "even though I wear the Crown in London here, not I will be Sovereign Gwledig of the Island of the Mighty in peace and war."

"Wherefore not?" said they.

"None is fitted to hold that office except Pryderi fab Pwyll at Arberth," said he.

"That is true," said they. "Crowned King shall you be in London, but the Sovereign Gwledig of the Cymry shall be Pryderi fab Pwyll during his lifetime; and he shall exercise his leadership from Arberth."

From that out for fifty years the world was full of the renown of Pryderi Wledig. At war-times he would go forth, year by year, with the hosted Dimetians and the men of the Island of the Mighty, righting wrongs and putting an end to oppressions in the four quarters of the world; conquests he made in Spain and Persia, in Greece and Byrgwyn, in Sach and Salach; in the Islands of Corsica, in India the Greater, in Llychlyn, and at the foot of the Alps. No bards in the world but delighted to sing his praises. "The like of him has not been known," they said, "since Arthur Emperor's time!" Neither in the Island of the Mighty nor in the width of the world was there anyone to compare with him: either for matchless might in sweeping through the battle, on the day when he rode in his chariot in the midst of his teulu to war; or for beauty and glory of mien; or for wisdom in kingcraft when he held council of lords and kindred at Arberth; or for skill at harping and narrating stories at feast-times; or, when he had a mind to, in the use of subtle consonance and assonance in the framing of melodious poems.

II. The Embassies Hu Gadarn Sent to the Gwldig when Pryderi's Destiny was to Change and Become Ennobled

AT THE time this branch of it begins Pryderi Wledig had been reigning a long time, and as men count it he was an old man: driving on his five score years, the rumor is. But the druids said, "He is immortal already!" – seeing him not growing old, but the hair of him golden as ever it was, and the limbs strong, and the face that of a hero in his prime. Was he not the son of Rhianon, and she a Goddess? And was he not therefore half immortal by nature?

Songs in his praise were going up and down the world. Among all the nations, there was none at that time to equal the Cymry of Ynys Wen; and of the Cymry, there was none to equal the Dimetians; and of the Dimetians there was no man nearly to equal Pryderi. None to equal him, or to dream he might be equalled. No arrogance was to be found in him, and no sloth, and no injustice: and there was no man to accuse him of any fault. There was no one, in all the western world, to accord him anything but praise and reverence and love.

Hu Gadarn was on his throne on the Wyddfa, and engaging in his deep cogitations, and devising plans for the welfare of the Cymry from that out through the ages of ages. It appeared to him that a cycle was coming to its close with them; and that if they were not to die, and their language to drift into silence, there must be quiescence in the Island of the Mighty now, and night and sleep must follow the sunlight of their glory. Also there were the needs of his armies, that wage war forever against Chaos along the borders of Space: he must consider those needs, and send them reinforcement, it seemd to him. "Where is Arianrod Ren?" said he.

"I am here," said Arianrod.

"Turn you the wheel in heaven, if it please you," said Hu. "Declare the immediate fate of the Cymry of Ynys Wen."

She turned her wheel, and read what was written on the thread. "The fate is rest and quiescence," said she. "It is the proper ending of glory, the natural coming on of night and sleep after day. The deed of Heilyn ab Gwyn has been atoned for: it is as if the door at Caer Walas had never been opened, that looks towards Aberhenfelen and Cornwall;

Pryderi the Gwledig has been what Bran the Blessed would have been."

"Yes," said the Mighty One. "Declare you now the fate of Pryderi Wledig, if it please you."

She turned the wheel again, and pondered on what was written. "Here it is," said she. "The fate of Pryderi is on the verge of change."

"Will the change be for the better of for the worse?" said Hu Gadarn.

"Oh, for the better," said she. "It will be expansion, and becoming glorified beyond any glory known to it heretofore."

"A marvel to me if it should be glorified further, and he remaining in the Island of the Mighty," thought Hu.

Then he fell to his musings and cogitations again. "Lord Manawyddan," said he at last; "go, if it please you, to your son the Gwledig of the White Island, and make known that it is permitted to him to take his place with us now in the Circle of the Gods."

Right glad was Manawyddan at that; right glad was the Family of Hu; right glad Rhianon Ren. And there was another that was glad, and none more so: that old impetuous Cymro made immortal, Pendaran Dyfed the Archer of the Lightnings. He had been the Penteulu of Dyfed in the old days, and he had been Rhianon's protector whilst Manawyddan was in exile; and because of the grandeur of his nature, Hu Gadarn had conferred immortality on him, and taken him into the Wyddfa, before Manawyddan's return, and made him, from Penteulu of the Dimetians, Penteulu of the Immortals, when they drove their battle against the hellions along the borders of space.

It was the morning of Calanmai, and Pryderi Wledig was on the throne at Gorsedd Arberth when Manawyddan dragon-guised came soaring out of the dawn, and gave him the greeting of heaven and man, pleasantly and kindly; having first taken human shape on the hilltop.

"Lord father," said Pryderi, "good it is with me, and very good; but far better be it with you."

"I come upon an embassy from the Mighty One," said Manawyddan.

"Make known the message, if it please you."

"Here it is," said Manawyddan. "The days of your mortality are ended, if you will. It is offered to you to forsake human existence in the Island of the Mighty, and to assume glorious Dragonhood with us."

"Yes glorious is Dragonhood," said Pryderi. "But offer it not to me, in the name of heaven."

Manawyddan was disappointed and amazed. "Wherefore not?" said he.

"On account of the race and kindred of the Cymry. It is the delight of my life to serve them and encourage them, and to assure them victory in the fray when the hosts go forth: and it would be the sorrow of sorrows on me to leave them, out of uncertainty as to their fate thenceforward."

"I will bring this message to the Mighty One," said Manawyddan.

A year passed; and it was the morning of Calanmai again; and Hu the Mighty was deep in his musings. "Lord Pendaran," said he, "is there remembrance with you of the land of the Dimetians, and of Pryderi Wledig their lord?"

"There is, lord Might One; and furthermore, hankering desire after them, day and night."

"Go you then, if it please you, to Pryderi on Gorsedd Arberth, and announce to him permission to take his place with us here and be immortal."

"Lord Mighty One," said Pendaran, "wonderfully apt is this decision; wonderfully wise and apt!"

Thereupon he went forth. Pryderi, watching from the throne on Gorsedd Arberth, saw the blue of heaven catch flame as it were from north to south with dragon travelling; and in a moment there stood Pendaran Dyfed before him, – stern of visage, immortal, glorious.

"Lord Pendaran," said Pryderi, "indeed and indeed, the greeting of the God and the Man to you, the best in the world and in Wales."

"Come you with me, Pryderi fab Pwyll, and no wasting words with you!"

"What now, in the name of heaven?" said Pryderi.

"It's Hu the Mighty has acquired wisdom at last," said Pendaran.

"He is sending for you to come to the Wyddfa, and quit wasting the foolish years of your life on mortality. Reverently I speak of him: he, heaven knows, the great captain of dragonhood in these worlds. Come you then with me, and learn what existence is, that you have not understood heretofore!"

A kind of darkness came over the face of Pryderi. "Is it commanding this the Mighty One is, or is it invitation and offering?"

"Offering? No! Do you forget whose son you are, and your office in these islands? An embassy from king to king I come; offering and courteous invitation I bring with me."

"Then ask it not of me, in heaven's name!"

"Heaven help thee better," said Pendaran, "with thy youthful hotheadedness and thy desire for argument and wilful and stubborn ways! Wilt thou be wiser than our Lord the Mighty One? Wilt thou shun the great warfare on the borders of space?"

Said Pryderi: "Were you hearing at any time of the Dimetians in Dyfed, or the kindred of the Cymry in the White Island?

"By heaven I have heard of them; and I have never heard evil of them!"

"Would none be needed to stand by them?" said Pryderi. "It is my delight to serve and encourage them, and to bring them prosperity, and ensure them victory when the hosts join battle. It would not delight me to leave them, and remain uncertain as to their fate when I was gone."

"Thou art the son of the Son of the Boundless, evil on thy stubborn ways! Thou art the son of my chieftain, and I have not found thy better on the Wyddfa! Proud will I be to bear thy haughty message to the Mighty One."

Pendaran returned to the Wyddfa, and came where Hu Gadarn was enthroned. "Is there news with you of the coming of the Gwledig?" said the Gods.

"There is not," said Pendaran. "Proud is that man, and glorious; he is not one to forget the Cymry. Miserable he would be on the Wyddfa, remembering them and their needs and occasions, and he not there to lead and comfort them. A wilful and a stubborn man he is, as it is fitting he should be; with the hotheadedness of youth on him, and the grand, magnanimous nature of his race. Not he will forsake the Cymry, whether to receive immortality or for another cause."

"It is a lovely quality in him," said Hu Gadarn. "Another year shall he be given to dwell among them."

But as for Pryderi, he had forgotten it before the third day of May was over.

When Calanmai came again, Hu Gadarn sent Gwydion to Pryderi. "Offer him the immortality again, and offer it more urgently than ever," said the Mighty One. And so Gwydion did; but for all his urgency, Pryderi was unwilling to go with him.

"Not well to reject what may be offered by the Mighty One," said Gwydion, when Pryderi had refused the immortality. "And there is this to consider," said he: "Manawyddan is there, and Rhianon Ren; and the men of the teulu of your father are there; and old Pendaran Dyfed is lacking full delight in his godhood until you shall come there also."

Pryderi sighed. "Lord brother," he said; "it was ever the custom of the Gods to make trial of the man who might have his place on the throne of Gorsedd Arberth here."

"That is true," said Gwydion.

"Three times they made trial of my father, offering him this and that," said Pryderi.

"There is no denying it," said Gwydion.

"Evil upon me if I have learnt nothing from his failure in those trials," said Pryderi.

"What message is there for the Mighty One?" asked Gwydion.

"There is praise and gratitude for him first," said Pryderi; "and thereafter there is this: Although I have met with many trials, never have I met the equal of this one. I declare to you that there is no part of me but yearns for the companionship of the Gods and of the Dimetians made immortal. But here in Dyfed are my people, and here in this island are the Cymry: and my life is due to them, and my love is due to them, and my protection and fostering care are due to them. Even though the offer is from Hu Gadarn, evil upon me unless I reject it."

"Well, well," said Gwydion, sighing; "I will take this message to him."

He came into the council hall on the Wyddfa, and made it known to the Gods. They all shook their heads gravely, sighing, when they heard it. "Dear indeed," said they, "there is but little perception, with mortality, of the nature of our calling and office!" But they all marvelled and experienced delight at the heroism and compassionate character of Pryderi.

"Lord Mighty One," said Rhianon Ren, "it will be necessary to put compulsion on my froward son."

But Hu Gadarn mused in his mind, considering it. "Not so," said he; "there will be no putting compulsion on him yet. Death will not come to him while he may be nourished with the food and drink that are nourishing him now. Go you, Lord Gwydion, and deprive him of the wheat of Amaethon your brother, and of the Cow Llefrith Laethwen."

But Pryderi had forgotten about it before the fourth day had passed.

III. The First Two Deprivations of Pryderi, and Old Age Coming on him

CAME GWYDION AB DON to Manawyddan on the day of the wheat harvest in the vale of Gorsedd Arberth. "Soul," said he, "is the Basket of Gwaeddfyd Newynog with you?"

"It is," said Manawyddan. "Do you require it of me?"

"I do, for the portage of wheat," said Gwydion. Thereupon Manawyddan gave it to him.

By the next evening the Dimetians had threshed the harvest of the valley of Gorsedd Arberth; and the grain was gathered in sacks in the barn. When the feast was for beginning there came a bard out of Ireland to the gates of the palace; and was brought into the hall, and had the best welcome in the world with Pryderi. For pleasantness of demeanor and skilful charm of address, all thought him without his equal among the bards of the four quarters of the world.

Nine kings were feasting with Pryderi that night: namely Sawel Benisel, and Aedd king of Ireland, and Paris king of France; and the kings of Llychlyn and Caer Ochren and Caer Sidi; and the king of Persia, and the emperor of Africa the Great, and the king of the Island of Appletrees in the west of the world. They were nine supreme sovereigns, handsome men, wearers of golden torques, proud breakers of battle; but compared with Pryderi Wledig they were all but striplings, and it was the greatest honor they had received in their lives, to be his guests in the hall.

It seemed to all that the feast that night was the most glorious that had ever been held in the Island of the Mighty since the days of the Emperor Arthur. Never had the splendor of Pryderi's reign seemed so splendid to anyone; never had he himself appeared so triumphantly courteous in the exercise of his power and dominion and glory.

On the dais with the kings sat the bard out of Ireland. Whoever looked at him was filled with delight: he alone was comparable, in his beauty and dignity and affability, with the Sovereign Gwledig of those islands. When it came to the narrating of heroic stories, the chief bards of the Island of the Mighty stood forth and exercised their art and science; and it appeared to everyone that they had never been excelled, and never would be. Then the bard out of Ireland told a story, and his art in narrating it was seven times better than the art of the others.

"Marvellous to me is this," said Pryderi. "Though I have heard stories from Gwydion ab Don himself, never has it been given to me to here such story-telling as this."

"Lord," said the bard, "there was nothing wonderful in it. The songs will be better, if it should please you to hear them."

So Pryderi requested him to sing.

If his story-telling had been good, his singing was as much as seventeen times better; and many thought it was even more than that. "I am unable to tell what reward would be fitting to requite you for this singing," said Pryderi.

"Name you what reward you will, if it please you," said the bard. "There was nothing wonderful in the singing."

"Not so," said Pryderi. "I set no limitation upon your merits. Ask what you may desire, and if it be within the boundaries of the south, you shall receive it."

"I ask that this basket may be filled with wheat: the wheat of Amaethon from the valley of Gorsedd Arberth," said the bard.

Pryderi looked at the basket. "The wheat shall be given you," said he, cheerfully and kindly. Then he called to his servingmen. "Bring you hither the whole of the harvest of the valley," said he. "Sack by sack, let it be emptied into yonder basket, and not three grains remaining on the floor of the barn."

All marvelled when he said *the whole harvest*; for the basket was not one that had the look of holding more than a bushel or so. But sack by sack they brought the harvest in, and poured it into the basket; and when the last sackful had been poured into it, the Basket of Gwaeddfyd Newynog, according to its nature and peculiarities, was no more than half full.

"Will treading it down be required of me also?" said Pryderi.

"No," said Gwydion ab Don; "I am content with it."

The feast went forward; and Pryderi Wledig was no less cheerful and courteous and hospitable than before; but inwardly he was aware of the loss it would be to him, losing the whole of the wheat of Amaethon.

The next morning Gwydion departed in the cold of the dawn; and none had discovered that he was Gwydion. No sooner was he gone, and the wheat of Amaethon with him, than the Cow Llefrith Laethwen made her way into the courtyard and came to Pryderi where he stood after his singing health to the one that had departed; all had thought she was on her travels in Lloegria or in Alban, or indeed beyond the sea. "The loss will not be irreparable while you remain with me," said Pryderi, stroking her. Thereafter she went wandering no more, but stayed at Arberth with Pryderi, or followed him from court to court when he made the circuit of the land.

At Calangauaf Gwydion came to Pryderi at Dinas Fawr on the Tywi, and saw that his hair was turning gray and that there were deep lines on his face that had not been on it formerly. "Lord Brother," said Gwydion, "are you willing to forgo your mortality now?"

"Heavens knows I am not willing," said Pryderi. "On account of the loss of the wheat of Amaethon the Cymry are in greater need than ever of the help I can give them; ill would it become me to leave them now."

"Alas for this answer," said Gwydion. "Unpleasing it will be to the Mighty One of the Wyddfa."

"Lord Brother," said Pryderi, "it appears to me that it will not be unpleasing to him. Well known is his love for the kindred of the Cymry."

Gwydion brought the news to Hu Gadarn. "The loss of the wheat is bringing old age on him," he said; "but it is not causing him to falter. While the milk of Llefrith Laethwen remains to nourish the life in him there will be no compelling him to leave the Cymry; and without compulsion he will not leave them."

The year went by; and old age came down upon Pryderi as it went: his hair gew gray; it appeared to him that the vigor of his limbs was not what it had been.

Now here is what happened on the Wyddfa on the day before Calangauaf in that year. Hu Gadarn rose up: "I must go forth," said he. "Lord Tydain Tad Awen, assume you the regency of heaven, if it please you." But he said to himself, "Evil will befall the Race of the Cymry, unless I work ruin upon them now."

Then he called Gwydion ab Don, and went forth with him, his hand on the shoulder of Gwydion. "Bring you the Lord Gwledig into the Wyddfa Mountain," said he. "Delay no longer with it."

"Will it be by compulsion?" said the Son of Don.

"It will," said the Mighty One. "And let the compulsion be such that he has never received any honor to equal it, and that renown of its glory will ring down among the Cymry till the end of the ages. Lovely, with me, I declare to you, is this unflinching love he has for them."

Then Hu Gadarn went down into the Island of the Mighty.

And here is what befell at Calangauaf, at the court of Pryderi:

The men of the south were accustomed to hold their fair every Eve of November at the town of Abercennen on the Tywi, and Pryderi would hold court at Dinas Fawr, high above the town and the river: at this time Calanmai was for Arberth and Dyfed, and Calangauaf for

Abercennen and Ystrad Tywi. The reason of this was that three days before Calangauaf Llefrith Laethwen would go down into the waters of the Tywi, under the bridge, to renew her beneficent nature, travelling for three days as a salmon in the sea, from the shores of Wales as far as to the Court of Nefydd Naf Neifion the Prince of the Sea. On Calangauaf she would come up from the river again, and into the town; and for the sake of getting milk from her it was customary for many to gather on that day in Abercennen from every part of the universe: kings and bards that had hospitality with Pryderi in Dinas Fawr, and multitudes that camped in the valley under his protection; and they would get their flame at midnight from the sacred fire of the druids at the head of Grongar Hill.

But this year there were rumors and apprehensions and uncertainty, for some reason, throughout the Island of the Mighty; and by reason of that few were encamped in the Vale of Tywi, and there were few guests from afar with Pryderi at Dinas Fawr.

Well might there be apprehensions and uncertainty! At midmorning a messenger came into the hall at Dinas Fawr. "Lord," said he, "there is disquieting news from London."

"Tell you the news without embarassment," said Pryderi.

"Here it is," said the messenger: "There is one come there whom all hold to be the Emperor Arthur; and the princes of Lloegria have appointed him Crowned King of London and Gwledig of the Island of the Mighty."

"It may be a cause for marvelling," said Pryderi; "but not for anger or grief."

"Will there be hosting the men of the south on account of it?" said Iestyn Benteulu, the son of Goronwy the son of Pendaran.

"There will not, dear soul," said Pryderi.

At noon a second messenger came into the hall. "What news is there?" said Pryderi.

"Lord," said he, "disquieting news."

"Tell it you, as if it were the best," said Pryderi.

"Here it is," said the messenger, "and evil be upon it! The men of Gwent and Morganwg have declared their allegiance to the one thought to be Arthur Emperor; and this declaration is equal to revolting against thee."

"Lord," said Iestyn fab Goronwy, "will there not be hosting the Dimetians now?"

"There will not," said Pryderi. "Of their own will they come to me; of their own will they shall go unhindered."

Between that and dusk the third messenger came into the hall. "Is the news disquieting?" asked Pryderi.

"Woe is me, disquieting it is, for the peaceable!" said the messenger.

"Tell it you, without fear or hesitancy," said Pryderi.

"The men of Gwynedd are hosted, and marching southward through Ceredigion on behalf of the one held to Arthur Emperor; and the men of Iscoed, Caerwedros, Gwinionydd and Mabwnion have joined them."

"Let the men of the teulu be gathered, and their swords sharpened and their equipment all in readiness," said Pryderi. There is no saying but that his heart was sore and heavy in him. "Dyfed was my father's, and I will protect it," thought he.

Iestyn went forth and gave the order to the men of the teulu – the six-score proud and valiant princes there were of them. Then said Ithel fab Einion Arth Cennen: "All this news is marvellous, and exceedingly disquieting and sorrowful."

"Old age has come on me, since the loss of the wheat of Amaethon," said Pryderi. "They will desire a younger man to be the Gwledig; but I will defend the borders of Dyfed and Ystrad Tywi."

"Miserable, ah me, is this ingratitude!" said Ithel. "There are Gods on the Wyddfa that will desire vengeance on the Cymry."

"Accuse not the Cymry, dear soul," said Pryderi. "They have been deceived by this appearance of white hairs on me; it will be seeming to them that I am no longer fitted for war and peace. In my deed they are far from knowledge of the truth of it!"

"Lord," said Ifor Ddistain ab Ceredig, "if the Cymry are deceived, let them be undeceived. Well known to us are the peculiarities of the Ring and the Fillet of the Family of Hefeydd Hen: renew you your youth with them, if it please you!"

These were treasures Rhianon brought with her from the God-land she was native to; and they had that power to renew the youth of the aged, if their owner desired to exercise it.

"They were entrusted to me for the benefit of the Cymry," said Pryderi. "While there is still vigor in the limbs and clear thought in the mind, there will be ability to protect the Cymry, and little need for youth-renewal."

They sat down to the feast; and as they did so there rose a great tumult from the town below. A man came running to the door of the hall. "What new is there from Abercennen?" said Pryderi.

"Lord Wledig," said the man, "the worse news in the universe. Llefrith Laethwen is stolen."

Pryderi rose up. "Let every warhorn sound the *Hai Atton!*" said he; "and let the teulu be prepared to ride out with me tonight, and the hosting of the Dimetians under the distain follow in the morning." Then he turned to the messenger again. "Let it please you to make clear the manner of the stealing," said he.

"Here it is," said the messenger. "The Milkwhite Milch-cow had come up from the river, and the men of Abercennen had obtained what milk they desired; and they were unarmed because of the druid peace of Calangauaf. Suddenly there rode six-score armed and glorious men into the marketplace; they had the appearance of being the teulu of the Gwyneddigion; the penteulu at their head a man of extreme resplendent glory. They dispersed the men of Abercennen and drove away Llefrith Laethwen towards the north."

Pryderi took thought. "There will be no breaking the druid peace for us," said he; "we will not rise forth until after the rekindling of the fires. Let the feasting go forward now, with curtailment of songs and stories. Let the teulu assemble in he marketplace after the rekindling."

From the end of the feast until midnight Pryderi was at his preparations for following the men of Gwynedd with the teulu that night, and for the hosting of Dyfed and Ystrad Tywi that should march the next day. "Let that host defend the banks of the Teifi," said he; "the teulu will be enough for the resucing of Llefrith Laethwen."

He rode down into the town before midnight; and there the women and children and the old men who were beyond fighting, came about him. Theretofore whenever their lord had ridden forth they had been filled with pride and delight; now there was uneasiness on every mind of them, and many of the women were mourning quietly, and many of the children wailing. Pryderi went among them on foot and spoke to all cheerfully and kindly. If there was a baby wailing, a word from him, or maybe his taking it in his arms from its mother, would be restoring its peace. The children that could walk he would comfort with patting their heads and reminding them of the heroic renown of their fathers. He would laugh with the old men over the battles they had fought under him of old time; to the women he would praise their husbands and their sons. By the light of the torches he went about the marketplace among them; and the crowds followed him and spoke of their love for him; and many would touch his mantle, and many would bend down and kiss his hands.

"We will have the Milkwhite Milch-cow with us tomorrow or the next day," said he. "Come you, dear souls! there will be no need of apprehensions."

But they saw the white hair on his head, and the lines of age on his brow; and grief weighed upon the hearts of all of them.

"Lord," said Ifor Ddistain, "will there be going up on to Grongar for you before the riding forth, to obtain flame from the holy fire for rekindling the hearth of the palace?"

"Go you up and obtain the flame for me, dear soul," said Pryderi. "I will remain here with my people until it is time to ride." Never had it happened to him before to leave the druid fire unvisited on the night of Calangauaf and Rekindling.

An hour after midnight the men of the teulu came riding into the marketplace. They had all obtained their flame on Grongar Hill, and rekindled their hearths with it. The townsfolk made way for them; they gathered, six-score men, the pride and flower of the Dimetians, in the midst of the marketplace: Pryderi fab Pwyll on his horse at the head of them.

As they rode forth he turned to the people he was leaving. "Fear you not that I shall be bereft of the power to protect and serve you!" he cried.

Wailing broke from the women and children; the old men bowed their heads and wept.

IV. *The Battle at Maen Twrog high above Melenryd, and the Imposition of Dragonhood on Pryderi*

PRYDERI WITH his teulu rode northward; at dawn they came to the boundaries between Ystrad Tywi and Ceredigion, and halted to take food. There came Gwydion ab Don to him, wearing his human and bardic guise.

"Lord brother," said Gwydion; "come you now with me to the Wyddfa; accept godhood; forsake this outworn mortality."

"Is it now you would ask it of me?" said Pryderi. "Lord brother, lord brother, not until now have the Cymry needed my protection! Evil upon me if I forsake the toils and weariness of mortality now."

"Glorious and compassionate is the answer!" said Gwydion, sighing. "As it will be, it will be," said he; and went his way.

They rode forward. They tracked the men of Gwynedd through Ceredigion, and through Ceri and Arwystli, and through a part of Powys. At Arllechwedd they saw the rievers of Llefrith Laethwen before them after. They hastened on in pursuit; at noon on the fourth day from their setting out they came up with them. Pryderi sent Iestyn Benteulu forward to demand peace and the restoration of the Milkwhite Milchcow.

"We will not give her up unless compelled by fighting," said the Chieftain of the Gwyneddigion. It seemed to Iestyn that he had never seen better men than these Gwyneddigion, not even among the Dimetians themselves — so beautiful and glorious they were. He wondered that such men could be.

The battle began, and went forward until dusk. With confidence the Dimetian heroes rushed into the fray. Never had it happened to them before to meet men who might hope to encounter them without defeat. They were the pride of the Island, unexcelled; the terror of the hostile in the four quarters of the inhabitable universe. Easily, it seemed to them, they would put compulsion upon these Gwyneddigion.

They left their horses in the camp: they had brought no chariots, on account of the need of swift journeying through the wintry mountains where chariots could not pass; and there were none with the Gwyneddigion. Proudly they rushed down into the valley, Pryderi their lord at the head of them: Pryderi the white-haired, better than the best of them still, when it came to waging war. Proudly they raised up the proud warshout of the Golden Dragon. "For the sake of the Gwledig of the White Island we make war," they said.

But who were these that came against them? Who were these that swords harmed not; that spears smote not, or smiting, did not wound? Proud and gloriously they fell: the flower of the proud Dimetians, the teulu of the Gwledig of Ynys Wen. Man by man they fell: Istyn fab Goronwy fab Pendaran fell; and the son of the Lord of Aberdaugleddau; and the three grandsons of Ceredig Call Cwmteifi, Ifor and Idris and Ithel. Again and again they rushed on the spears of the Gwyneddigion: they were men accustomed to victory; often they had obtained it even at the foot of the Alps. They were tall and handsome men, wearers of golden torques; ruddy golden their hair; pleasant their voices; pleasant and gleaming their eyes, inspiring love; unknown to them, theretofore, had been the hosts that could stand gainst them. Man by man they fell about their lord Pryderi. Who were these supreme ones that withstood them – whom no sword could wound, nor well-cast spear destroy? Man by man the Dimetians fell. Three score of them were dead at sunset; yet were they not driven back. Pryderi fab Pwyll in the forefront of them: Pryderi the White-haired: terrible the blows of his griding sword. Proud were the Dimetians that fell; proudly and gladly they died. Gay, exultant, singing, they sped westward wind-borne, or in dim flame over the waves in their ghostly boats toward the Island of the Blest. "Fortunate are we, truly," they said, "this day at last we have seen Pryderi fab Pwyll make war."

At dusk the Chieftain of the Gwyneddigion sounded truce upon his horn, and the two armies went back to their camps on the hills. Pryderi watched by the campfire, looking out over the valley where the men he loved had fallen at his side. Weariness was on his limbs, sadness upon his spirit; "Old age is coming on me," he said. He thought of the ones that had fallen in the valley. They were all heroes: even in the Island of the Mighty where were there men who could equal them? They were the grandsons of heroes; Iestyn fab Goronwy fab Pendaran was the penteulu at the head of them: a man worthy to be the grandson of old Pendaran Dyfed. No one had had more of Pryderi's love than he; and he lay slain in the valley, and the half of the teulu with him. Pryderi sat by the campfire; evil upon him unless he mourned.

At dawn as they made ready to go forth there came a messenger from the Gwyneddigion. "Lord Gwledig," said he; "I come upon an embassy from my chieftain: summon you, if it please you, the chiefs of your teulu to hear the message."

"They are summoned from me already," said Pryderi. "Speak you the message without concealment."

"Here is is," said the other. "The Gwyneddigion have no enmity against the men of the south, and desire friendship with them."

"They shall have it," said Pryderi, "when the Milkwhite Milchcow is restored to us uninjured."

"She will never be restored," said the messenger. "This day she grazes in the meadows of the mightiest chieftain in Eryri."

"Nor will there be peace between thy chieftain and me," said Pryderi.

"Between you and him let there be war," said the messenger; "and between the Dimetians and the Gwyneddigion let there be peace. It pities my chieftain that the men of the south should be destroyed."

"Yes," said Pryderi; "it shall be between him and me. Body against body and soul against soul we will decide it; and there shall be peace between the two armies."

"At Maen Twrog high above Melenryd he will wait for you," said the messenger.

"At Maen Twrog I will come to him," said Pryderi.

He armed himself with the subtle equipment his father had made for him of old. Eagerly the Dimetains sought to dissuade him from going; it was sorrow to them to remain at peace on the mountain while their lord might be making war in the vale, but they had no fear or doubt as to the result. It was well known in those days that no mortal would achieve the slaying of Pryderi in battle or even the wounding of him, if the wound was to be grievous. But there was no dissuading Pryderi. "Too many of you I have lost already," said he.

He armed himself with sword, shield, and shoes of subtle making, beyond what helmet he may have had; what twisted torque of gold he may have had about his neck; what golden breastplate of a king he may have worn on his breast. Then he went forward alone to the hilltop of Maen Twrog in the midst of the circle of the mountains, between the two hosts.

The Chieftain of the Gwyneddigion gave him the most courteous greeting in Wales or the world.

No less courteously Pryderi greeted him again, and praised the skill and prowess he had shown in the battle.

"They were nothing wonderful," said the Chieftain. "Incomparable, to me, has been the honor of opposing you; incomparably glorious was your warfare. It was for the sake of experiencing it that I came against you."

"It will be a delight to me to make conflict this morning with one so warlike and courteous," said Pryderi.

Therewith they began to fight.

And all that day they fought upon the crag-top, – the vast ring of mountains around them, and the two hosts watching from afar. All that day the Dragon of Dyfed maintained the combat: he old and white-bearded, and the one that opposed him in the prime of his strength and vigor. Fierce, relentless, vehement was his attack; proudly indomitable the defense of Pryderi; unremitting the warfare until noon.

"Lord Gwledig," said the Chieftain then, "it is time now for rest and truce."

"Rest and truce let there be, if you desire it," said Pryderi. "Better with me would be continuation of warfare."

"If it would be better with you, let it continue," said the Chieftain.

Therewith they went forward with it again even more regally than before. Swift and vehement the attack and counter-attack; proudly unconquerable the defense and counter-defense until the evening.

"Let it be renewed at dawn, if it please you," said the Chieftain.

"Yes yes," said Pryderi, sheathing his sword.

"Proud were the Immortals if you made war in their ranks with them," said the Chieftain.

"I have fought in many battles," said Pryderi; "but the best of them was peaceful in comparison with this. Puny, beside you, was the best of my foes of old time."

With that they returned to their camps for rest.

Pryderi sat watching beside the fire that night. Weariness was on his limbs, sadness on his spirit on account of the glory of the men he had lost. Old age, he was aware, was growing on him hourly. Suddenly there stood before him one whose form had the full splendor of godhood – all of flame and extreme magnificence, intensely radiant under the wintry stars.

"My son Pryderi!" said the God.

"My father!" said Pryderi, rising up.

Said Manawyddan: "The Gods make war upon Chaos along the borders of space; and they have need of equipment for their wars. Therefore I desire a gift from you, my son, Pryderi."

"Name you the gift, lord father, if it please you."

"It is the Sword, the Shield and the Shoes of the Subtle Making, that I made for you of old, and that the Gods need now."

"Proud I am that you should ask them of me," said Pryderi; "delightful to me it is, to give them." So he brought out those treasure; and Manawyddan, taking them, assumed dragon form, and sped away through the night sky with them.

Dawn came grayly over a world gloomy with fine rain. Pryderi armed himself with such equipment as there was for him: sword, shield and shoes that were but of mortal and unsubtle making – ungifted with divine peculiarities. He went forth to the fight again. On Maen Twrog high above Melenryd the Chieftain of the Gwyneddigion met him; prouder of mien seemed that one than the day before: stronger of limb; more exultant of spirit. But Pryderi felt the old age upon him: it was in his mind that he was not now as once he had been.

They gave each other noble and courteous greetings; they lauded each other's valor and exalted demeanor; each acknowledged proudly the honor it was to him to be opposing the other; with sincere admiration each contemplated the heroic bearing of his foe. Very tenderly the Chieftain regarded Pryderi; every tenderly, and with reverence.

They prepared to fight, and began to fight; and fought. Never had either of them fought so magnificently before. Until noon they dealt out mutually fierce and griding blows; splendid attack and defense; indomitable counter-attack and counter-defense. For all the vigor of the Chieftain, and his stainless prime of manhood, there was no obtaining for him advantage over old, war-worn white-bearded Pryderi. At noon he drew back.

"Rest you now, in the name of heaven, lord brother!"

"Not so, unless you desire it," said Pryderi. But he felt the old age weighing on his limbs.

They went forward with the fighting; and it was even better between noon and dusk than it had been during the morning. Clouds drifted over the mountains; they waged their warfare in the midst of dark clouds and drizzling rain. Old age grew upon Pryderi: slowly the Chieftain was gaining the advantage.

At sunset the rain ceased and the clouds drifted from above Maen Twrog. Heavy purple were the heavens eastward; at the early setting of the sun, a passionate flame of glowing scarlet low down over the hills and the sea. Suddenly the aspect of the one that was against him seemed to Pryderi to change: he flamed up and towered over Pryderi, a moment majestic with compassion; then awful in beauty, terrible in immortal grandeur, unhuman as the glory of the dawn, as the sombre glory of the night dragon. Pryderi gathered his strength and raised once more the warshout of the Cymry, and swept out at the Chieftain with his sword; and equal the vigor of the blow to the best vigor of his youth and early manhood. But what sword can wound the flame of Immortality? Pryderi beheld the one that was against him stretch forth an arm into the darkening immensity of heaven, and pluck a spear out of heaven that had the awful semblance of the lightning. A great cry broke from the Dimetians where they watched from afar on their mountain. They saw the wound given that no physician could ever heal. They saw the Dragon of Dyfed fall.

He fell; dimness came upon his vision; through the dimness he saw the splendor of godhood shining above him. "Who art thou, O Glorious One that hast slain me?" he panted.

"I am Gwydion ab Don, lord brother," said he.

In that manner Pryderi Wledig passed from mortality. In Maen Twrog high above Melenryd he was slain; in Maen Twrog is his grave to this day.

But the Dimetians, watching from their mountain, beheld two shining Dragons rise up from the crag of Maen Twrog, and launch their glory on the night, and scintillate forth and drive through the heavens towards the Wydffa Mountain.

"Dragonhood has been imposed on him," they said. "Our lord Pryderi is made one with the Immortals."

And thus it Ends.

NOTES

ABRED [Ah'-bred] Inchoation: this material universe, one of the three worlds or states of existence

ADEN-FWYNACH [Add'-enn Vooeen'-akh]: one of the three birds of the Goddess Rhianon sent as guides to Manawyddan

ADEN LANACH [Add'-enn Lan'-nakh]: one of the three birds of the Goddess Rhianon sent as guides to Manawyddan

ADEN LONACH [Add'-enn Lawn'-akh]: one of the three birds of the Goddess Rhianon sent as guides to Manawyddan

ALAWN BRIF-FARDD PRYDAIN [Al'-own Brieve'-varrthe Prud'dine]: one of the three Prif-fardd

ALBAN: Scotland

AMAETHON [Ah-my'-thon]: one of the sons of Don

ARIANROD [Arr-yan'-rod]: one of the Goddesses

BACH, little: term of endearment

BENDIGAID FRAN [Ben-dig'-ide Vran] or Bran Fendigaid [Fen-dig'-ide]: see Bran the Blessed

BRAN THE BLESSED: once Crowned King of London

BRYTHON [Bruth'-on]: the ancient Britons

CADAIR IDRUS [Cad'-ire Eé-dris]: a mountain in Wales

CAER [Care]: a Castle

CAER ODORNANT: Bristol

CALANGAUAF: Halloween

CARIAD BACH: A term of endearment, as 'little sweetheart.'

CEINION GRYDD [Kine-yon Greathe]: Ceinion the Cobbler. Crydd, a cobbler

CELFYDDWR CLOD CLEDDYFAN [kel-voth'-oorr claud cledh-uv-igh]: the swordmaker

CERIDWEN [Care-id'-wen]: one of the Goddesses

229

CEUGANT [Kigh-gant], Infinity: one of the three worlds or states of existence

CHILDREN OF BEAUTY: the Fairies

CYMRAEG [Cum-rygue]: the language of the ancient Britons

CYMRY [Kum'-ree]: the Welsh, *see also* Brython

CYNGHANEDD: an intricate scheme of alliteration used in Celtic verse.

DIENW'R ANFFODION [Dee-enn'-oorr An-fod'-yon]: *see* Manawyddan

ENGLYN [Eng'-lyn]: a verse form

EWINWEN FERCH YR EIGION [A-win'-wen Vairrkh er Ygue'yon]: the daughter of the Sea Wave

FACH: A diminutive expressing endearment, etc.

GALANAS: *see* King's Galanas

GLANACH [Glan'-nakh]: see Aden Lanach

GOFANNON [Go-van'-nonj: one of the sons of Don

GORSEDD: "throne" — a session of the bards, hence of the Gods

GWERDDONAU LLION [Gwairr-thonn'-igh Lhee'-on]: the Islands of the Blessed in which the seven found Bran

GWIAWN Cat's-Eye the Sea-Thief [Gwee'-on] one of the three Persecuting Kinsmen of the Island of the Mighty

GWIAWN LLYGAD CATH [Gwee'-on Lhug'-gad Cahth]: *see* Gwiawn Cat's-Eye.

GWLEDIG: National: i.e., a nationality elected Over-king, appointed chiefly in times of crisis. If you can't put a *w* in between the *G* and the *l*, by all means pronounce it Glay-dig.

GWRON BRIF-FARDD PRYDAIN [Goo'-ron Brieve'-varrthe Prud'dine]: one of the three Prif-fardd

GWYDION [Gwud'-yon]: one of the sons of Don

GWYNEDDIGION: the men of Gwynedd, a kingdom in the north of Wales.

GWYNFYD [Gwun'-vud]: the World of Bliss, Heaven: one of the three worlds or states of existence

GYRRU'R GWYNTOEDD: the Wind-driver

HAFREN [Have'-wren]: the River Severn

HAI ATTON [High At-ton]: a war-shout — 'A nous!'

HARP OF ARTHUR (The): the Constellation *Lyra*

HENFORDD: Hereford. Loegria (Lloegr): that part of Britain which is rightly called England

HIREWIN FRITH [Here-ray'-win Vreeth]

HU GADARN [Hee-Gad'-arrn]

HWYL [Hooeel]: a chanting tone in speech, like the sound of the wind in a pine-forest or in the rigging of a ship

"If I shall," etc. — i.e., "If I am permitted"

ISLAND OF THE MIGHTY (The): the name most commonly used for Ancient Britain in the Welsh romances — Ynys y Cedyrn. Other names were Ynys Wen, the White Island; Ynys Fel, the Honey Island; Ynys Prydain, Prydain's Island — whence Britain: Prydain was a legendary king

KING's GALANAS: the fine exacted under the Welsh laws for the murder of a king

LLWYD AB CILCOED [Lhooid ab Kil'-coyd] one of the three Persecuting Kinsmen

LLONACH [Lhawn'-awn]: *see* Aden Lonach

MANAWYDDAN [Man-ow-oth'-thanj: the name of the hero of this story, first known as Pwyll, later as Dienw'r Anifodion, and lastly as Manawyddan

MIL GWELL ANGAU NA CHYWILYDD, a proverb: "A thousand times better death than shame"

MWYNACH [Mooeen'-akh]: *see* Aden Fwynach

NWYFRE [Nooee'-vray]: the ether of space

PENNILLION: verses of a certain kind

PENTEULU [PEN-til'-ey]: chief of the teulu, or king's body-guard.

PLENYDD BRIF-FARDD PRYDAIN [Plen'-neathe Brieve'-varrthe Prud'-dine]: one of the Prif-feird

PORTH DINAS GWRON [Porth Deen'-ass Goo'-ron]: the Gate of Gwron's City

PRIF-FARD, *also* Prif-feirdd: the three primitive Bards of Britain; the Three Dragons

PUMLUMON [Peem-leem'-on] — *anglice* Plynlimmon: a mountain in Wales

PWYLL [Pooeelh]: see Manawyddan

RHIANON [Rhee-an'-non]: Manawyddan's wife

RHYDYCHEN: Oxford

TARIANWR TADWY [Tarr-yan'-oor Tad'-wyj: the shield-maker

TATHAL TWYLL GOLEU [Tath'-al Tooeelh Go'-ligh]: one of the three Persecuting Kinsmen

TEULU [til'-ey]: a special body of 120 nobles that formed the bodyguard of the Welsh kings

TYLWYTH TEG (The) [Tull'-ooeeth Teg]: the Fairies

"White your world," a benediction

TYR'D TI!...CWYD!...TRYR'D TI!...CWYD!...CWYD!: Teerd tee – Cooeed, etc.

WYDDFA (The) [With'va]: the peak of Mt. Snowdon in Northern Wales: the Olympus of Celtic Britain

YNYS FEL [Un'-nis Vel]: *see* Island of the Mighty

YNYS PRYDAIN {Un'-nis Prud'-dine]: *see* Island of the Mighty

YNYS WEN [Un'-nis Wen]: *see* Island of the Mighty

YNYS Y CEDYRN [Un'-nis ce Ked'-irrn]: *see* Island of the Mighty

About the Author

Kenneth Morris (1879-1937) was one of the great fantasy writers of the 20th century. Born in Wales, he spent 22 years in California. In 1930 he returned to Wales, where he died in 1937 at the age of fifty-seven. In addition to *Book of the Three Dragons* (1930), he is also the author of *The Fates of the Princes of Dyfed* (1914), *The Secret Mountain and Other Tales* (1926), and a novel published long after his death, *The Chalchiuhite Dragon* (1992). His collected short stories were published as *The Dragon Path: Collected Tales of Kenneth Morris* (1995).

ℭold 𝔖pring 𝔓ress

An Imprint of Open Road Publishing
P.O. Box 284
Cold Spring Harbor, NY 11724
Jopenroad@aol.com

Nonfiction:

The Science of Middle-earth, by Henry Gee, $14.00

More People's Guide to J.R.R. Tolkien, by TheOneRing.net, $14.00

The People's Guide to J.R.R. Tolkien, by TheOneRing.net, $16.95

The Tolkien Fan's Medieval Reader, by Turgon, $14.95

Tolkien in the Land of Heroes, by Anne C. Petty, $16.95

Dragons of Fantasy, by Anne C. Petty, $14.95

Myth & Middle-earth, by Leslie Ellen Jones, $14.95

The 100 Best Writers of Fantasy and Horror, by Douglas A. Anderson, $16.95 (Spring 2005)

Fiction:

The Sillymarillion, by D.R. Lloyd, $11.00

Book of the Three Dragons, by Kenneth Morris, $11.95

Lud-in-the-Mist, by Hope Mirrlees, $11.00 (Spring 2005)

Thin Line Between: Book One of the Wandjina Quartet, by M.A.C. Petty, $11.00 (Spring 2005)

———————————

For US orders, include $5.00 for postage and handling for the first book ordered; for each additional book, add $1.00. Orders outside US, inquire first about shipping charges (money order payable in US dollars on US banks only for overseas shipments). We also offer bulk discounts. *Note:* Checks or money orders must be made out to **Open Road Publishing**.